Praise for the reigning queen of romance,

"Palmer's talent for character development and ability to fuse heartwarming romance with nail-biting suspense shine in *Outsider.*"
—*Booklist*

"A gentle escape mixed with real-life menace for fans of Palmer's more than 100 novels."
—*Publishers Weekly* on *Night Fever*

"The ever-popular and prolific Palmer has penned another sure hit."
—*Booklist* on *Before Sunrise*

"Palmer knows how to make sparks fly… heartwarming."
—*Publishers Weekly* on *Renegade*

"Readers who enjoy stories by authors who know how to pack an emotional wallop will add Palmer to their list."
—*Booklist* on *Renegade*

"The dialogue is charming, the characters likeable and the sex sizzling."
—*Publishers Weekly* on *Once in Paris*

"This story is a thrill a minute—
one of Palmer's best."
—*Rendezvous* on *Lord of the Desert*

"Diana Palmer does a masterful job of
stirring the reader's emotions."
—Lezlie Patterson, *Reading Eagle* on *Lawless*

"Sensual and suspenseful…."
—*Booklist* on *Lawless*

"Diana Palmer is a mesmerizing storyteller who
captures the essence of what a romance should be."
—*Affaire de Coeur*

"Nobody does it better."
—Award-winning author Linda Howard

"Nobody tops Diana Palmer when it comes to
delivering pure, undiluted romance. I love her stories."
—*New York Times* bestselling author Jayne Ann Krentz

DIANA PALMER

OUTSIDER

ISBN-13: 978-0-373-77234-6
ISBN-10: 0-373-77234-3

OUTSIDER

This edition published by arrangement with Harlequin Books S.A.

www.HQNBooks.com

Printed in U.S.A.

Also by Diana Palmer

Lacy
Heart of Winter
Night Fever
Before Sunrise
Renegade
Lawless
Diamond Spur
Desperado
The Texas Ranger
Lord of the Desert
The Cowboy and the Lady
Most Wanted
Fit for a King
Paper Rose
Rage of Passion
Once in Paris
After the Music
Roomful of Roses
Champagne Girl
Passion Flower
Diamond Girl
Friends and Lovers
Cattleman's Choice
Lady Love
The Rawhide Man

Look for Diana Palmer's new hardcover
Lawman
Coming in June

OUTSIDER

CHAPTER ONE

IT WAS AN UNUSUALLY COLD morning for October in Houston, Texas, and Colby Lane's left arm ached. There wasn't a lot left of it, thanks to a stint as a covert specialist in Africa. He'd been too drunk to take proper precautions and it had been shot off, then amputated from just below his elbow. The state-of-the-art prosthesis he wore was classified technology, very advanced, and the hand at the end of it looked real enough to fool most people. He even had sensation in it, thanks to implanted computer chips. He was, he mused, a walking, talking lab rat with stealth capability. He grinned to himself at the mental picture that thought produced.

But the smile faded rapidly. He was in a foul mood. It was only his second full day on the job as new assistant chief of security for the Ritter Oil

Corporation's Houston branch. He'd taken the job as a favor to his old friend, Phillip Hunter, who was training him to be his replacement. The Hunters were considering a move back to Tucson, Arizona.

Meanwhile, Colby was trying to get used to new surroundings and at least two department heads who thought they knew how to do his job better than he did. He'd formerly worked for the international Hutton Corporation as another friend's assistant chief of security. Then the Hutton Corporation gave notice that it was moving overseas. He didn't want to go with it. Colby knew Hunter from his childhood on the reservation. Like him, Colby had Apache blood. But Colby also had an innate dislike of tight schedules, corporate politics and wearing a suit. His background in covert operations as a mercenary soldier, not to mention a brief stint in top-secret intelligence work for the government, made this routine job an uncomfortable fit. Office politics was a far cry from going after the enemy with weapons. The amputation of his arm had cost him the work he'd done all his life. He was bitter about that; in fact, he was bitter about a lot of things. Life had failed him. One old friend had voiced the opinion that Colby's growing array of wounds stemmed from a death wish. He hadn't admitted it aloud, but the accusation hit a nerve. He was tired of aching wounds, broken dreams, shattered illusions. He was tired of life itself.

Here in Houston, he was trying to settle down for the first time in his life, with two failed marriages behind him and a past history of alcoholism. He'd overcome the drinking problem years ago. He was sober as a judge these days. But he no longer had the physical means to continue in demanding special operations work overseas. He resented forced retirement from his vocation of choice. His aching arm reminded him of all that he'd had to give up.

He'd tried hard to put his past to the back of his mind. He had enough to worry about, getting used to this new job. His background, however, predisposed him for security work. He was an expert in martial arts and small arms, not to mention counterterrorism. He was a past master in interrogation techniques and he'd almost learned diplomacy. He had credentials that had even impressed Hunter—not to mention Eugene Ritter, the head of Ritter Oil Corporation. Now he had to find a way to exercise diplomacy with words when he was used to doing it with firearms. It wasn't easy.

He walked in the front door of the sprawling modern building in an industrial complex outside Houston, absently displaying his ID on a card clipped to his lapel as he passed the security guard at the desk. Ironic, he thought, that he was chief of security and still had to flash his own badge to get into the building he protected. The guard seemed to see the same irony, because he couldn't resist a grin. Colby returned it.

He was an impressive figure in his navy-blue business suit. He was tall, handsome, lean, and physically formidable, with thick, shining black hair that held a slight wave. He had deep-set black eyes and an olive complexion, and he wore his hair conventionally cut. He never discussed his Apache ancestry. It wasn't immediately apparent, anyway, because there was a comfortable amount of white blood in his lineage. He was wearing his newest prosthesis, linked not only to muscle remnants in his left arm, but to his brain as well. It looked quite real, even up close, and he could do almost anything with it—except lift. He could even "feel" hot and cold. The sensors were incredible.

As he turned the corner toward the executive offices, he noticed two children playing in the corridor. Both were dark-haired and dark-eyed. Both were girls. He'd almost forgotten that it was bring-your-daughter-to-work day for Ritter's employees. Just what he needed, a floor full of hyperactive children to contend with at the beginning of a new job. It wasn't that he didn't like children. But he was bitter because he had none of his own. He'd wanted them badly.

His ex-wife, Maureen, had taunted him with his sterility before she left him. It was just as well, she'd said, because she didn't want mixed race children. She hadn't realized that he was part Apache when they'd married, or he might have been saved a lot of heartache.

She'd been an obsession with him, in those days. When she walked out after only two years of marriage, he thought he'd die. When she'd divorced him three years later, he was devastated and turned to the bottle. It had taken him months to dry out and get his life back, with some help from friends and a psychologist. He'd conquered his demons. But children still reminded him of the pain.

One of the children ran laughing down the hall. The other, who looked about six years old, stopped and stared at Colby from a pretty, intelligent face dominated by big brown eyes. She had long brown hair that reached her waist in back. She was lovely; Hispanic in appearance. Or perhaps she had Native American ancestry. He knew that Hunter had a little girl who was on the premises today. Perhaps this was her.

The little girl came right up to him and reached up to touch the sleeve where the prosthesis protruded. "I'm sorry your arm got hurt. You shouldn't have been drinking. You weren't quick enough, so you couldn't get out of the way in time. But this hand looks very real, doesn't it?" She touched the hand, which he jerked back at once. "Does it still hurt you?" she asked matter-of-factly, staring up at him with dark eyes that seemed oddly familiar.

His eyes exploded with rage. What had possessed Hunter to tell his daughter so much intimate information about him? How dare a child criticize Colby for not being quick enough to save his arm! In fact, how dare she make such a personal comment to a total stranger? He was touchy enough about missing part of his arm in the first place, without having attention drawn to it. Even close friends, whose interest he didn't mind, knew better than to say such things to him. It made him furious that a child should be so forward.

"What business is it of yours?" he demanded in a soft tone that nevertheless cut like a whip. Added to the fierce scowl on his unsmiling face, it made him look very intimidating. "I don't answer to kids for my actions. And it's my arm!"

"I…I'm sorry," the child stammered, shocked.

"Who told you about it?" he demanded. "Answer me!"

She shook her head nervously and ground her teeth together, tears threatening.

He cursed harshly under his breath. "Get back to whoever you're with today, and stay out of the corridors!" he snapped at her. "This is a business, not a nursery school!"

She backed away from him with wide, hurt eyes. She turned suddenly and ran back the way she'd come, her voice breaking on a sob.

He ground his teeth together. He hadn't meant to attack the child like that. It had shocked and offended him that a child would be so personal, and so critical, with him. He didn't like remarks about his handicap. But he shouldn't have been so aggressive toward her. She'd been really upset.

He started after her down the hall. Hunter came out of a side door, his eyebrows arching at the look on Colby's face.

"What's eating you?" he asked.

Colby grimaced as he faced his friend, the same height and build as himself, but a few years older. Hunter had a few gray hairs these days.

"Is your daughter here today?" he asked Hunter.

"Yes. Why?"

He felt worse than ever. "I upset her. She made a remark about my arm and it hit me the wrong way." He glared at Hunter. "Why did you tell her how I lost it?"

Hunter's eyes narrowed. "I've never told Nikki about your arm," he said curiously, puzzled.

He blinked. "Maybe it was somebody else's kid. She had long, dark hair and dark eyes. She looked Hispanic, I thought."

"Oh, that might be Marie Gomez's little girl. Was she wearing an embroidered dress?"

"No."

Hunter hesitated.

Colby grimaced. This was not a good way to start a new job. "I didn't mean to make her cry," he bit off, averting his eyes. "I'm not used to kids. What she said hit me the wrong way. But how would a stranger's child know such personal things about me?" he wondered aloud. He glared at Hunter. "I didn't sign on as a babysitter."

"It's only for today," Hunter said. "The kids will all be gone tomorrow."

Colby ground his teeth together. "I'd better find the little girl and apologize. She went down that way," he added, and moved reluctantly along the corridor.

Hunter stood still. He was remembering something a friend and coworker here, Sarina Carrington, had said once about Colby Lane. She and her daughter and the Hunters were good friends from Tucson. She'd transferred here recently from Arizona. She was working with Hunter on a project he hadn't yet told Colby about—in fact, he couldn't tell him about it. But Colby was about to get a very unpleasant shock. There was a connection that Colby didn't know about yet, and the child might figure in it. He wondered if he should stop the other man. He wasn't sure how he could, now.

Colby noticed an open office door and he heard a child sobbing. He'd have to find a way to apologize for making her cry. He was no good with kids, and he hated women. Probably the child's mother would be out for his blood. He was new here and already he was making enemies. Old man Ritter wouldn't like that. He'd better try to smooth things over. But this was going to be difficult. And he had questions about the child's source of information about him, as well.

He walked into the office in time to see the little girl folded close to a slender woman's breasts, cradled and kissed. Sleek pale blond hair was tamed in a neat French twist at the woman's nape. Her voice was tender as shè comforted the child, rocking her in her arms. There was something familiar about that voice…

The little girl pulled back, as if she sensed Colby's presence. She looked at him from red, angry eyes.

"*¡Matador de hombres!*" she raged at him in Spanish. "*¡Hijo del Diablo!*"

"*¡Lengua como una serpiente!*" he shot right back, dark eyes blazing.

He was just getting over the shock of being called a man-killer by a child in perfect Spanish, when the blond woman rose gracefully to her feet and turned to face him, and a nightmare vision corded his powerful body like a drop from a sudden height at the end of a rope. It was Sarina Carrington. Sarina, whom he'd hurt and rejected. Sarina, the first wife nobody even knew he had. Ex-wife, he corrected at once. But the shock still had him speechless. And he wasn't the only one.

The woman stared at him, silently, with wide, shocked eyes, and her full mouth suddenly flattened. She bent and clutched the child to her and stood up, lifting her in her arms, her own nightmares darkening her eyes. Colby Lane! For a few seconds, she thought she might faint. Her heart skipped like a wet engine. The years fell away and she was a teenager, hero-worshipping the handsomest, sexiest man she'd ever known. Just the sight of him had been enough to leave her tongue-tied and gasping. The first time he'd kissed her, the rapt pleasure in her face had amused him and he'd laughed. She'd loved him more than her own life. It had been almost seven years since she'd seen him. She hadn't even known where he was. And then, suddenly, out of the blue, he was here…!

Slowly she forced herself to remember that she was twenty-four years old, and in a very responsible position. In the past seven years, she'd grown far away from that sensitive, lovesick teenager who'd inadvertently ruined Colby's life—and her own.

Circumstances had forced him to marry her, and he'd made her pay in a terrible way during the one day their marriage had lasted. Perhaps he'd had reason to treat her so terribly. Nevertheless, he wasn't taking out old hurts on her child! Her dark eyes narrowed and she glared at him with real hatred. "What are you doing here?" she asked coldly. "And what did you say to my daughter?"

He was on shaky ground, but it didn't show in his hard face. He glared back. "You should tell your child not to be so forward with strangers. She insulted me."

She frowned, looking into the child's face so close

to her own. "Bernadette, is that true?" she asked quietly.

The child's arms tightened around her neck. She glared at Colby. "No, ma'am," she said politely.

"She made a personal remark. My life is none of her business," he replied in a voice dripping like ice.

"I can't think why your life would interest anyone except you and your wife, Mr. Lane," she said coldly. "Certainly it doesn't interest me."

He let that slide. She didn't know that he and Maureen were divorced. His pride wouldn't let him admit it. He'd gone straight from Sarina after the annulment to marry Maureen in a civil ceremony. Maureen, the love of his life, who'd made his life hell.

He was trying to reconcile seven years of distance with the woman he saw before him. She had a child. She'd married, then. He'd wondered how she'd coped with the nightmare of their wedding night. He hadn't meant to hurt her so badly, even though he blamed her for everything that had happened.

"Does your husband work here, too?" he asked, hating himself for the question.

"I don't have a husband," she replied after a minute, putting the child back on her feet. "Bernadette, why don't you look for Nikki and go down to the canteen together?" she said to the child, her eyes and voice tender. She smiled, a little uneasily. "Are you okay, now, baby?"

"Yes, Mama. Don't worry." Bernadette hugged her. The affection was returned generously. The child gave Colby a second cold glare and walked out of the office past him without another word. Her breathing sounded odd. Probably she was hoarse from the tears, he thought, and felt guiltier.

His mind was in turmoil as his eyes went back to the slender woman from his past. "I didn't mean to upset the child so badly," he bit off.

Sarina went back around her desk and sat down, looking very mature and businesslike. She studied Colby like a museum exhibit. "Why are you here?" she asked. "The annulment was completed seven years ago, as I recall, even though I never got the paperwork."

Until that moment, he'd never realized that he hadn't gotten a final copy of it. He'd not kept track of it and he'd never had to prove that his former marriage had been annulled. Odd, he thought irrelevantly, that he didn't have a copy of his second divorce papers, either. But Maureen had them somewhere, he was sure.

He blinked, brought back to the question. "Hunter wants to go back to Tucson. I'm his replacement."

That was news to her. Hunter's wife, Jennifer, was her best friend, and the other woman said they loved it in Houston. She lifted one thin eyebrow. Her eyes, dark as night, were her best feature, next to those soft, sensual lips. She wasn't pretty. She had a beautiful complexion, and thick, silky blond hair. Her breasts were small, like her waist, but she had flaring, nice hips and pretty, long legs. He'd seen her without clothing only once, but he'd never managed to banish the memory. Sarina, laughing with him as they walked in the park. Sarina, in his arms, dying for him. Sarina, crying out in pain when he couldn't stop, Sarina, shuddering in the aftermath of a passion that he couldn't control…

He pulled himself back to the present. She didn't know how tortured he'd been afterward, or to what depths he'd sunk trying to forget what he'd done to her. She didn't know. He couldn't tell her, even now.

"How long have you been working for Ritter?" he asked abruptly.

"Seven years," she replied without raising her eyes. "But I'm only in Houston temporarily, working on a special project. Bernadette and I live in Tucson."

Bernadette. That name rang a bell. He recalled the happy months he'd spent with Sarina in the old days, while he was guarding her millionaire father from a kidnapping attempt by people who wanted the location of his secret mines which produced a priceless strategic metal. Colby, who worked for military intelligence, was assigned to keep tabs on him. In the process he'd met Sarina, who was living at home. They'd become close at once. She was in college, so he assumed she was in her early twenties.

He still didn't know that she'd graduated a year ahead of her class in high school and done two years of college in one. He didn't know, either, that she'd been only seventeen at the time of their forced marriage. They'd been caught by her father and two of his business associates and their wives in a compromising situation. Her father had literally forced Colby to marry her, using his career as a threat, to save face with his social set. At the time, Colby had been working for the CIA, and he loved his job. The old man could have cost him his profession, and Colby knew it, so he'd given in with bad grace. Carrington had assumed that Colby and Sarina had been intimate. They hadn't.

Their wedding night was payback for Colby. He still regretted it. Of course, a day later annulment papers were filed, the minute the millionaire found out from the private detective he'd hired that Colby had considerable Apache blood and that his total worth was somewhat shy of the impression his luxurious style of dress had led the older man to believe it was. Colby didn't know how Sarina had responded to her father's demand that she lie about her wedding night and sign the annulment papers. He'd left her in tears in the early hours of the morning, so angry and full of self-contempt that he didn't even look at her as he left the room.

Before that final meeting, in the early days of their friendship, they'd talked about children in a casual sort of way. She'd always wanted children. A girl, she told him dreamily, and she'd name her Bernadette. There was an old movie she'd seen, and that was the heroine's name. She thought it was beautiful.

"We'd heard that Hunter wanted an assistant," she said, glancing at him. "There was some sort of drug raid and an arrest last night," she added without meeting his eyes. "They said Hunter was in on it."

"So was I," he replied.

That was a surprise, but she was good at hiding her emotions. "Were some of our people here involved?" she fished.

He closed up. "I don't discuss ongoing cases with civilians," he said.

She gave him a long look. "You haven't changed," she said. "You're just as enigmatic and cold as you were then."

"Well, you've changed," he said flatly. "I wouldn't have recognized you."

"I've grown up," she replied. "Children do."

"You were no child when you followed me around like a lost puppy," he said, wanting to hurt.

She hesitated, but she didn't want to admit how young she'd been. Or how stupid. "It was just a bad case of hero worship. I don't do it anymore," she replied sarcastically. "I took the cure. Remember?" she added with pure venom.

He didn't reply, but he avoided meeting her eyes. "Life goes on."

"So they say." She took a disk out of the drawer and fed it into her CD-ROM drive. "I have some paperwork to finish. I'm sure you have duties of your own."

He hesitated. "About the kid…"

She looked up. "Bernadette isn't used to strangers being harsh with her, even if she does have mixed blood."

"Hispanic," he agreed, assuming that she meant the child had Hispanic ancestry. He didn't notice the faint flicker of Sarina's eyelids. The little girl certainly spoke Spanish with some fluency. His eyes blazed with anger. "My own blood is mixed, if you remember," he retorted.

"As I recall, you did your best to hide your Apache ancestry. But, then, I remember as little about you as I possibly can, Mr. Lane," she said with a cool little smile. "Now, if you'll excuse me, I'm quite busy." She turned her attention back to her computer, ignoring him completely.

He turned on his heel and stalked out. He could have chewed tenpenny nails.

SARINA LET OUT THE BREATH she'd been holding since he walked into her office. She felt drained of life, exhausted, burned out. She'd loved Colby Lane. But her relationship with him had destroyed her life. One look into those black eyes had resurrected memories that were much better left dead.

She wondered what Bernadette had said to him to provoke such a reaction. The child had odd little flashes of insight, almost like precognition. Sometimes she frightened other children with her predictions. She frightened her mother, too. Bernadette's grandfather had possessed the same sort of mental insight. There was a Comanche uncle in Oklahoma who also had it. She hoped it wasn't going to cause Bernadette trouble as she grew older.

Right now, though, her concern was how she was going to manage her job with Colby Lane in such proximity. He didn't know anything about her, least of all why she was here, and she couldn't let him find out. She hoped Bernadette didn't slip and say anything to him in Apache. Apparently he spoke Spanish, because he'd answered Bernadette in the same tongue. She'd have to talk to Hunter. He and Jenny missed Tucson but it was news to Sarina that they were planning to go back, because Jenny was pregnant with their second child and in the care of a local obstetrician.

Bernadette and Nikki, the Hunters' daughter, were best friends. The two families were close. That was going to make the situation more difficult. There were things that Sarina didn't want Colby to find out. She'd have to caution the Hunters to keep quiet about her background—and Bernadette's special gift. The last thing in the world she wanted Colby Lane to know was who Bernadette's father was. What a tragedy that he should turn up now.

Another problem presented itself as she thought about Bernadette's violent upset in Colby's presence. The child had been diverted to go find Nikki, and she seemed all right. But often it took a few hours for the symptoms to appear, and she had sounded very hoarse as she left Sarina's office…

She turned her attention back to the computer. She didn't even want to think about it until she had to. Maybe, maybe, it would be all right! Damn Colby and his hot temper!

COLBY STALKED INTO HUNTER'S office with black eyes blazing. He closed the door sharply, bringing the other man's surprised gaze to his face.

"What's biting you?" he asked Colby.

"That little girl, the one who knew about my arm…her mother is Sarina Carrington," he said harshly.

Hunter eyed him cautiously. "So?"

Colby glared at him. He hesitated. "Sarina's my ex-wife."

Hunter actually dropped the pen he was holding. He and his wife had known Sarina for seven years, and they were aware that she knew Colby Lane. But she'd never mentioned a prior marriage.

Colby barely noticed. He went to the window

and looked out, his hands jammed into his pockets. "It was a long time ago," he said. "We were only together one day before she filed for divorce."

"What a smart woman," Hunter murmured dryly.

The memory of the brief marriage was like a knife through Colby's gut. He didn't say anything for a minute. "She was in college when I left," he said aloud. "I thought she'd go into teaching or some profession. She's a clerk here, I gather."

Hunter averted his eyes from his friend's piercing gaze. "A records clerk," he said, hoping he still had a poker face. "I understand she dropped out of college. She wanted a job with less pressure so that she had time for her daughter."

That was a laudable goal, and Colby couldn't fault it. But he was upset. He'd never expected to see Sarina again, much less find her working in a corporation that had just hired him. The job would necessarily foster contact between them. He didn't want a daily reminder of his cruelty.

"Why isn't she working in Tucson? I know you've got a branch office there now. You were working in it at one time."

"Yes. She was briefly reassigned here to fill in for another employee," Hunter said, grasping for any reasonable explanation. "They'll probably go back to Tucson in the near future."

Colby relaxed, just a little. "That's probably a good thing."

"Listen, I've got a meeting with Eugene. Want to come?"

"Do I need to?"

It would be tricky if he did. Hunter was keeping secrets. He couldn't let Colby in on them.

"Not really. I'll brief you. Just routine stuff. You can skip this one," Hunter said with a smile. "If you want something to do, you can go around and introduce yourself to the department heads. You know. Practice diplomacy."

Colby glared at him. "My gun's in my desk drawer."

Hunter gave him a wry look.

Colby shrugged. "All right, I'll work on my people skills."

"Good idea." He picked up his notes. "Did you make up with Bernadette?"

Colby shifted his arm uncomfortably. "Her idea of making up would involve a skinning knife, from what I saw."

Hunter almost bit his tongue trying not to make a joke about similarities between the child and the man. "She likes most people."

"She hates me," Colby said shortly. "And I'm not keen on kids who make personal remarks to total strangers." He scowled. "But how in the hell did she know about my arm?" he asked angrily. "I haven't had any contact with Sarina for seven years, so the kid couldn't have found out from her mother. And if you've never told Nikki," he finished, letting the remark speak for itself.

"Bernadette knows things," Hunter said. "I don't know how. Maybe there was a shaman in her ancestry somewhere."

Colby frowned. "I thought she was Hispanic."

"Sarina doesn't talk about her ancestry," Hunter said, hoping he could avoid any revelations about Bernadette's background. He didn't dare let on. Sarina would kill him.

"Do you know who her father is?"

Hunter turned toward the door. "No," he said. It was true that he hadn't, and he'd never really thought about it…until now. This was dangerous territory. The whole Apache nation was small enough to make it easy to find relatives on the reservations. He couldn't tell Colby that Bernadette's ancestry was Apache, and he'd almost let it slip with the shaman remark. Hunter didn't want Colby asking questions. He still had cousins at a reservation back in Arizona. "I'll be back in an hour or so. Hold down the fort."

Colby patted the cell phone at his belt. "If there is an attack, I'll ring you."

Hunter made a face on his way out.

Colby made the rounds of the executives. One made an immediate impression, and it wasn't a good one. He was assistant head of human resources, a real jerk named Brody Vance who had delusions of importance. He had an administrative assistant who was very nice. She was going with a local DEA senior agent named Cobb, according to Hunter. Colby had met her during a raid at the company warehouse the previous night, when she'd driven a car through machine-gun fire to save Cobb's life—and his and Hunter's. She was quite a woman.

He rounded a corner, and there was Sarina. But she wasn't alone. There was a tall, dark, handsome Latin, about Colby's age, with her. He was leaning lazily against the wall with his arms crossed, and the two of them were in earnest conversation. They were so engrossed, and he was so intent on them, that he didn't notice the little girl running toward them until she called to the man.

"Rodrigo!" she laughed. "Are you coming to my birthday party when we have it?"

"Of course!" he replied, holding out his arms. He caught her up and whirled her around, laughing deeply. "How could I miss all the cake and ice cream?"

"You'd miss me, too," she chided. She kissed him and linked her arms around his neck. "Dear Rodrigo, whatever would me and Mommy do without you?"

"I'll make sure that you never know!" he teased, hugging her back.

Sarina checked her watch. "We'd better go. We still have to stop by the grocery store on the way home. Are you coming over for supper?"

He shook his head. "Thanks, but I have a meeting."

"I forgot."

He shrugged. "Another time."

She smiled at him in a way that made Colby's teeth set. "Another time," she said.

The man she'd called Rodrigo bent and brushed a careless kiss across her cheek. "Take care of my best girl," he told Sarina, winking at the child.

"I always do," she replied warmly, waving as he went off down the hall.

Sarina and Bernadette turned together and there was Colby, blocking the aisle, glaring at both of them.

"There's that awful man again," Bernadette said with a cold glare.

"Bernadette, we don't make rude remarks about people we don't know," Sarina said gently. *Not even when they're richly deserved,* she thought silently.

"Sorry, Mommy," Bernadette muttered under her breath, but she didn't stop glaring at Colby.

Sarina took her hand and walked toward Colby. She stopped when he didn't step aside.

"Who's the guy?" he asked, nodding toward where Rodrigo had disappeared.

"A friend," Sarina said before she thought that it was none of his business. "Rodrigo Ramirez. He works here, too. Would you move, please?"

"Is he the girl's father?"

Sarina's eyebrows arched. "I've only known him three years."

He looked at Bernadette with a narrow stare. "I hope you don't have any plans to try to blame her on me," he said out of the blue, without a clue why he'd made the outrageous remark. "I'd rather be shot than lay claim to a child that rude."

She wasn't a violent woman, but the sarcastic remark hit her in a raw spot. She'd had years of anguish, from her troubled pregnancy to a dangerous delivery, and all the health problems that had come afterward. The comment made her furious. Without pausing to count the cost, she drew back her foot and kicked him in the shin as hard as she could.

He groaned and bent over to rub his leg with a muffled curse.

"Good for you, Mommy," Bernadette said gleefully. "That's the one that got hit with the baseball bat, too!"

Colby gaped at her. Only the month before, he'd had to apprehend a man at his former job for Pierce Hutton who was armed with a baseball bat. He'd been hit in the leg trying to subdue the perpetrator. How the hell did the kid know that?

"Come on, Bernadette," Sarina said, almost dragging the child along with her past the small café downstairs.

Colby walked after them, hobbling a little. "That child is a witch!" he raged in Apache. Sarina didn't respond to the insult, but the child looked back at him with cold, angry eyes as he followed them down the hall. If his leg hadn't been hurting so badly, he might have noticed that she understood what he'd said about her.

Inside the small café overlooking the corridor, maintained for Ritter employees, Alexander Cobb was buying a cappuccino for the young woman Colby remembered from the shoot-out. Colby grimaced as he noticed Cobb watching him with an unholy amused grin. His new job wasn't starting off on the best of feet.

CHAPTER TWO

IT BOTHERED SARINA that Colby had warned her not to accuse him of being Bernadette's father. Of course, he had no reason to think it was true. He'd said it in a sarcastic manner and was probably trying to score points. He didn't bother to mention her frantic call, and his chilling response to it, all those years ago when she was pregnant with Bernadette. He'd told Maureen to tell Sarina that he was sterile and the child couldn't possibly be his. What a joke.

But not a funny one. She'd called him in her ninth month of pregnancy, desperate for help. She'd been totally alone, with no money, unable to work, and at the mercy of bill collectors and the obstetrician who was trying to save her baby. Colby had told his wife Maureen to tell her that she was lying, it couldn't possibly be his child, that he never wanted to speak to her again. She was a filthy little liar, Maureen had quoted, and he hated her for trying to ruin his marriage to Maureen. If she accused him again of fathering her child, Maureen added, Colby would take her to court.

After all these years, it was still painful to remember his rejection. He didn't believe he could have a child and he'd made sure she knew it. That was something of a relief, but it was disturbing that he'd even alluded to it just now. She loved her daughter. She didn't want to take any chance of losing her.

But perhaps she was worrying for no good reason. Colby was surely still married to that horrible woman, Maureen. It was obvious that he didn't like children. And if he truly believed he was sterile, perhaps his rude remark about Bernadette's parentage was a defensive posture to protect his pride.

It was a sad fate that had landed him in her path, especially now, when she was already in so much danger. Her job entailed risks that were becoming more and more unacceptable now that Bernadette was in the line of fire. She was a patriot and she could do a job that not many other people wanted. But was it fair to put Bernadette at risk? If something happened to her, the child would have no living relative save one. And he didn't even know about her. Worse, there was the terrifying health issue which would make the child's chances of adoption unlikely. More and more she was regretting her choice of careers.

A few days later, she was washing dishes at the kitchen sink when she heard a gunshot. Bernadette had been sitting in a small cloth chair on the front porch, but she came running inside.

"Mommy, there's a boy with a gun!"

She caught the child up in her arms. "Are you all right? You weren't hit?"

"No, Mommy. I'm okay."

"Stay down!" Sarina said, tucking the child beside the refrigerator. She took down the key from above the door, the one that fit the drawer by the front door, in case she needed what was inside. Then she went carefully to the front of their small apartment and looked out through the curtained window. Old Señora Martinez was standing on her porch with both hands to her mouth, staring after three young men in bandanas who were running wildly toward a waiting car. A fourth man yelled curses after them. He was holding his arm, from which blood poured. Sarina knew the man; he was Señora Martinez's grandson Raoul. He went to the old lady and soothed her, kissing her forehead. She took his good arm and drew him, fussing, into the apartment and closed the door.

No doubt the shooter was the old lady's nephew, Tito. He was fourteen and headed for jail, as sure as the world. He used drugs and he was violent when he was under the influence. Not that this grandson, Raoul, who'd just been shot defending her was any prize—he was, in fact, the leader of one of the more notorious project gangs. She liked old Señora Martinez. She didn't want her idiot nephew to kill her in a drug-crazed stupor. She was going to mention the incident to a friend in law enforcement. Right now, she didn't dare call the local police because her name would go on the report. At least, she wasn't required to take any action. She closed the drawer back and locked it, putting the key over the door as usual.

"Is it over, Mommy?" Bernadette asked from the kitchen.

"For now," Sarina assured her, holding out her arms. She hugged her daughter close. "You must always be alert. You shouldn't sit on the porch alone, baby."

"I know. I'm sorry."

"We live in a bad place," Sarina said worriedly. She hadn't wanted to opt for an apartment in this low-rent area of town, but it had been necessary. Medical bills had forced her to seek such accommodations. She watched her daughter carefully, hoping that the upset wasn't going to trigger an attack, as Colby's harsh remarks had earlier in the week. But Bernadette wasn't upset at all. In fact, she was smiling.

"I like it here," Bernadette said surprisingly. "The

other kids play with me, and they don't make fun of me. Mommy, am I a person of color?"

Sarina laughed delightedly. "Well, yes, baby, you are," she had to admit. "You have Apache blood. Remember, what your grandfather told you about the Apache Women Warriors? You come from brave people!"

"Was my daddy brave?"

Sarina bit her tongue. "Of course he was," she said, forcing a smile.

"Why didn't he want me?" Bernadette asked.

"Bernadette…"

"I know, we don't ever talk about him. But my granddaddy loved him. He said my daddy was troubled and didn't know who he was."

"Those are deep observations, my darling," Sarina said.

"I saw that awful man get shot," Bernadette said out of the blue. "But when I asked him if his arm hurt, he was hateful to me."

Sarina frowned. "You saw which man get shot?"

"That awful man you kicked," she said. "He doesn't like me. Well, I don't like him, either. He's a horrible man!"

Sarina averted her eyes. Bernadette had made these strange comments about a dark man from time to time. Sarina knew she had visions, which very often were accurate. It was a gift she'd shared with her late paternal grandfather, who could also see things before they happened. But she hadn't known until today that Bernadette had that mental link with Colby Lane. It was vaguely terrifying.

She sat down heavily on the sofa. "What else did you see, Bernadette?" she asked seriously.

"He drank a lot of bad-smelling stuff from a bottle and a man he worked for hit him real hard," the child recalled. "Then he shot somebody and got shot back and his arm was all bloody. It was a place called Africa."

Sarina was stunned. "You saw that?"

Bernadette nodded. She pushed back a strand of long hair. "There was this woman, too. She went away and he got real upset."

Sarina's heart jumped. Maureen left him? She hated herself for the joy she felt, even momentarily. He'd never get over the other woman. That was a fact she had to face. He didn't want Sarina. He never had and he never would.

"What do you say we have a pizza tonight?" Sarina asked the child.

"Could we? With mushrooms?"

"You bet!" Sarina got up and looked out the window again, worriedly. "I guess it's safe to ask a defenseless pizza guy to come here."

"It's safe," Bernadette said with a grin. "I'll protect you, Mommy. Granddaddy said his father was a shaman, and that he had a brother who could see things before they happened, just like Granddaddy and me could."

"Well!" She hesitated, wondering how to bring up a worrying subject. "Bernadette, I want you to promise me something."

"What, Mommy?"

Sarina chewed her lower lip. "That man, today, the one you saw shot. I want you to promise me that you'll never, *never,* speak Apache in front of him."

The little girl frowned. "But, why?"

Sarina drew in a slow breath. "You mustn't ask me that. But you must promise. I know you'll keep your word."

The child nodded. "My granddaddy taught me that I must always do that." She looked at her mother quizzically, but finally she nodded. "Okay, Mommy, I promise."

Sarina smiled and hugged the little girl warmly. "I love you."

"I love you, too." She drew back. "Do you think Santa Claus would bring me a microscope for Christmas?"

Sarina laughed. "It's two months until Christmas. I suppose it isn't too early to be thinking about it. But the microscope you want is very expensive, baby," she added gently.

Bernadette laid a gentle hand on her mother's shoulder and looked very adult. "I know it costs a lot for my medicine," she began. "Maybe I could do without it..."

"No!" Sarina said at once.

"But it costs so much..."

Sarina hugged her close, her eyes closed as she imagined life without the new drugs, the way it had been. "I don't care what it costs."

Bernadette laid her head on Sarina's shoulder. "I wish I was like Nikki," she murmured. "She never gets sick."

Sarina's eyes closed. She wished, not for the first time, that she'd been able to take better care of the child in the beginning. The doctors had said that it made no difference, but Sarina didn't completely believe them. If anything happened to Bernadette, she'd die!

The child pulled away and looked into her parent's worried eyes. "Mommy, I'm all right," Bernadette assured her. "Really." She smiled. "I'm going to be a detective one day, working in a big city, and there's this very handsome man who's going to marry me. I dreamed it."

Sarina's eyes closed and she shivered. The child could truly see ahead. It was a relief, in a way.

"So you mustn't worry," Bernadette continued. She bit her lower lip. "I'm going to be fine." She didn't add that she had worries about her mother that she didn't dare share. She forced a smile. "Maybe Santa Claus will bring me that microscope anyway," she added, grinning. "In fact, I'm almost sure he will!"

"I don't know."

"It never hurts to ask. Right?"

Sarina got up, chuckling. "We'll see. Now, let's order that pizza!"

COLBY LANE went home to his small rented apartment and fixed himself a frozen dinner. He had a sudden urge for pizza and couldn't understand why.

He checked his telephone messages while the microwave cooked. There were no messages. He wasn't surprised. The only people he knew in town were the Hunters. He had no social life to speak of, no close friends except Tate Winthop. Tate was in D.C. now, with Cecily and their son, working for the government again—although not in any dangerous situations. Colby's father had died two years ago, although he hadn't known until he'd made a trip to the reservation the year before. He still had cousins there, but they were oddly reluctant to speak of his late father. All they'd told him was that the old man had lived in Tucson until his death. His body had been buried at the old Apache cemetery near his former home in a small, private ceremony. His cousins had been oddly reticent to speak of the ceremony.

He and his father hadn't spoken since he married Maureen. The old man hadn't approved of her, and

Colby had overreacted to the criticism. He and his father had never been really close. He'd loved his mother, but she'd died when he was very young and his father had started drinking and become brutal. He blamed the old man for everything. Now that he was older, and had been obsessed with a woman himself, he began to understand his father's behavior. He wished he'd made an effort to see the old man while there was still time. Now he was alone in the world. No wife, no kids, no parents. He had an uncle in Oklahoma and a cousin or two. He wouldn't have recognized them if he'd seen them on the street. It was a lonely sort of life.

When he and Maureen had married, he'd envisioned them being together for life with a houseful of kids. But she didn't want mixed blood kids. Just as well, he thought bitterly, since he was infertile. He thought about that little girl Bernadette, Sarina's daughter, who was Hispanic. He wondered who her father was, and how Sarina had managed to conceive a child after the nightmare of pain he'd given her on their wedding night. He'd had a couple of neat whiskies. He'd hoped it would be enough to leave him incapable. It wasn't. Long afterward, he'd left her in their hotel room, shivering under the covers, and he'd been eloquent about how he felt about the wedding that had been forced on him.

He'd gotten himself a separate hotel room afterward, ordered a whole fifth of Cutty Sark and finally passed out, dead drunk. He didn't awaken until the next day, and when he went to look for her with an uneasy conscience, she'd left. A letter had been sent to him the day after the quick wedding by some attorney, with a terse note from her father. Annulment papers would be mailed to him as soon as they could be drawn up, and they wanted an address to send them to. He gave them Maureen's. Obviously Sarina had been willing to lie about the marriage being consummated and he didn't give a damn. He'd sign their stupid papers. Maureen had called him the day he'd married Sarina to tell him she wanted to get married at once. He'd made some excuse and then he'd taken out his fury on Sarina. His conscience still troubled him.

He'd had a rushed assignment overseas before he and Maureen could get married. When he came back, she told him that she forged his name on the papers and the annulment had been granted, so they could get married right away. She had a friend who was a minister and he was willing to marry them. She had the license and everything. All he had to do was say the right words. Odd, that ceremony, he recalled. Maureen even kept the license. He hadn't seen it since. He assumed that she'd used it to get her own divorce. He'd signed some sort of papers, on tacky legal stationery. He didn't remember much of it. He'd been drinking back then, too.

He and Maureen had a feverish wedding night after their quickie wedding. She'd kept him at a distance all the time they were dating. The abstinence had been one reason he'd fallen on Sarina like a starving wolf, he recalled with shame. But Maureen had been an obsession. Once she was truly his, he'd had to leave her behind in Washington, D.C., for several months because he'd been given a new assignment overseas. Sarina's father had pulled strings to get him out of town. Right after that, he'd left military intelligence and gone to work with a group of mercenaries. The money had been fantastic, and he'd loved the adrenaline rushes. But that was over now.

He felt regret about Sarina. It must have taken a great deal of courage for her to risk intimacy with a man again, he thought. He hated the memory of what he'd done to that gentle young woman whose only crime had been to love him. None of what happened had really been her fault, even if he'd blamed her for it. The fault had been his own, for having too much to drink at the party they'd both attended, and letting them be discovered by her father and his associates in a compromising situation. He'd blamed her for that, but he shouldn't have.

She was still as attractive as ever, he mused. She was more mature, more independent, more spirited than the woman he'd once known who was owned by her rich father. He was surprised that she was working for a living. Her father had been worth twenty million dollars, and she was his only heir. He'd heard that Carrington had died six years earlier. He hadn't grieved, but he'd thought about Sarina finally being out from under his thumb, and with money of her own. He frowned, remembering how she dressed, how her daughter dressed. If there was money now, it didn't show in their clothing, or in the lowly position, probably poorly paid, that she held now.

The microwave buzzed and he pulled the instant dinner out of it. He had a small store of dinnerware and silverware that he'd brought from his apartment in D.C. He still lived like a Spartan. Old habits died hard. He didn't have possessions. A man who was constantly on the move couldn't afford to lug a houseful of stuff around with him.

Hunter had been, like himself, in the CIA, and then in freelance covert ops before he settled into security work. It had surprised him to find Hunter married and with a child. His wife was a knockout—a gorgeous blond geologist named Jennifer who was a cousin to the wife of old man Ritter's son, Cabe. The way Hunter and Jennifer felt about one another was obvious to a blind man. They'd been married for years, but the passion hadn't burned out, not by a long shot. Perhaps, he considered, some marriages did work out.

He thought about his own two failed marriages

and winced. He'd chosen badly. Maureen had nothing in common with him and she hadn't loved him. She'd loved what he could give her materially. Theirs had been an obsessive physical relationship that burned out a year down the road. He'd been determined to hold on, but in the end, he had to let her go. Admitting failure had cut up his pride. Maureen had been an obsession, but he'd learned that obsessive desire was no substitute for love. Sarina had loved him with all her heart, and he'd pushed her away brutally. Perhaps, he thought philosophically, he deserved the misery he'd endured. Certainly it had paid him back for the hurt he'd caused Sarina.

He finished his supper, had a shower, and went to bed early. In his youth, he could go night and day. Now, with his war wounds hurting like hell in the darkness, he had to take advantage of any drowsiness he was lucky enough to get. None of his comrades would recognize this worn-out soldier who made his living by protecting an oil company from thieves and drug smugglers. He felt far older than his years. Perhaps he should be grateful that he was still alive. Many of his friends no longer were.

JUST BEFORE LUNCH, Colby was walking by Sarina's office when he saw her in earnest conversation with the Hispanic man, Rodrigo Ramirez. Funny, they were obviously close but they didn't act like lovers. There was nothing like physical attraction in her regard, and her body language was interesting—she folded her arms tight around her chest and her expression was completely businesslike. If she was involved with the man, she was good at keeping things discreet.

Rodrigo was a puzzle as well. Colby had asked Hunter about him, only to be told that the man, a Mexican national, worked as a liaison between Eugene and an equipment company owned by Eugene's son, Cabe Ritter. It seemed a thin sort of connection, and an odd sort of job. For some reason, he didn't see Rodrigo at a desk job. He had the strangest feeling that he'd run across the man somewhere.

Sarina passed a file to Rodrigo and stood up. "That's all I've got so far," she said, her voice carrying in the deserted offices—it was lunchtime and most everyone else was already gone.

"I have more. I'll put it on a CD for you," Rodrigo replied in softly accented deep tones. "On a more personal note, you need to consider a move. Bernadette's too conspicuous a target."

"I can take care of Bernadette," she replied quietly. "I can't move. You know why."

"I could help you," he began.

She held up a hand. "Bernadette and I will manage. It's better now, anyway."

"Why can't I ever convince you to do the safe thing?" the Latin asked, his accent growing more prominent.

"Safe is for old women," she replied with a laugh. "Besides, this job is more important than any we've ever done."

"That it is," he had to agree. "I just don't like having you take point on the firing line."

"You never do, but it's my choice."

"You and your independence—" He broke off when he noticed Colby Lane approaching the door. He stood up and lifted an eyebrow. "Can I do something for you, Mr. Lane?" he asked formally, his deep voice faintly accented.

Colby glanced at Sarina. "I had a question for Miss Carrington," he replied. "Nothing urgent. It can wait."

"I have to go," Rodrigo replied, noting the time. "I'll call you," he told her.

She nodded.

When he left, she looked at Colby icily. "Yes?"

"What did he mean, about your daughter being at risk?" he asked.

Both thin eyebrows went up. "Is my daughter's welfare your business, Mr. Lane?"

"Drop the formal line," he said coldly. "We were married."

She laughed mirthlessly. "I've had headaches that lasted longer than our marriage did."

He stuck his hands in his pockets and stared her down. "What risk?" he repeated.

"We live in government housing," she said.

"There are gangs and last night there was a running gun battle while Bernadette was sitting on the porch. A neighbor boy was shot."

He scowled. "Why do you live there?"

She didn't share Bernadette's condition with outsiders. She didn't want to think about the night before, when she'd been awakened from a sound sleep and had to rush with Bernadette to the emergency room. It was Colby's fault, but he didn't know it and she wasn't going to tell him. "My daughter doesn't exactly blend in a white community," she said instead.

One eye narrowed dangerously. "Why are you living in such a place?" he persisted. "Your father was worth millions when he died, six years or so ago, and you were an only child."

"I'm not worth millions," she informed him.

"He must have left you something."

She just stared at him.

"Your child's father should be paying child support," he said, changing tacks.

"Chance would be a fine thing," she replied.

"Hunter said he was Hispanic," he persisted. "He must have relatives, or even friends. It shouldn't be hard to track him down."

God bless Hunter for that white lie, she was thinking. "Why don't you just do your job, Mr. Lane, and leave me alone to do mine?" she suggested, sitting back down.

"How did the child know about my arm?" he asked out of the blue, hoping to shock her into an answer. What Hunter had told him hadn't made sense.

She frowned. "What about your arm?" she asked, diverted.

She didn't know? He straightened. "She knew I was…wounded," he prevaricated.

"Oh." She studied his face curiously, but it gave away nothing. "I don't know," she lied. "Maybe somebody mentioned it to her."

Colby wondered who might know about his injury besides Hunter, but he let it slide. "Why can't you get something in a better section of town?"

"Bernadette's had enough prejudice already," she said reluctantly. "She's accepted in the Chicano community."

"Are you?" he chided.

"Surely you know that Chicanos can be fair as well as dark?" she taunted. "Besides, I fit in quite nicely. I'm literate in Spanish."

"You can read and write it as well as speak it?" he asked.

She nodded.

No wonder the child was fluent in that language. He was thinking about what she'd said, about prejudice. He'd hidden his ancestry most of his life to avoid it. Sarina didn't try to hide Bernadette's. But she was protective of the child, and obviously loved her. Why would she live in so dangerous a place?

"I'm sure Hunter could help you find a better apartment," he said.

"We're happy where we are. Or are you going to assure me that guns are only found in the minority communities?" she chided.

"They're not as likely to be used in a better neighborhood."

"Ha!" She turned on her computer.

"You're avoiding the issue."

She looked up at him, trying not to let her mind wander back to happier times. "You have no right to make it an issue," she said quietly.

He drew in a breath. "Fair enough."

She turned her attention back to the computer.

"Why did they send you here from Tucson, instead of just getting someone from Houston to fill in?"

"Are we doing an interview?" she asked, exasperated.

"Your daughter likes the Mexican. What's his name? Ramirez?"

She smiled deliberately. "I like Rodrigo, too," she said. "We've been friends for over three years. He's been good to us."

He didn't like that. He didn't know why. Perhaps he still had a faint sense of possession about Sarina. They had been married once, if only for a day and a night.

"You were in college," he said, remembering. "Didn't you finish?"

She had, but she wasn't telling him. "I dropped out," she lied.

"So this was the only job you could get, I suppose."

She nodded, glad that he couldn't read minds.

"You were your father's only child," he said, frowning. "I still don't understand why you're living like this."

"My father had emphatic ideas about what he wanted to do with his money," she said without resentment. She'd long since accepted her fate. "I don't mind working for a living."

He folded his arms across his chest. "I suppose you knew that Maureen and I divorced two years ago."

She looked up with a carefully blank expression. "How would I know that?"

"Hunter knew." He saw the faint flush in her cheeks. "He was my friend from childhood. I can't believe he never mentioned my name to you."

She didn't like remembering the shock the first time she'd heard Phillip mention his old friend Colby, when she and Jennifer were taking natural childbirth classes together. She'd admitted that she knew him, but she'd managed to keep their connection a secret. Phillip only knew that they'd dated and that Colby had provided security for her father. She'd asked Jennifer to tell Phillip not to mention Bernadette's real heritage to Colby, but she hadn't said why. Hunter was intelligent. He probably knew the truth.

Her eyes were even and cold. "He mentioned it only once. You were the one subject that the Hunters knew never to mention in front of me."

His eyelids flickered. That shouldn't have come as a surprise. But it did. "Point to you, Miss Carrington," he said quietly.

"This seems an odd sort of place for you to be working," she said suddenly, lifting her eyes. "It's a far cry from the military, isn't it?"

The past few years flashed before his eyes. He saw his wounds, his conflicts with political counterparts, his disillusionment with his life. "I don't like hospitals," he said, compromising with the truth.

She arched both eyebrows.

"I spent a lot of time in them between overseas assignments," he replied coolly.

Her eyes searched over him. "It doesn't show."

Obviously she didn't know that he wore a prosthesis, even if her daughter did. He was oddly reluctant to tell her.

"You wanted to be a diplomat as I recall," he said instead.

She shrugged. "We make choices, and then life gets in the way. I'm happy enough with the work I do."

He stared at her for a long moment, remembering happier times, camaraderie, even her quirky sense of humor. She was so staid now, so dignified, that he couldn't reconcile the woman he saw with the woman he'd once known so intimately.

"Take a picture," she said with a glare.

"You were like a bonfire seven years ago," he said absently. "Bright and glowing with life and fun."

She looked up, the anguish of the past years in her dark eyes, visible pain. "I grew up," she said.

He frowned. "How old are you now?"

She laughed hollowly. "What a question!"

"Answer it."

"I'm twenty-four," she ground out.

He stared without speaking. In his eyes was a shadow of pain. He actually winced. "You were seventeen when we married?"

His expression and the outburst were surprising. "You were in military intelligence," she pointed out. "I assumed you knew everything about me."

He didn't challenge her mistake about his military background. "I never checked you out, for Pete's sake, there was no reason to!" He pushed back a strand of faintly wavy black hair. "God! Seventeen! I thought you were older, experienced…!"

Her face closed up. She couldn't bear to remember the pain and humiliation of her first intimacy. She flushed as she fiddled with papers on her desk, for something to do.

"Sarina," he began, trying to find the words to

apologize. "You were in college. I thought you were in your early twenties. Considering your social status, and your background, and the age I thought you were—it never occurred to me that you didn't have some sexual experience."

"You didn't care what I had," she accused darkly. "You were furious that I'd, how did you put it, tricked you into marrying me by setting you up for my father to find us in a compromising situation. You couldn't do anything to him, so you made me pay for it."

His eyes darkened with anger. "I was upset, yes. But I didn't hurt you deliberately."

"Really?" She got to her feet, almost vibrating with anger. "It took four stitches!" she added with helpless venom.

That didn't register at first. Then it did. He vaguely remembered blood on the sheets, and had assumed that her period had started. But if it hadn't…

His face colored. He'd had a couple of neat whiskies to try to stop himself from touching her. It hadn't worked. His control had been precarious at best, and he'd blamed her for putting Maureen out of his reach with their unwanted wedding.

But he hadn't meant to hurt her physically. He drew in a long breath. Alcohol had been responsible for so much tragedy in his life. He hadn't realized it until he got into therapy and had his sins laid out by a psychologist.

His tortured expression disturbed her. Sarina sat back down, avoiding looking directly at him. "It was a long time ago," she ground out. "Never mind."

He searched for words to explain it, to tell her that Maureen had deserted him for weeks, for no reason that he ever knew. He'd been hurting inside and Sarina's presence was like a healing balm. Then, the very day he found himself married to her, Maureen had tracked down his friend Tate Winthrop and got his number. She'd called to tell him that she was ready to get married now. He'd been livid. Sarina had tricked him. He wanted revenge…but even so, he hadn't deliberately hurt Sarina. Or so he'd thought, all these years.

He blinked. The psychologist had told him that most of his problems had resulted from a guilty conscience, but not to do with Maureen. He drank to forget how he'd treated Sarina. The shame was so great that he'd never told anyone about her, not even his best friend, Tate.

Even now, when he looked at her, he remembered all over again how bright and lovely she'd been in those days. For one insane moment, in the midst of explosively delicious foreplay, he'd been tempted to let the marriage stand and let Maureen go her own way. The obstacles would have been impossible ones, though. He hadn't known how old Sarina really was. But he did know that she was the sheltered daughter of a multimillionaire, while he was mixed Apache-Comanche and poor, to boot. Besides that, he was in a profession that could cost him his life any day. She thought he was in the military. He wasn't. He worked for the CIA as a paramilitary contractor, a freelance agent who hired out as a counterterrorism and small arms specialist, to any government willing to meet his price. He'd been working for the American government when he met Sarina. He and Hunter had similar backgrounds, which was why they got along so well together. Sarina didn't know.

"There were obstacles you didn't know about at the time," he said finally, jamming his hands into his slacks pockets.

She didn't answer him. She was remembering those terrible days after he walked out of her life. Her father had demanded an annulment, and Sarina had been too hurt and angry to refuse. She'd had to lie about their one intimacy. Colby hadn't ventured a single objection. After one reluctant phone call, full of recriminations and not even one apology, Colby had left her.

"You must have hated me," Colby ventured with narrowed eyes.

She didn't look at him. "It was wasted energy. I very soon learned how to channel it into more positive areas."

"Such as working as a clerk for an oil company?" he replied, irritated.

"It pays the bills."

"Not very well, considering that piece of salvage you call a car."

She lifted her head and glared at him. "Don't you have something to investigate?"

He shrugged. "I suppose so."

She turned back to her work, ignoring him.

He watched her for a few seconds, with more misgivings and sadness than he was willing for her to see. He turned and walked out.

HUNTER WAS WAITING for him in his office when he got there. The other man was preoccupied.

"Something wrong?" Colby asked.

Hunter shrugged. "Something. Cobb's just found out that the DEA's got two undercover agents in place here."

"Who are they?"

"Damned if I know, and he won't tell me. He was hopping mad when he found out. He says they came in from another district, following a suspect who works for us. Nobody told him a thing because he told the drug task force that he had a leak in his department."

"That's probably for the agents' safety, if there's a leak in his department," Colby suggested.

"No doubt. There's something else. We've got an employee who's involved with the woman who took over Manuel Lopez's empire."

"That would be Brody Vance," Colby said easily, smiling when Hunter looked surprised. "I was with you when we invaded the warehouse with Cobb and his task force," he reminded the other man. "Vance bailed Cara Dominguez out of jail later."

"Yes, he did." Hunter's lips compressed. "I should have had Cobb get a warrant to wiretap his office."

"He's smart," Colby replied. "He probably thinks that's already been done."

"Could be. But we need to keep our eyes on Vance."

"I could rig a wire in his car," Colby mused aloud. "I can do it in a way that he'll never suspect, and stick a homing device in as well, so that we can track his movements."

"I don't know if we can get a judge to let us do that," Hunter said.

Colby stuck his hands in his pockets. "Suppose I do it without your knowledge?"

"Creative thinking," Hunter replied with twinkling dark eyes.

"Do we know anybody in the office that he's close to?"

"He was hitting on Cobb's girlfriend. But he's given her up, apparently, since she's been seen so much with Cobb. Which brings to mind something else Cobb told me. He says she has great skills as a cybertech."

"If she's that good at it, she's wasted on working for Vance."

"True. Why don't we make use of those skills, then," Hunter suggested. "Perhaps Mr. Vance is doing something sneaky with his e-mail. We retain the right to inspect all company e-mails here, including personal ones. It wouldn't be illegal."

Colby smiled, showing perfect white teeth. "In which case," he replied, turning, "I'll just go and have a word with Jodie."

"And I'll check the employee dossiers and find out which employees came here from out of town," the other man murmured to himself, because Colby had already left.

He did that, his eyes widening with surprise when he realized how many secrets their friend Sarina had been keeping from them. He knew that she didn't want Colby to know about her past, and he wouldn't tell. With an efficiency that would have surprised Colby, he changed the records in the master computer so that Colby wouldn't luck upon a connection that would reveal too much to his old friend. He didn't even feel guilty for doing it.

CHAPTER THREE

COLBY HAD JODIE start looking for anything incriminating in Brody Vance's e-mails, cautioning her to say nothing about the assignment. She agreed readily and seemed to look forward to the challenge.

Meanwhile, Colby waited near a canteen window at lunch and watched to see which car Vance got into. As he'd suspected, the personnel manager had just traded cars, probably to throw any interested persons off the track, since his car had been seen at the warehouse the night of the drug raid. Now he was driving a late-model Lincoln, gray in color. He thought back wistfully to the days when he had contacts at the DMV and could have someone run a tag for him anytime he liked. Now that he was working in the private sector, he was limited—especially in this new job in a new city. Probably he could have had Hunter do it for him, but his pride wouldn't let him. He felt his status keenly in these early days. He had to prove himself. That meant doing his own investigating.

At midafternoon he paused for a cup of coffee and a sweet roll in the canteen while he formulated ways and means of getting into the man's car without being seen. At least he wouldn't have to have help with that. Covert action was his stock in trade. He became aware of activity near him. It was just after school and Rodrigo walked in with Sarina's daughter by one hand, and a box of colored pencils and a small pad in the other. He seated her at a table, put the art supplies on the table, whispered something that made her smile, and left.

The child made Colby uneasy. She glanced at him with a mutinous pair of dark eyes and an expression that made him feel guilty. He didn't like it. He was sorry he'd made her cry. She didn't have to rub it in. Worse, he didn't understand his own bad attitude toward the child. He'd always thought he loved children. Perhaps it was the knowledge that he couldn't father one that affected him so blatantly.

He finished his roll and sipped black coffee, his eyes idly studying the child while she drew and colored on sheets of white paper. He wondered if Eugene Ritter knew that his workplace was being used as a day care center for his employees. Or one of them, at least. It wasn't any of his business, really.

But it felt as if Sarina was making a point, at his expense; she was showing him that she could use the canteen as her daughter's private playground and Colby couldn't stop her. The thought was irritating.

He drifted off for a few minutes, thinking about bugging Vance's car and the equipment he'd have to pick up at a local electronics store. He missed his former job. It had been dangerous, but never boring. He wondered, and not for the first time in the past two years, how he was going to adjust to daily routine. His time as security chief for Hutton had been interesting, but there were few challenges. At least bugging a car gave him a little taste of the old life.

He finished his coffee, cold by now, and popped the cup into a trash can near the door. The child was intent on her coloring, ignoring him. She irritated him almost as much as her mother did, he thought bitterly. He didn't understand why. Then he got a glimpse of what she was drawing and his whole body clenched. She really did have talent. The figures, despite their childish creator, were recognizable. She'd drawn a jungle scene, of a figure wearing dark glasses and a camouflage uniform manning what looked like a machine gun on a trail between two large trees. They were plane trees. African plane trees. Colby had more reason than she could ever know to be upset by the drawing.

He glared down at her, tall and intimidating. Bernadette looked up at him, and her former accusing gaze went into eclipse when she saw his expression. She sat very still.

"Who told you about this place?" he demanded, as he swept the drawing up in his hand. "And this man?" he added, turning the drawing toward her. "Answer me!"

He was scary like that, she thought. Nobody had ever been so harsh with her. The resentment and anger she felt translated into fear as he glared down at her. "No…nobody told me," she said in a hurt whisper. He was really mad. She didn't know what to say.

"Nobody, the devil," he ground out, his eyes pained as they went back to the drawing. It made his whole body tense. He remembered Sarina saying that the child had visions. He hadn't believed her. But what other explanation was there for the drawing? His arm throbbed just looking at it.

She sat watching him, gnawing on her lower lip.

His hand clenched on the drawing as he became aware of her unblinking scrutiny. "You don't belong in here, anyway. This is no day care center," he added icily. "It's a business."

She swallowed hard, her eyes as big as saucers. She didn't speak. She strained to get a decent breath of air in her lungs. Her eyes grew brighter with the struggle.

That made him angrier.

His dark eyes narrowed and he didn't smile. "Go

to your mother's office and stay there," he said in a cold, commanding tone.

She got up quickly, grabbing at her paper and pencils, dropping one in her haste. She scrambled to pick it up. When she turned to go quickly out of the room, Colby saw tears on her cheeks. Her breathing was actually audible.

He cursed under his breath. The child had feelings of glass. He hadn't meant to sound that threatening. He wasn't used to children and this one disturbed him. How did she know where he'd been shot? How did she know what the man who'd shot him looked like? His arm throbbed again as he stared at the scene that brought back so many painful memories of Africa. He glared at the drawing and started to crumple it. Then, involuntarily, he folded it and put it in his shirt pocket instead. The child knew more about him than anyone except Hunter and his friend Tate Winthrop, and she knew it in ways that were eerie and disturbing.

Every time he saw her, he remembered that he couldn't father a child. He felt less than a man. Sarina's presence upset him more, bringing back all his failings with a vengeance. But that was no reason to take it out on the little girl. Nor was her uncanny gift for seeing into his private life. He shouldn't have been so curt with her. He felt guilty all over again as he watched her scrub her eyes with a little fist. It was like a knife through his heart. He could almost feel the pain…

Cursing under his breath, he started toward the retreating child just as Rodrigo Ramirez came back into the canteen. He stopped dead when he saw Bernadette. His black eyes flashed angrily as he connected Colby's stern expression with Bernadette's tears. He bent and picked her up, cuddling her close. Colby could hear her rasping sobs all the way across the room. The sound went through his tall body like a bullet.

Rodrigo tucked the child under his chin and walked straight at Colby with a stride that meant business. His black eyes were murderous. The mild-mannered clerk Colby had found vaguely pathetic was suddenly somebody else.

"If you have something to say to Bernadette, you can say it to me," Rodrigo said icily, his Spanish accent thicker in anger.

"The canteen isn't an appropriate place for a child to play," Colby said curtly.

"Eugene Ritter gave Sarina permission to bring Bernadette here in the afternoons," he replied. "She can't afford day care—it would take her entire weekly salary to put Bernadette in care." It wasn't the whole truth, but it was all Rodrigo felt comfortable telling this stranger.

Colby frowned. He hadn't known it was that expensive.

"If you have a problem, I'll inform Mr. Ritter," Rodrigo continued in a soft, threatening tone. "But if you say one word to Bernadette about her presence here ever again, rent-a-cop," he added with deliberate insolence, "I will kick your ass from one end of this building to the other."

"You're welcome to try, Ramirez," Colby replied just as coldly. Like the Latino, he didn't back down an inch, even when he knew he was in the wrong.

"That day may come sooner than you think," Rodrigo said in a soft, dangerous tone.

Colby's eyes narrowed. "Gee, see me shaking with fear!" he drawled contemptuously.

Rodrigo bit off a word in Spanish that made Bernadette's eyebrows lift. He flushed when he realized what he'd said to Colby, his lips making a thin line as he turned abruptly to carry the child out of the canteen.

Colby watched them go. He hadn't expected such a threatening stance from a man he'd considered one step below a filing clerk. Colby wondered again why Ramirez seemed so familiar. That scene Bernadette had drawn, quite competently, was a landscape in South Africa. Colby remembered the location well. It was where he'd lost his arm. There was no way on earth the child could have known that. So how could she have drawn it?

He couldn't get the sound of her raspy sobs out of his mind. It was unnatural, the way she sounded, and familiar. He'd had asthma as a child. He'd outgrown it, but there had been many trips to the local clinic before then, especially when he was upset.

He went back to his office in a daze of misery. He sat down behind his desk and stared blankly at the wall. His arm hurt like hell. The doctor who made the prosthesis said that the phantom pain was incurable. He could still feel his hand, even though it was no longer there. The doctor explained that the nerve endings in the brain that controlled that hand were still intact. So to his brain, he still possessed his hand. It was something he'd had to learn to live with. It hadn't been easy.

The door opened and he looked up into Hunter's dark eyes.

"Ritter wants to see you," he said.

Colby got up. "It won't take much imagination to know why," he said heavily. "I didn't mean to make her cry again."

Hunter's eyebrows arched. "Excuse me?"

"Bernadette," he said, seeing again the small face covered in tears. "I said the canteen wasn't a day care center. She didn't even fight back this time, she got up and left." He grimaced. "Sarina's friend Rodrigo said that Ritter gave her permission."

Hunter nodded. "He did. For more reasons than I can tell you right now," he added. His eyes narrowed. "Just a word of advice. You don't want to give Rodrigo an excuse to make an enemy of you. He's not what he seems."

"I noticed that. He's not my idea of a liaison officer. So, who is he?" Colby asked shortly.

Hunter hesitated. "I can't tell you that, either. I know." He held up a hand when Colby's lips thinned. "It's frustrating for me, too. I trust you. But Cobb and Mr. Ritter don't know you as well as I do."

"How the hell am I supposed to work security here when I don't know what's going on around me?"

"You'll have to trust me to keep you pointed in the right direction until I can fill you in. But stop picking on Bernadette or even I won't be able to save you," Hunter added firmly. "You used to be able to recognize a hornet's nest before you stuck your head into it."

"I used to have a real job, too," he returned with impotent fury. "When I was faster, younger, stronger...when I had two arms!"

Hunter let out a long breath. "It wasn't easy for me, either, at first," he said in a softer tone. "I had hell fitting into a private sector job. But I managed, because I had to. You'll manage, too. Just try not to take everything so seriously. One child in a canteen for a couple of hours isn't going to bring down the corporation. Is it?"

Colby grimaced. "She throws out challenges without saying a word. She knows things she shouldn't know. It occurred to me that her mother might have sent her into the canteen on purpose, to get under my skin. She's antagonistic."

"Sarina isn't petty," Hunter replied. "She fights face-on, not behind your back. She's had a hell of a hard life. Cut her some slack, Colby."

Colby glowered. "Some hard life! Her father was a multimillionaire..."

"Her father," Hunter said furiously, "put her in the street when she refused to have an abortion," he bit off, noting Colby's sudden stillness. "He didn't want a mixed-blood child to dilute his perfect bloodlines. He cut her off without a penny. Later, when she had complications and wasn't able to work, he refused any help, knowing that she couldn't even afford food and rent and had nobody else to turn to! She almost lost Bernadette. It's a miracle she didn't die in child-birth!"

Colby stared at him blankly. The revelations shocked him. "There are government agencies that help people in trouble," he argued.

"Right. A millionaire's daughter whose face is familiar to people on the street walks into a welfare office and asks for financial aid and they're going to cut her a check," Hunter scoffed. "They laughed her out of the office. They thought it was a joke."

"Then, what about the child's father?" Colby persisted.

Hunter hesitated. He averted his eyes. "The father wouldn't do anything. He denied that the child was his. He told Sarina never to call him again." He wasn't supposed to know that. Sarina had told Jennifer in confidence. But Jennifer had no secrets from Hunter. Hunter could have bitten his tongue. He shouldn't have told Colby.

"The cold-blooded son of a bitch," Colby breathed harshly. "Why didn't she file charges against him? A simple blood test would have confirmed paternity. At least he owed her child-support!"

"Nobody could find him."

"Don't hand me that," Colby muttered. "Any half-baked detective could have tracked him down through his relatives!"

"The father lived out of state," Hunter said shortly. "Sarina didn't try to find him after that one attempt. She said that if he didn't want his child, it didn't matter, because she did. Bernadette is her whole life." Hunter checked his watch. "We'd better get cracking. Ritter doesn't like to be kept waiting."

Colby had a suspicion that Hunter knew a lot more about Bernadette's missing father than he was willing to say.

"Rodrigo looks familiar," he murmured as they walked down the hall.

"Does he?" Hunter asked in a deliberately light tone.

Colby stuck his hands in his pockets. "He loves that child," he said, thinking aloud. "He was ready to deck me for what I said to her."

"He'd marry Sarina in a minute if she'd have him," Hunter replied. "She won't. She has nothing to do with men."

Colby's high cheekbones flushed with embarrassed guilt. He was glad his friend was looking the other way. He knew, as Hunter didn't, why Sarina had nothing to do with men. But it raised another question. How had she managed to get involved with Bernadette's father, after the pain he'd caused her?

WHEN HE GOT TO RITTER'S office, the silver-haired elderly man wasn't alone. He had Alexander Cobb's family friend, Jodie, in his office as well. The young woman was flushed and traces of anger were still visible in her eyes.

Ritter gave Colby a look that promised retribution at a later date, but he didn't say a word about Bernadette at the moment.

"Miss Clayburn has just quit her job as Brody Vance's assistant," Ritter said with a wry smile, "so we're rehiring her as a computer expert. Cobb says she's on a par with cybercrime experts in his agency," he added. "I'd like to put her to work doing extensive background checks on certain employees."

"We've got a member of the drug lord's team working here, haven't we, sir?" Colby asked Ritter.

"Almost certainly," Ritter replied. "After what happened in our own warehouse, I'm convinced that we've still got an illegal shipment of drugs hidden somewhere as well. We had a close call."

"Colby and I had a closer one," Hunter murmured dryly with a smile at Jodie Clayburn. "If Miss Clayburn hadn't driven that car right into one of the drug smuggler's accomplices, Colby and I would both be dead right now—and so would DEA senior agent Alexander Cobb."

Jodie smiled. "I still can't believe I did that," she pointed out. "I'm much better at fighting crime with computers than cars."

"That's what you'll be doing from now on," Ritter told her, and outlined her salary and responsibilities.

She accepted the new job at once, and thanked Eugene. Hunter walked her out to her car. She could finger the female member of the drug smuggling team, who was Brody Vance's girlfriend, and she'd actually planted a bug for Cobb under the woman's table at a local coffee house and obtained evidence of drug smuggling. Cara had been arrested, but Jodie was in danger. Cobb was taking her down to his ranch in Jacobsville for a few days for safekeeping. It was Brody Vance who'd let Cara Dominguez into the warehouse parking lot in the first place. He'd bailed Cara out of jail, and pretended innocence. But Ritter knew he had to be involved somehow.

Ritter sat back in the conference room chair and glowered at Colby Lane when they were alone.

"I know," Colby said on a sigh. "I've been unreasonable about the child. But there's an excuse, even if it isn't much of one." He got up, pulled the drawing Bernadette had made out of his pocket, unfolded it and placed it on the polished wood surface of the boardroom table in front of Eugene Ritter.

"So? It's a drawing," Ritter said, puzzled, as his blue eyes met Colby's dark ones. "The child has talent. Why are you showing it to me?"

Colby's face tautened. "That—" he put his finger on the man in fatigues with the machine gun in the drawing "—is the SOB who shot my arm to pieces in Africa! And this," he added, indicating the path between two tall trees, "is where it happened."

Ritter frowned. "You told the child?"

"I told her nothing," he returned curtly. "I've told no one. There were eight other people with me in Africa, including Hunter, who saw it go down. None of them ever discussed it with anyone else, much less a little girl!"

Ritter sat back in his chair heavily. He didn't know what to say.

"The day I first saw her, in the hall here, she came right up to me and said that if I hadn't moved so slowly, I wouldn't have lost my arm," Colby added heavily.

"I...don't understand," Ritter murmured.

"Neither do I," Colby said flatly. "I'm sensitive about my handicap," he added. "I don't discuss it with anyone except Hunter and my old comrades."

"Perhaps her mother told her...?"

"I haven't seen her mother for almost seven years," Colby interrupted, and then clamped his jaw shut, because Ritter hadn't known there was a prior relationship.

Eugene's silver eyebrows arched. "You knew Sarina before you came to work here?"

Colby picked up the drawing and took his time refolding it. "We were married once. Briefly."

"The child..." Ritter began at once.

"...is not mine," Colby said firmly, in a tone that didn't invite further speculation.

"You're sure of that?" Eugene plowed right ahead.

Colby's eyes lowered to the boardroom table. "I'm sterile," he said in a haunted tone.

Ritter's indrawn breath was audible. "I'm sorry. I have two sons. I can't imagine not having them." He stood up. "But none of this is a reason to make Bernadette's life difficult. She takes enough heat from other students without getting it here where her mother works as well."

Colby scowled. "Heat from other students?" he asked blankly, before he remembered what Sarina had said about putting the child in a predominantly Hispanic school.

Eugene's eyes were old and wise. "Didn't you have problems in grammar school?"

"I went to a grammar school on the reservation," he replied. "All Apache."

"Well, Bernadette isn't so lucky," the old man told him. "She's had her problems with prejudice, in Arizona and now here. It's one reason Sarina moved into a heavily Hispanic district. Bernadette fits in there better than she does in a predominantly white school. In fact," he added, "Hunter's daughter, Nikki, goes to the same school. They've had their own problems."

Colby put the drawing back into his pocket. "That doesn't explain why she has to stay in the canteen in the afternoons," he said slowly.

"Day care costs as much a week as Sarina makes," Eugene said flatly.

Colby stared at the older man. "What if a woman had two or three kids?"

"It would cost more than she made at most clerical positions to put them in day care, I suppose."

"That's not right," Colby said harshly.

He shrugged. "Tell the government. Meanwhile, I let Bernadette sit in the canteen, where she's no trouble. It's my corporation. I can do what I like in it, within reason." His blue eyes narrowed. "And you won't cause her any more problems, will you, Lane?"

"No, sir, I won't," Colby replied quietly. "I didn't understand the situation at all."

"None of us understands it," Eugene muttered, turning. "How any man could turn his back on a beautiful child like that is beyond my comprehension."

"I know what you mean."

"Well, let's go through the warehouse one more time," he told Colby, "and see what we can turn up."

"Right behind you, sir."

THE SECURITY GUARD who'd let the drug smugglers into the warehouse was in jail pending arraignment. Ritter and Colby talked to the other two security guards, who maintained that they hadn't seen anything suspicious. They did a cursory search, but turned up nothing that looked like drugs.

Ritter contemplated having the warehouse searched inch by inch, but Colby felt that constant surveillance would yield better results. He recommended the placement of additional hidden cameras and recording devices, which would be unknown even to the security guards.

The suggestion made Eugene grin. He agreed at once, and Colby felt better about his earlier faux pas.

BUT HE WENT BACK to his office feeling vaguely uncomfortable, still, about the way he'd upset Bernadette.

He'd taken out his .40 caliber automatic Glock, checked the clip, and was cocking it when Sarina walked in without knocking. She stopped dead in the doorway as he put on the safety and stuck the pistol back into its holster on the opposite side of his belt.

Sarina stared at the gun. She hadn't realized that Colby would carry one on the job, but it was stupid not to have anticipated it. The Glock was the preferred weapon of many law enforcement agencies. You could drop one in a mud puddle and it would still fire.

But she wasn't supposed to know that, so she kept her mouth shut and folded her arms over her chest.

"I know why you're here," Colby said without preamble. "Your friend Ramirez and Mr. Ritter have both had a bite of me. So go ahead."

He'd taken the wind out of her sails. He didn't even look hostile.

"Why did you upset her this time?" she asked instead.

He pulled the drawing out of his pocket, unfolded it, and handed it to her.

She blinked. She didn't understand it. She frowned up at him. "It's a jungle," she began.

He shucked his jacket, unbuttoned his sleeve and shot it up.

She actually gasped when she saw where the prosthesis met the remaining portion of his left arm, just below his elbow, and all the blood ran out of her face.

Her reaction made him uncomfortable. Maureen

had found the prosthesis repulsive, too, not that it had mattered. He'd lost his arm after they'd separated. He'd given in to her decision to maintain a separate residence with bad grace and stayed drunk for a long time afterward. She'd lived with the man she later married, and became pregnant in defiance. Colby had given in to the divorce at once when he knew that, but she'd been oddly careless about it, and she'd never shared the final papers with him. She'd acted as if her marriage to Colby didn't even exist.

It was during that separation that he'd lost his arm. He hadn't touched a woman intimately since the shooting. Obviously Sarina found him distasteful as well. It shouldn't have bothered him, they were worlds apart now; but it did.

He dragged the sleeve down savagely and refastened it. "I was on assignment in Africa a few years ago, one of several assignments I took there. That—" he gestured toward the drawing "—is where it happened. It was just after Maureen moved out. I developed a serious drinking problem. Our unit ran into an ambush that all our intelligence hadn't prepared us for. I wasn't quick enough to get out of the way. My arm was shot to pieces, although one of our team walked right into the machine gun nest and took it out. If he hadn't, I'd be dead. We had a doctor in our group who did the amputation. We were miles from a hospital and blood poisoning set in. If there hadn't been a small clinic nearby where our doctor had access to surgical instruments and antibiotics, I'd be dead. It isn't a memory I particularly enjoy."

She stared again at the drawing. "Nobody told Bernadette about any of that," she said.

"I'm not totally stupid," he shot back. "I do realize that."

She bit her lower lip, hard. "I'm sorry. I'm certain that she didn't mean it to be upsetting."

"Are you?" He laughed curtly. "She doesn't like me. I've already made an enemy of her. She gave me a look that could have fried bread, and then she drew this."

She frowned worriedly. "She isn't vindictive," she said, but without real conviction. Her daughter had a regrettable temper.

"Maybe she isn't, consciously." He studied her curiously, remembering what Hunter had said about her life. "You could have hired a private detective and found Bernadette's father, forced him to pay child support," he said bluntly.

Her eyelids flickered, but she didn't betray the unsettling feeling that remark provoked in her. Her arms folded tighter. "I had all the trouble I could handle, at the time," she said quietly.

"Things are different now." He perched on the edge of his desk, his black eyes narrow and thoughtful. "I can find him, if you want me to."

Her face went pale. "I don't," she said firmly, and wouldn't look him in the eye. "It's ancient history."

"Not when you can't even afford day care," he retorted.

Her eyes blazed. "That is none of your business," she said hotly.

"Anyone who comes into the building is my business, especially now." He stood up. "We've got drug smugglers running around here with automatic weapons," he said.

"Yes, I heard about the shoot-out," she replied. "Miss Clayburn saved your life." She didn't add that her heart had almost stopped beating when she realized he could have died before she even knew he was here. All those years of pain and heartache, and she couldn't stop worrying about him.

"Mine and Hunter's and Cobb's," he agreed. "If they're in the right sort of mood, drug smugglers will take out anything moving—including a child."

She knew more about that than he realized. "I hardly think they're likely to attack the canteen," she pointed out.

"A week ago, I might have agreed with you." He moved close to her suddenly, and she gazed up at him, too surprised to react.

He stared down at her with angry dark eyes, memory haunting him as he recalled how she'd looked that one night, with her long blond hair around her head on the pillow, her brown eyes shocked as he touched her intimately, her gasp of pleasure followed by a moan so graphic…!

He groaned under his breath as he saw the helpless attraction on her face. Amazing, he thought, after what he'd done to her.

His right hand went hesitantly to her soft, flushed cheek and rested there gently. His dark eyes were full of shadows. "I've made a hell of a lot of mistakes in my life," he said quietly. "I guess I didn't think about the damage I did."

She stared back at him, a little unnerved by the contact, but too helplessly enthralled to move away from it. His touch still had the power to make her hungry. "You and Maureen left a trail of broken lives behind you and never looked back," she accused huskily. "It's a little late for an attack of conscience."

"What do you mean, broken lives?" he asked curiously.

Her face closed up. "Maybe you'll find out one day," she said. Her voice shook as his thumb smoothed gently over her lower lip.

He watched her reaction with almost clinical curiosity. "I drank like a fish," he said unexpectedly. "I got into fights. I lost jobs. I ended up as close to the bottom as a man can get without dying. Then my best friend's girl got me into therapy and I began to realize that I was self-destructive. Even so, it took a long time for me to get my life back together. I was obsessed with Maureen."

She drew away from the pressure of his hand. Maureen, again. It was always Maureen. Why did it still hurt, after all those years? "Perhaps if you'd stayed sober, you'd still be with her."

His voice was thick with pain when he said, "She didn't want my children. She didn't approve of racial mixing."

She almost bit her tongue trying not to react to that statement.

"So I suppose it was just as well that I was sterile," he concluded heavily. "My lifestyle wasn't conducive to fatherhood, anyway."

"Lots of kids grow up in the military without major problems," she pointed out.

He hesitated. His eyes narrowed. "Sarina, I wasn't exactly in the military."

She blinked. "But you were, when you were guarding my father. You were in military intelligence…"

"That was my cover story. Actually I was working for the CIA," he interrupted, "as a specialist in counterterrorism, private security and hostage negotiation. Hunter and I worked together for the Company for a few years, just after I met you."

She stared at him, trying to reconcile what he was saying with what she thought she knew about him. "You were a… spy?"

He shrugged. "In a manner of speaking. Your father had clandestine ties to a foreign government and threats had been made. We were called in."

She was speechless. She hadn't known that.

"Afterward," he continued quietly, "I was in a…conflict overseas, helping support a small African government against a potential military coup when I got drunk, got careless and lost my arm." He didn't mention that he'd worked in Africa as a mercenary. He didn't want her to know everything about his past. Not yet.

She leaned against the door facing. "Bernadette saw it," she said uneasily. "I didn't realize at the time that it was you. But she saw it happen. She told me about it the first day you were here."

"Yes," he replied, searching her eyes. "And she'd never seen me in her life. So my question is this—how did she know such an intimate thing about a total stranger?"

CHAPTER FOUR

SARINA WASN'T TOUCHING that question. Bernadette had a solid link to Colby and she didn't dare elaborate on why. "I don't know," she said evasively.

"Has she done this before?" he persisted.

She hesitated. She didn't want to tell him how proficient Bernadette was at reading the future. She remembered that Colby's father had the same gift, and that Colby must certainly know about it. She didn't dare risk having Colby know so much about the child. "She did dream that her grandfather was going to die," she said, downplaying her daughter's amazing gift.

"Your father?"

"No. Her…father's father."

He scowled. "You knew him?"

She turned away. "It's none of your business now," she said. "My private life is just that—private."

"Why couldn't he find Bernadette's father, then?" he demanded.

"Because his son hated him," she returned, glaring at him over her shoulder. "They'd had no contact for years."

He understood that situation. He and his own father hadn't spoken for years before the older man's death. He searched her face, noticing the lines, the dark circles under her eyes. She looked older than her years. He recalled what Hunter had said about the life she'd had.

"Everybody turned against you," he said softly, frowning. "You were a sweet, loving woman. You never deserved such treatment."

Her expression was unreadable. "What was it you used to say? That whatever doesn't kill you makes you stronger? I got stronger."

His gaze slid down her body. She was just as desirable as she'd been when he first knew her. But he'd cheated her. He couldn't blame her for hating him. He drew in a long breath. "Of all my mistakes," he murmured, "you're my biggest. I should never have touched you."

"I never understood why you did," she added coldly.

He couldn't admit that he'd been feverishly hungry for her, despite their forced nuptials. Even the anger hadn't stopped him. He hated knowing that he'd hurt her that badly. His face hardened. "Know what the psychologist said? She said that Maureen wasn't my problem…my problem was you. What I did to you drove me right into a downward spin. I thought you were experienced. I do have some memory of the things I said to you when I left you."

So did she. She couldn't manage to meet his eyes when she recalled them.

"Maureen was just an excuse I gave myself for drinking," he said heavily, "because it hurt too much to dig deeper into my past."

She wanted to believe him. She couldn't. His passion for Maureen had been too much a part of their lives. And apparently he still didn't know what Maureen had done to get Colby. She turned away.

"You don't believe it."

She shook her head. "I was never more than a footnote in your life. We both know that. Anyway, it doesn't matter now. Move on, Colby," she said with a trace of humor in her voice. "I have."

He actually winced as she walked away from him.

THE QUESTION OF HOW Bernadette knew about his arm haunted him. His behavior toward the child did, too. She had spirit. He couldn't forget those black eyes spitting fire when she called him a man-killer. She was no coward. She was back in the canteen the next day, but Colby was careful not to go near it. He didn't want to upset her again. It had hurt him that she cried. She seemed to be a tough, intelligent child. It wouldn't do to hurt her proud spirit. He'd been very much like her at her age.

Things had progressed in the drug smuggling case. Colby and Hunter were privy to a piece of tape on which Cara Dominguez met with an associate in a retro coffeehouse called The Beat, courtesy of DEA agent Alexander Cobb's friend, Jodie Clayburn. It turned out that Cara did know something about the missing shipment of drugs, but she was careful not to tell her associate very much. Perhaps she suspected that Jodie's presence in the coffeehouse wasn't totally innocent. She'd been out of jail on bail on drug smuggling charges, but she suddenly skipped town and vanished. Cobb subsequently fired one of his agents, a man named Kennedy, for passing information to the smugglers. Kennedy had been arrested, along with the warehouse security guard. Cobb knew that was one of the leaks he'd been searching for. But Cy Parks had said that there were a couple of leaks among government sources. Colby knew that Cobb wasn't dead certain that Cara didn't have any more "moles" in his office, so he kept a lot of information from Colby and even from Hunter.

Colby and Hunter were still looking for that shipment of drugs, certain that they were somewhere in Ritter's warehouse. But they couldn't find them, not even when they had drug-sniffing dogs brought in covertly by a member of Cobb's drug task force. The dogs walked around the rows and rows of boxes on pallets, but they didn't give any signal at all. One of them nosed the wall a time or two, but Colby figured out why easily—some male dog had managed to get into the place and hiked his leg on it. If one dog left a urine trail, every other male dog who came along would add his scent to it. The drugs had to be in one of the higher boxes, but it would require a lot of lifting and a lot of examination to find anything at all. Considering the size of the warehouse, it would have given several employees job security for half a year. Ritter couldn't spare the manpower or the time to go through every box on the place.

"I know the drugs are here, damn it!" Hunter muttered late Friday.

"We'll find them," Colby assured him.

"Think so?" He glanced at his watch and grimaced. "I've got to leave."

"It's half an hour until quitting time," Colby pointed out.

"Nikki's in a play tonight at her school," the other man replied. "She and Bernadette have major parts in a play for the Harvest Festival."

"Ritter said that they go to the same school."

Hunter nodded, his expression wry. "She and Bernadette are best friends. Nikki likes the school a lot. So do we and Sarina."

They passed by the canteen, where Bernadette was busy drawing.

"She's really good with an art pencil," Colby said with reluctant praise.

"And not only with pencil and paper," Hunter replied. "You should hear her sing. She has the voice of an angel."

It was odd, Colby thought, that he should feel pride in the child, when he'd given her nothing more than hostility. There was a disturbing link between them. Few knew about his private life; he seldom shared it. But the child was, somehow, right inside it.

"Is she singing tonight?"

Hunter glanced at him curiously. "As a matter of fact, she has a solo."

Colby shifted his weight restlessly. "Where is this school?" he asked. "And can anyone go to see the program, or do you have to be a parent?"

Hunter smiled to himself. "You can go with Jennifer and me if you'd like to."

Colby hesitated. He didn't know how Sarina or the child would react to his presence. But he was curious. Very curious. "Yes," he said after a minute. "I would."

"I'm going home early because we've got plumbers coming. Jennifer has to drop Nicole off at five, to get ready for the program. Come over to the house about six and we can go together. That suit you?"

Colby nodded. "I'll be there." He turned back toward his office. He didn't look at the older man. "Thanks."

"No problem."

Colby went back to his office and opened the lower drawer. There was a bag in it from a local art supply store. It was an impulse purchase he'd made, one that he didn't really understand. Before he could talk himself out of it, he took out the bag and walked back to the canteen.

The child looked up when he entered. Her big, brown eyes were eloquent. She stilled at once, her expression uncertain and apprehensive, as if she expected a new frontal attack.

Colby put the bag down on the table in front of her. He pushed it toward her. Then he just stood there.

Bernadette reached out with a small hand, curious, and opened it. Inside were a real artist's sketch pad, several charcoal pencils, a professional eraser, and a whole big metal container of pastel pencils. There was even a book on preliminary sketching.

"Wow," she said softly. She looked up at him quizzically. "They're for me?"

He nodded.

She smiled shyly. It brightened her whole face. Her dark eyes glowed as she met his. "Thank you."

He shrugged. "You have real talent."

The smile grew. Then it faded. She looked guilty. "I'm sorry."

He frowned. "For what?"

She shrugged. "That picture I drew. It wasn't a nice thing to do."

He moved a little closer, his expression curious. "How did you know about that place...about what happened there?"

Her dark eyes were troubled. "I don't really know," she said honestly. "I've always had it. I see things. I dream things that come true. I saw that happen to you," she added, pointing toward his left arm. She grimaced. "It was...it was terrible."

He swallowed. "Yes."

"My granddaddy said it was a gift, and that I shouldn't be afraid of it, but I am," she confessed, her eyes lowering to the art supply bag. "I don't want to know bad things."

"Is it only bad things?"

She nodded. "There's a new one. I can't talk about it. I can't tell Mommy."

He frowned. "Tell her what?"

She looked up with pain in her small face. "Something bad is going to happen to her," she said.

He had a curious sinking sensation in his stomach. "Do you know what it is?"

"No, I don't," she told him. "But Mommy's going to get hurt. I don't know what to do. I can't stop things from happening, I just know about them sometimes."

The thought of something happening to Sarina was disturbing. He moved closer and knelt beside her chair. He was so tall that his eyes were on a level with hers. "Where is it going to happen?" he asked softly.

Her dark eyes met his. They were bright with worry and fear. "In a big place with boxes," she said. "At night."

He frowned. The only place he knew that had boxes was the warehouse. But Sarina had no business that would take her in there, at night or any other time.

"You work with Nikki's daddy," she said. "Taking care of people who work here."

He nodded.

"Can you take care of my mommy, too?" she asked. "So that she doesn't get hurt?"

He searched her eyes. "Yes, I can. I won't let anything happen to your mother," he assured her in a calm, confident tone. "I promise."

She swallowed. "Thanks," she said shyly, laying a soft hand tentatively on his broad shoulder.

Her touch made him feel odd inside. He shrugged. "You're welcome."

"You don't like me," Bernadette said suddenly.

He felt guilty all over again. He frowned. "It isn't that," he said hesitantly. "I'm not used to kids. And besides that, I don't…share my life with people," he tried to explain.

She nodded, as if she actually understood. "Me, neither," she said, sounding much more adult than her six years would allow. "The other kids think I'm spooky. Or they pick on me on account of I'm…" She hesitated, remembering that she wasn't supposed to tell him she was Apache. “Different,” she added after a short pause.

“Even the Chicanos?” he asked with a smile.

She smiled back. “No. Not them. They get picked on, too, just like me.”

He knew how she felt. He had no special gifts, but he’d been an outsider all his life, in one way or another. First from his people, then from his father, then from society itself. Maureen had taught him never to trust a woman. The world had taught him never to trust people. He was locked up inside himself. He couldn’t get out.

“Hunter says that you sing,” he said after an awkward silence.

She nodded. “I’m going to sing tonight at our play.”

“I’m coming to the play with Hunter and Jennifer,” he said.

“You are?” Her eyes were wide and soft, and she reminded him suddenly of his own mother, whom he remembered with love and sadness. It was something about the expression…

She made him uncomfortable. In many ways, she was a potent reminder of all that he’d missed out on in life, of his flaws, his inadequacies. He got to his feet, vaguely uneasy, aware of an odd sensation, as if he were being watched.

He turned, and there was Sarina in the doorway, her face troubled and curious.

Discovered, she wiped the expression from her face and tried not to show how much Colby's tenderness with her child had disturbed her.

"Time to go, pumpkin," she told her daughter with a warm smile.

"Okay, Mommy. Look what he got me!" she exclaimed, opening the bag.

"Art supplies?" She looked at Colby with open curiosity.

He stuck his hands in his pockets. His expression gave away nothing. "If she's going to draw, she should have proper equipment," he said gruffly.

Sarina pursed her lips and peered in the bag again. "At least it doesn't tick," she murmured. "Are you sure you didn't slip any poison into the pencil points?"

"That wasn't nice, Mommy," Bernadette told her. "You said we must always be polite to people."

"Yes, we should," Colby replied with a mischievous smile. "Your daughter needs to teach you some manners."

Sarina glared at him. "Sometimes we can choose which people we want to be polite to," she hedged.

"Is that any way to treat a person who was hired to keep you safe?" he asked, tongue-in-cheek.

She grimaced. "All right, I'll be polite," she said curtly. She wasn't comfortable with his changed attitude toward Bernadette. He'd been eloquent about her in recent days. There were good reasons why he couldn't spend too much time around the child.

"Thank you," Bernadette told Colby as she took her mother's hand, after putting her drawing and pencils in the bag he'd given her.

He shrugged. "You're welcome."

Sarina nodded, uncertain of what to say. She turned and let Bernadette out of the canteen.

Bernadette's excited voice floated back to him as they walked away. "He's coming to hear me sing tonight!" Bernadette told her mother excitedly. "And he said I could draw very well! He isn't a bad man at all, Mommy!"

It was like being hit in the stomach. The child's enthusiastic response to him was disturbing. He felt a warm glow inside, like nothing he'd ever known. He felt as if he knew her, and he didn't understand why.

It made him feel even guiltier that she was so receptive to him, after he'd been cruel to her.

Sarina, listening to the child, was concerned, more than ever. If Colby got too close to the child, he might learn things she didn't want him to know. Bernadette was obviously fascinated by him, and it seemed that Colby was discovering feelings for her as well. It was going to complicate things.

THE SCHOOL PLAY was a new experience for Colby. He'd never seen one, except when he was a child. They were doing something called a Harvest Celebration. Apparently it was politically incorrect to mention Halloween these days. There were no spooky decorations like the ones they'd had at his school when he was a child, no Halloween carnivals with children all dressed up going from room to room to explore haunted places or fish for prizes or play games. He was amazed at how much an outsider he felt.

The children were dressed in regular, but nice, school clothes. They told about the harvest of the first Thanksgiving, and how people had gathered crops in the fall, and they recited poems about autumn. There were pumpkins on the stage, but they weren't carved, and they didn't have candles in them.

Nikki Hunter recited a poem about apples being gathered in an orchard. Then Bernadette came up to the microphone, looking very nervous. A large woman sat down at the piano and began to play an introduction. Bernadette, her dark hair straight and shiny around her face, wearing a pretty brown dress with a white collar, searched the audience until she found her mother and then Colby and the Hunters. She smiled.

The pianist nodded, and Bernadette sang "Bless this House." Colby felt chills run down his spine. The child was incredibly gifted. Her voice was high and clear as a bell. It was painfully familiar. He closed his eyes. He could hear his mother singing to him in the late evening, smiling as she tucked him gently into bed.

The last of the song faded away and there was applause. Colby came back to the present and joined in, smiling at Bernadette. She saw him and smiled back.

The curtain closed. Apparently the play was over. The Hunters moved forward into the crowd to look for Nikki. Bernadette was already running down the aisle to be swung up against a broad shoulder. Rodrigo Ramirez! Colby's teeth clenched. He hadn't seen the man, or Sarina, for that matter. They'd been a few rows ahead of him and on the other side of the auditorium.

He hesitated, but he couldn't see any reason not to tell the child how beautifully she sang. If Ramirez didn't like it, tough.

He walked up to the couple. Bernadette saw him and beamed.

"You did come!" she exclaimed.

He smiled, ignoring Rodrigo. "Hunter was right," he said gently. "You do sing like an angel."

"Thanks," she replied shyly.

"Where are the carved pumpkins and ghosts and witches and black cats?" he wondered, looking around.

"Be quiet or you'll get us thrown out," Sarina said in an undertone. "It's controversial to celebrate Halloween these days."

He made a sound under his breath. He glanced at Rodrigo. "Not in your country, it isn't," he mused. "Of course, there it's the first day of November when you celebrate El Dia de Los Muertos."

Rodrigo's dark brows shot up. "Indeed we do. How would you know that?"

"I get around."

"I'm surprised to see you here," he commented.

"He got me lots of pencils and stuff," Bernadette told Rodrigo. "He's not a bad man after all."

"Have you checked the wall at the post office?" Rodrigo asked under his breath, with a cold glare at Colby, who returned it with interest.

"We should probably go," Sarina said, feeling the tension grow. "Rodrigo's had a long day."

"Oh, I can see that being a liaison officer would wear a man out, all right," Colby replied blithely. "All that hard labor..."

Rodrigo's black eyes flashed. "Yes, it must be as tiring as doing security work. Checking all those doors to make sure they're locked...?"

Colby took a step forward and Sarina moved between the two men to grasp her daughter's small hand and Rodrigo's arm.

"Time to go. Good night, Colby," Sarina said at once, almost dragging Rodrigo along with her.

Bernadette clung to Rodrigo's neck, smiling back at Colby. "Good night," she called.

He nodded, glaring at the other man. He shoved

his hands into his pockets and stood there, glowering. Hunter had to speak twice before he realized they were leaving.

Jennifer, blond and gorgeous, smiled to herself as Colby drove away from their house. Nikki was in her room, finishing up her homework before going to bed.

"He and Rodrigo are going to bump heads at some point," she told her husband.

Hunter smiled down at her. "They just did," he reminded her. He gathered her close in his arms. "But that's his problem, not ours."

She smiled back, tugging his head down so that she could kiss him. "I'm two months along today," she whispered.

One of his lean hands went to the slight swell of her stomach. "I can hardly wait," he said softly. "You've brightened all my dark corners, just by being in my life. I never dreamed I could be so happy."

She grinned at him. "And you spent all those years glowering at me and pretending to hate me."

He shrugged. "I finally had the good sense to look twice."

She chuckled. "Sure, after I got shot."

He hugged her close. "Don't remind me," he bit off. "That was a near thing. If the marksman had slipped, you'd have been dead. There we were, in the Arizona desert, miles from a doctor or a clinic. Good thing it was only a flesh wound. But it scared the hell out of me. I knew then how I felt about you," he confessed in a deep, husky tone. "That's why I lied about how I felt and ran."

"Didn't do a bit of good, did it?" she teased. "You came back."

"My life was empty." He bent and kissed her tenderly. "I was so afraid I'd lost you. Eugene almost sent me back to Arizona, did he ever tell you? He thought I'd hurt you enough."

"He told me. But he was happy with the way things turned out." She stared up at him in the light from the front porch. "I miss my cousin Danetta."

"I know. We can go back to Tucson when I get Colby properly settled, if you like."

She hesitated. "You know, Houston really isn't so bad. Nikki loves this school, and she and Bernadette seem to really fit in, for the first time."

He frowned. "You'd like to stay here?"

She gnawed her lower lip. "Let's wait another month or two before we make a final decision, can we?"

He smiled slowly. "Whatever you like. Colby may not be too happy, having to play second banana to me."

"Colby's not like that, and you know it. He was perfectly happy working under Tate Winthrop in Washington, D.C."

"I suppose he was at that. Well, we'll wait a bit and see what happens."

She smiled and kissed him again.

THE NEXT DAY, Colby was walking past Hunter's office when he saw Ramirez strolling beside an old friend whom he hadn't seen in years, Cy Parks. He grinned and his eyes sparkled.

"Cy! Long time no see," he said at once, reaching out to shake Cy's hand.

"That's your fault," Cy chuckled. "I tried to keep in touch. I didn't know you were working here until Alexander Cobb phoned me. How's it going?"

Colby shrugged. "I'll get used to civilian life eventually." He glared at Ramirez. "What are you now, the official greeter for the company?" he drawled. "Of course, they usually are older people…?"

Rodrigo's dark eyes flashed. "If you'd care to step out back with me, I'll show you how old I am!"

"It would be a pleasure," Colby agreed, black eyes flashing.

Cy stepped between them. "Sorry, but I'm pressed for time," he said with a speaking glance at Rodrigo. He caught Colby's good arm. "Come on, Colby. Cobb asked me to stop by. I've got some information for Hunter."

"How do you know each other?" Rodrigo asked, curious.

Cy gave him a blank stare. Colby caught Cy's eyes and gave a silent warning. He didn't want Ramirez knowing about his past. He didn't want anyone knowing, especially Sarina.

"Colby's an old friend of Micah Steele, who lives

in Jacobsville now," Cy hedged. "They used to work together years ago, with Hunter, in an unrelated field," he added, to throw Rodrigo off the track. "I met Colby in Washington, D.C., when Micah worked there," without adding where Colby had been working at the time.

"Micah's good people," Colby drawled. "I owe him my life." It was true. Micah had amputated his destroyed arm.

Hunter came down the hall, having spotted the small group.

"Parks!" Hunter chuckled, joining them. "Good to see you."

"Good to see all of you, too. It's been a long time," he added, wincing inside as he realized what he'd just said. He didn't dare let on that he and Rodrigo were old acquaintances, too.

"Why, exactly, are you here?" Colby asked suddenly, frowning at Cy.

"I had Cobb ask him up," Hunter explained. "He knows more about Lopez's old operation than anyone."

"Well, not more than…" Cy began.

"Loose lips sink ships," Hunter interrupted with a firm stare.

Cy was quick. He realized that he wasn't supposed to let anything slip about Rodrigo's undercover work in Lopez's organization. He wondered why Hunter was keeping that secret from his coworker, but he let it drop.

"I might have some helpful information," Cy conceded, smiling. He deliberately didn't look at Rodrigo, who managed to seem disinterested and excused himself abruptly.

HUNTER LED CY and Colby into his office and closed the door. He was grateful that he'd been in time to stop Rodrigo from questioning how Cy knew Colby. It was going to be tricky now, keeping the two men from making awkward connections about the past. He couldn't blow Rodrigo's cover, no matter what he had to do. While Rodrigo hadn't actually been with them during the time Colby lost his arm, he had been in on a related operation with Micah Steele. He and Colby had seen each other in a staging area, but no names had been exchanged and they got no more than a glimpse of each other. That was a lucky break for Hunter. Rodrigo obviously didn't recognize Colby, and vice versa.

Cy had his foreman, Harley Fowler, watching the warehouse on the edge of Cy's property, which late drug lord Manuel Lopez had built to use as a distribution center for his cocaine shipments. Just recently, there was some new activity there. He was going to enlist another ex-merc, Eb Scott, to help with the surveillance. Eb had a state-of-the-art facility in Jacobsville where he taught tactics and combat and interrogation counterterrorism techniques to military personnel from all over the world.

Two years earlier, Cy and Eb Scott and Micah Steele had shut down Lopez's operation, along with local law enforcement and DEA agent Cobb's inter-agency drug unit. There had been a firefight, but many of Lopez's people went to prison. Lopez subsequently snatched Micah Steele's stepsister and took her to Cancún; Micah had mounted a commando unit of mercenaries to rescue her. Rodrigo had been one of them, having worked undercover to help bring down Lopez. The drug lord had died in a mysterious explosion near Nassau. Colby didn't know about Rodrigo's part in it, and he couldn't be told. Cobb had been insistent.

But what Cy Parks was able to tell Hunter and Colby about the organization of Lopez's former empire gave them more leads to run down. Colby was still curious about the apparent rapport between Cy Parks and Rodrigo, but he was diverted enough by the new information not to pursue it. Perhaps the Mexican was just good with strangers. After all, Colby reminded himself, the man did work as a liaison officer. He had to have good communication skills. Of a sort.

Before Cy left, he invited Colby down to his ranch. "You still ride, don't you?" Cy asked, "In spite of that?" He indicated the prosthesis.

Colby didn't take offense. Cy's left arm was badly burned from the fire that had killed his first wife and his son years ago. He smiled. "I mount offside, but I can ride anything you can saddle. I miss having horses."

"You ran quarter horses in the old days," Cy recalled.

"I had to give them up when I went freelance," he said, knowing Cy would understand he meant his mercenary work. "Thanks for the invitation. I'd love to get on a horse again."

"Any Saturday you're free will do," Cy said, smiling. "Just give me a call. You can meet Lisa. We're expecting our first child in a few weeks. Lisa lost our first one."

"You landed on your feet, though," Colby remarked.

"And how! See you."

ONE OF THE LEADS he and Hunter got from Cy Parks were the names of two Ritter personnel who had ties to Cancún. It didn't make them guilty, but it was suspicious that both of them would be new employees. Gary Ordonez was assistant supply clerk for the corporation and had a father with a shady background. Daniel Morris was an equipment operator whose background included jail time for distributing drugs—Ritter was gung-ho about helping rehabilitate ex-cons.

Colby wondered if the two had anything in their files that would point to a connection with Cara Dominguez. The obvious place to find that out was in the personnel office. So he dropped by Brody Vance's office to make enquiries.

He expected it to be easy. After all, he was assistant security chief and he had a legitimate right to search the files if any employee was suspected of having criminal ties. He also wanted to see how Vance reacted to the names, both of which he was certain had a connection to the local drug trafficking.

Brody Vance, however, balked at even the thought of disclosing confidential information about anyone who worked for the company.

"I'm sorry," he told Colby bluntly, "but my department doesn't make a habit of dishing out personal information about our workers, to anyone, even in security."

Colby looked at the man as if he suspected his sanity. "We're looking for a drug smuggler," he told Vance, and he didn't smile. "We can't allow the corporation to be brought up on charges of aiding and abetting criminal activities."

Vance shifted and looked uncomfortable. "I'm sorry, that's my rule."

Colby cocked an eyebrow. He opened his cell phone, dialed Hunter, and waited. Watching Vance, he began speaking in Apache.

"This guy won't let me look at the files," he told the other man. "I think he's hiding something."

"Want me to come down and help you convince him?" Hunter asked amusedly.

"Why not?"

He closed the flip phone and pocketed it.

Vance stared at him nervously. "What language was that?"

"One of several," Colby replied nonchalantly, "that I learned while I was working for the CIA." He didn't identify the language.

The look on Vance's face was priceless. "You worked for the CIA?" he stammered.

Colby didn't reply. It was a deliberate snub, giving Vance time to consider how dangerous it might be to deny the other man access to those files. He couldn't afford to bring suspicion down on his own head.

Vance was obviously reconsidering his position about the time that Hunter opened the door without knocking and walked in.

Hunter handed the man a sheet of paper which contained the names of the suspicious employees and some damaging information about criminal acts in their pasts. Vance ground his teeth as he read them.

"Now you'll open those files," Hunter said quietly. "Or you can explain your reluctance to the DEA. I can have one of their senior agents over here in five minutes, along with Eugene Ritter and one of our corporate attorneys."

Vance swallowed. Hard. He cleared his throat and sat down at his computer. His hands were unsteady on the keyboard.

"I'll print them out for you," Vance said meekly.

Hunter looked at Colby and had to fight a grin. "See how it works?" he asked Colby in Apache.

"Yeah, well the mighty warrior there looks as if he might need to change his trousers when we leave," Colby replied.

Vance, in the dark because he didn't speak the language, retrieved two sheets of paper from his printer and handed them over.

"Naturally," he told the men, trying to backpedal, "privacy is a great concern to us here."

"And I'm sure the drug dealer's employers will thank you for your efforts to shield them," Colby said. But he said it in Apache.

Hunter caught his arm and propelled him out the door before he had the opportunity to say it in English.

"Nice going," he told Hunter with a grin.

"When you've been in the security game as long as I have, you learn to deal diplomatically with hardheads like Vance," Hunter told him, grinning back. "It isn't much different from interrogation technique, but it works well on white collar types. I'll tutor you. Now, if you'll pick up two cups of coffee from the canteen, I'll go down to the warehouse and check this information out with the supervisors."

"I'll meet you in your office," Colby replied with a chuckle. Despite his background, he wasn't much more than a beginner in this sort of civilized verbal warfare. Most of his work had been done with an automatic weapon.

MINUTES LATER, Sarina was walking past Brody Vance's office when she heard him curse.

"You can't do that!" he exclaimed. "I'm already under suspicion…"

Sarina kept going, her eyes on a file that she'd opened, appearing oblivious to everything except the paper she was reading.

Vance noticed her passing by his door and suddenly broke into fluent Spanish and continued, unabashed. "I had to give them the information! I can't afford to get fired, and they're suspicious of me already. No. No, you can't get into the warehouse. They have it under constant surveillance. Yes, of course there are cameras!" He paused. "What do you think I am, an electronics engineer?" Another pause. "Well, I'm not sticking my neck out again. You ask Chiva. No, she's in Corpus Christi. Yes, you do that." The phone went down.

Sarina was excited. She knew she'd overheard something crucial, but how was she going to exploit it?

"¿Ha oido algo de que hablaba yo?" Vance said at her back.

She did understand what he'd said in Spanish, but she didn't dare react to the question. She kept walking.

"Miss Carrington?"

She turned, faking surprise, to find Brody Vance standing at his office door. "Yes, Mr. Vance?"

"Did you want to see me about something?"

She blinked. "Sorry?"

"Did you hear what I was saying?" he persisted.

She managed a dumb look. She held up the file. "I was going over this material because I have to get it to Mr. Ritter by quitting time. Sorry, but I wasn't paying attention. Did you call to me?"

He seemed to relax. "No. It was nothing. I just wanted to make sure you were happy with your job."

"Very happy," she said, smiling. "This is a nice place to work."

"Yes, it is. Well, don't let me keep you," he added. He smiled and went back into his office.

Sarina hurried down the hall, her eyes darting behind her to make sure she hadn't been followed by Brody Vance. She'd tell Hunter. He could notify the appropriate people. She was excited. Their first break!

But he wasn't in his office. She went toward the small cubicle where Rodrigo usually worked, but he wasn't there, either! With a muffled groan, she turned and started back around the corner when she ran, literally, into Colby Lane.

"Just the man I'm looking for," she said, taking him by the sleeve to tug him along into her own office.

"What's going on?" he asked, surprised.

"I overheard Brody Vance on the phone," she said at once when she'd closed the door behind them. Her dark eyes were sparkling with intrigue. "He was talking to a woman, by the sound of it. He said that he'd given information to somebody, that he couldn't help it, and that she couldn't get into the warehouse because there were surveillance cameras! He also said that he wasn't an electronics engineer, so I gathered she wanted him to disable them!"

He smiled. "Damn, you're sharp!" he exclaimed, delighted to know that they'd spooked Vance into using his phone. They could get a trace and find out who he was talking to. He caught her by the waist and pulled her against him, grinning as he bent to catch her soft mouth under his in a quick, hard kiss. He laughed at her surprise. "Sorry. Couldn't resist it," he said softly, letting her go. "I'm proud of you."

She flushed helplessly. The soft, quick contact rattled her.

He saw that, and his dark eyes began to glitter. "You're wasted on clerical work," he mused. Then he frowned. "Vance must be gutsy to make a statement like that out in the open, especially after what Hunter and I did to him."

She didn't understand what he meant. He didn't elaborate.

"He was speaking in Spanish," she corrected, and he recalled that she was fluent.

"Did he see you?"

"Yes. But he doesn't know I speak Spanish," she replied with a grin. "I was apparently reading a paper and didn't even look at him."

"You've put us ahead of the game," he said with genuine praise. "I'll get Hunter and we'll see what we can do with that tidbit of information. Maybe we can flush him out. Thanks, Sarina," he added gently. "You're a wonder."

"No problem." She hated the pleasure the praise gave her.

He cocked his head and studied her. "You might consider coming to work for me," he murmured, not altogether joking. "It's more exciting than typing up requisition forms."

She averted her eyes. "That's not a bad idea. Maybe I'll think about it."

"You do that." He left her in her office and went looking for Hunter. This might be just the break they needed to find that drug shipment.

CHAPTER FIVE

HUNTER WAS TALKING to an accountant near the front entrance when Colby found him.

"Something wrong?" Hunter asked.

Colby grinned. "Nothing major, just a little snag we need to discuss."

"Sure." Hunter excused himself and joined Colby farther down the hall.

"We spooked Vance," he said with barely contained glee. "Sarina heard him talking to a woman. He switched to Spanish when he saw her, unaware that she's fluent. He said he had to give us the names, and she asked if she could get into the warehouse. He said no, because it's under constant surveillance."

"Good for Sarina!"

"She's wasted in clerical work," Colby scoffed. "What a dead end job for a woman with her potential!"

Hunter groaned inwardly. He couldn't give her away. "Well, she does like the work," he said evasively. "We can have the number that Vance called traced," he added, working out strategies.

"Do you know someone at the phone company?" Hunter asked wistfully.

"I have my contacts. Later on, I'll share them," he promised when Colby looked frustrated. "Listen, I know you feel like I'm deliberately keeping you in the dark. But I can't buck Cobb. This is his operation. He's been working on it for a long time."

"That's not a problem," Colby assured him. "I've been in the same position you are, from time to time." He pursed his lips and frowned. "I really need to stick that wire in Vance's car, in case he decides to meet personally with his evasive girlfriend."

"There's going to be a staff meeting this afternoon," Hunter mentioned. "He'll be tied up for at least an hour."

Colby's dark eyes twinkled. "What a lucky break."

HE HAD THE WIRE in Vance's car in minutes, as well as a homing device under the trunk. It would be a backup, in case Vance somehow discovered the wire. But since Vance didn't think he was under suspicion, Colby mused, he probably wouldn't even look. Now, all they had to do was wait.

He'd planned the next day to spend some time

monitoring Vance's movements on his way to work. The weather put a hitch in the plan. Rain started coming down in buckets and didn't stop. Parts of Houston were prone to extreme flooding. Fortunately Colby's apartment house wasn't near a river.

But when he got to work, Hunter met him in the hall.

"You've got an SUV, haven't you?" he asked the younger man.

Colby nodded. "Why?"

Hunter hesitated. "I know you and Sarina have your problems, but she and Bernadette are stuck at their apartment and can't get to Sarina's car. The water's up to the fenders. I can't leave because Ritter's coming over with Cobb to discuss a new development. We're all supposed to meet in the conference room later this morning, including you. Can you go and get them and drop Bernadette off at her school?"

"Sure," Colby said easily. That kiss he'd exchanged with Sarina had rattled her. He still felt it on his mouth. Bernadette was warming to him as well. He thought that Hunter could have as easily asked Rodrigo to fetch them, and he grinned. He was one up on the Mexican. He hated knowing how close the man was to Sarina and the child. He didn't quite understand why he felt that way.

"Don't forget the staff meeting at ten," Hunter cautioned.

"I'll be back in plenty of time for that," Colby assured him.

IT WAS TRICKY getting near the apartment's parking lot. Most of it was underwater. Colby parked several yards away on the narrow paved road above the apartment complex and got out the hip-high wading boots he used when he went fishing. He pulled them on. He had a feeling Sarina and her daughter would have to be carried out or spend the day with wet feet.

The building was old. Sarina's apartment was badly run-down. The steps were cracked and there was peeling paint on the door. One screen on a window was loose. The unit needed painting. Some of the other apartments were in worse shape, though. It was really a low-rent area. His keen eyes caught signs of gang graffiti on the side of an adjacent unit, marking their territory. Hunter had taken him around town and alerted him to the different markings, just in case they had any gang involvement in the smuggling operation. This was not a good place for a woman and a little girl to be living. The only attractive thing about it was probably the low rent, he considered. It made him uncomfortable to see the poverty in which the two of them lived. The child was sweet, and had such promise. This area had running gun battles, gang graffiti, and probably drugs as well. Sarina had to cope with all that as well as supporting her child alone. He was furious when he considered how little Bernadette's absent father had done for them.

He waded up to the door and knocked.

There was a pause, before Sarina opened it, her dark eyes wide and curious.

"Hunter said he was coming," she faltered.

"Not his fault," Colby replied. "Cobb's on his way there with Eugene Ritter. Hunter couldn't get away, so he sent me."

"Oh." She seemed disoriented for a minute. Her eyes were bloodshot, as if she hadn't had much sleep.

Colby's black eyes lingered on her slender figure in the beige suit she was wearing with high heels and a very becoming flowered scarf around her neck. Her hair was long, draping over her shoulders like corn silk. He remembered suddenly, reluctantly, the feel of it against his bare chest…

"We'd better get moving before the water gets any deeper," he said curtly, trying to curtail the memory. It was arousing.

"Come on, Bernadette," she told the child. "Got your raincoat?"

"Yes, Mommy."

The child was wearing a yellow slicker. It was stained and looked as if it had come from a yard sale.

Sarina didn't have a raincoat, apparently, because she was clutching a ratty-looking umbrella. Odd, he thought, how the sight of their financial condition hurt him.

"Oh, hello," Bernadette said, brightening when she saw who'd come to rescue them.

"Hello," he replied, trying to sound pleasant. He smiled, too. He'd given the child enough heartache as it was. He had a lot to make up to her. "I'd better take her first," he told Sarina.

She hesitated. "She has to go in the backseat, if you have a passenger-side air bag," she told him.

He looked blank. "I beg your pardon?"

"If the air bag deploys for any reason with a small child in the front seat, it could be fatal," Sarina explained.

He shook his head. "We learn something new every day." He bent down. "Ready?" he asked the child.

She nodded, holding her book bag over one shoulder.

He swung her up easily with his right arm. The feel of her small arms clinging to his neck trustingly made his heart melt. "Hold on," he said softly, smiling. "I won't drop you."

"I know that," she told him, grinning. Her arms tightened.

He turned and walked up the slope past the parking lot to where his black SUV was parked.

"That's a very big truck," Bernadette pointed out. "Can you carry a horse in it?"

He chuckled. "I don't think so. Why?" he teased. "Are you thinking of buying one?"

She laughed, too. "I wish I could. We go to Jacobsville to see a friend of Rodrigo's who has a ranch there. He lets me ride his horses. I just love them!"

"I have a friend in Jacobsville who has a ranch myself," he murmured without naming Cy. "I used to have horses, too, when I was younger," he recalled. "I still love to ride."

They reached the truck. He opened the door and put her gently inside. "Fasten your seat belt," he told her.

"I always do. Mommy said I must always wear it."

He smiled at her. "Mommy's right. Watch your fingers." He closed the door gently and went back for Sarina.

The rain had slackened to a mist. She closed the umbrella and looked at him uncertainly. She knew that the prosthesis he wore, however high tech, would never support her weight.

He hesitated, feeling grim. He hated his disability.

"I could take off my shoes and walk," she said, gently so that she didn't bruise his ego. He looked so wounded. She moved closer to him, her dark eyes eloquent. "It's all right," she said softly.

He hated the compassion. He hated his weakness. His eyes blazed.

She looked up at him. He was a stranger, for all that they'd been close years ago. She didn't know what to say, what to do, to make things easier for him. "One of my coworkers lost his legs in Iraq, back in Desert Storm," she said. "He has two artificial ones. They're not high-tech, like your prosthesis," she continued gently, "but they're so functional that nobody in the office can outrun him in intra-unit competition."

He focused on that at once. "Intra-unit?" he wondered, because he knew there was no such competition at Ritter's business.

Her eyes flashed at the slip. She cleared her throat and thought fast. "Back in Tucson," she said quickly, "we had team competitions in sports."

"Oh." He drew in a slow breath, his eyes steady and curious on her hair in the elegant upswept hairdo, her body clothed in a simple beige suit with an off-white cotton blouse. He remembered her in silk. His hand went to the collar of her blouse and touched it lightly. "The first time I saw you," he said absently, "you were wearing a blue silk blouse with white slacks. Your hair was in a pigtail. You were playing with that golden retriever you had…"

Her gaze fell as she recalled with bitter pain what had happened when her father kicked her out of his house.

"What's wrong?" he asked, sensitive to her moods.

"My father had her put down, when he threw me out," she bit off.

He remembered her love for the sweet, obedient animal. Her father had been a monster! The remembered pain was visible in her eyes. Involuntarily his arms slid around her, pulling her close. He wrapped her up tight in his embrace, and rocked her. The expression on her face had hurt him, as so many things did now. His eyes closed as he drank in the faint rose-scented cologne she wore, the clean herbal scent of her hair under his cheek. "I'm sorry," he whispered deeply. "I know how much you loved her."

The tears came more easily because she was tired. She hadn't slept last night after the harrowing trip to the emergency room with Bernadette. She drew in a harsh breath and wiped angrily at the tears as she pulled away.

"Sorry," she murmured. "It's been a long night. I haven't slept much."

He frowned. "Why?" he asked angrily, immediately concluding that her friend Rodrigo had something to do with her weariness. "Do you and Ramirez have pajama parties?"

Her dark eyes opened wide. "In front of Bernadette?" she asked, shocked at his lack of perception.

Dark color flushed his high cheekbones and his lips made a thin line. He hadn't meant to say that.

"Here," he bit off, bending. "It will have to be a fireman's carry. I can't lift with the prosthesis."

He sounded so bitter. "I don't...don't mind, Colby," she whispered, still unsettled by what appeared to be jealousy.

His eyes met hers and held them. He felt his breath suspend deep in his chest as emotion shivered through him like electricity. He hesitated, his big hand going to her cheek, his thumb sliding tenderly over her full, soft lips.

"Seven years," he whispered unsteadily as his mouth slowly, hesitantly, covered hers. He nibbled her upper lip with tender, sensuous skill, the prosthesis hard at her back as he tugged her closer.

She felt like a girl again, uncertain of herself, too easily overcome by the need to be held by him, kissed by him. The years fell away as his mouth opened, pressing her lips apart so that he could deepen the kiss.

He groaned softly under his breath and suddenly swallowed her up whole against the lean, hard wall of his body, kissing her so hungrily that she couldn't even get enough breath to protest.

His hand tangled in her hair, disarranging hairpins as his mouth became insistent, devouring her there on the porch of her apartment as the rain suddenly increased. Neither of them noticed it, until a small voice called from the back.

"Mommy, we'll be late for school!" Bernadette reminded her from the open back door of the SUV.

Colby pulled back as if he'd been slapped. He looked into Sarina's wide, shocked eyes with a feeling of disbelief. His heartbeat was shaking him. His body was taut with desire. He moved back a step to keep her from feeling it.

"We...uh, we'd better go," she managed.

Her mouth was swollen from the heat of his kisses. Her hair was falling down. She was flushed. Her eyes were wide and dark.

He liked the way she looked. He smiled slowly, the way he'd smiled at her seven years ago, before the tragedy of their marriage.

That smile took her breath away. She couldn't even manage words.

"Doesn't he kiss you?" he taunted.

While she was trying to find a suitably cutting reply, he bent and lifted her gently over one shoulder, pocketbook, umbrella and all.

"Off we go," he mused, heading for the steps in the bank. "Hold on, now. We wouldn't want you to go headfirst into a nasty mud puddle, would we?"

She could barely breathe at all, and her mouth was sore. She hadn't remembered how expert he was, how sensuous. That horrible night they'd spent together had begun as a veritable feast of the senses when he started kissing her. She'd been on fire for him, until the pain started...

He was up the steps in a flash, his powerful body still in prime condition, despite his war wounds. He put her down gently, grinning at Bernadette, who grinned back and closed her door.

He opened the passenger door and guided Sarina's cold, trembling hand to the handhold just above the door, helping her boost herself up into the high vehicle and into the seat. He paused to take off his wading boots and throw them in the back of the truck.

Sarina was still dazed, sitting in the front seat but with the door still open. He grinned widely as he fastened her seat belt and then closed the door before he went around to his own side. He climbed in with a lighter heart than he'd had in years.

"Everybody settled and buckled in tight?" he asked, looking at Bernadette in the backseat.

"Roger, wilco," she said, giving him a thumbs-up.

His eyebrows lifted and he chuckled. "Good to go," he replied, flashing a dark, smiling glance at Sarina, who was trying to redo her hair. He reached over and pulled down the visor, which automatically lit up at both sides. His eyes met hers at very close range, dropping sensuously to her swollen mouth. "There you go," he said softly.

"Thanks," she whispered, almost choking on emotion.

He started the SUV and backed out into the parking lot. He glanced at the map Hunter had given him, but it didn't include the school. "Somebody will have to direct me to the school," he pointed out.

"Turn right at the stop sign," Bernadette said at

once. "Then you go through three traffic lights, and it's on the left."

He smiled. "Okay." He turned where she indicated, but at the bottom of the hill, the water ran across the road in a flood. He turned right onto another, smaller road.

"But..." Bernadette began.

"You never drive through standing water, when you can't judge the depth," he told her gently. "When I was a boy, they had to rescue five construction workers from a truck that stalled in the middle of the road in what looked like a trickle of water. They had to stand on the roof to keep from drowning."

"He's right," Sarina said, smiling over the seat at her daughter as she struggled to speak normally. "Remember how quickly the dips in the road filled up in Tucson, even when the rain was miles and miles away?"

"Yes, Mommy," Bernadette agreed, smiling. "I forgot."

Colby glanced mischievously at Sarina, who was still struggling with her hair. "Sorry," he said softly. "You don't even have a brush, do you?"

She grimaced. "Not with me."

"We'll manage something before we get to the office."

HE PULLED UP IN FRONT of the school, under the shelter, so that Sarina could climb out and get Bernadette out of the backseat, with her book bag.

"Aren't you going to come, too?" the child asked as Sarina started to close the doors.

He hesitated. The question was unexpected.

"You have to come in with us," she persisted.

Colby cut off the engine like a sleepwalker and came around the SUV. He'd probably have a parking ticket when he emerged. Bernadette caught his good hand in hers and held on tight, grabbing her mother's at the same time, her book bag slung over the back of her tattered raincoat.

He couldn't explain the way he felt, having that soft little hand clasped so tight in his own. It actually hurt him. He'd missed so much in his life, but the most noticeable and painful omission was children. He'd wanted them…!

They went into the office first. Sarina smiled at the clerk, a woman wearing no makeup and a frown. She perked up when she saw Colby and grinned widely.

"Hello, Bernadette," she said, but she was staring at Colby.

"I know we're late," Sarina said quickly. "We were flooded, and Mr. Lane had to come get us…we work together at Ritter Oil Corporation. Mr. Lane is…our assistant chief of security."

"I'm Rita Dawes," the other woman purred. "*So* nice to meet you, Mr. Lane."

"Can you give Bernadette a slip for her teacher?" Sarina asked gently.

"Certainly!" The woman wrote quickly on a slip of paper, which she handed to the child. "There you go, dear."

"Thank you," Bernadette said. She hugged her mother. Then, without hesitation, she turned and lifted her arms to Colby.

He swung her up and returned the hug, smiling. "Have a good day," he said, letting her down again.

She grinned up at him. "You, too."

She turned and went out into the hall, but she stopped suddenly as a blond boy with two companions spotted her and smiled with pure malice. Sarina saw the boy and held her breath. Colby didn't know, but it was no secret at the school that Bernadette's ancestry was Apache. She held her breath, hoping against hope that the boy wouldn't let the cat out of the bag.

"There's the Arizona aborigine," the boy drawled. "Why don't you go home to your mud hut and take your backward culture with you..."

He stopped suddenly because Colby was towering over him, glowering dangerously.

Colby went down on one knee, so that his black eyes were on a level with the boy's. "Bernadette comes from a long line of shamans," he said in a cold, soft tone, without realizing exactly what he was saying in the heat of anger. Subconsciously he'd noted her ancestry as Apache with the reference to medicine men. "Her people were on these shores long before yours landed. When your European culture was hiding in caves, hers was building canals and irrigated farms. I wouldn't call that inferior. Would you?"

The boy reddened while his two cohorts looked on, embarrassed. "Uh, no. No, sir," he added.

Colby stood up slowly, putting the boy at an even greater disadvantage. "Have a good day, sweetheart," he told Bernadette in a softer tone than he realized.

She looked up at him with pure hero worship. She smiled. "Thanks!"

He shrugged, glaring at the boy. "I thought bullying was against the rules," he added, his black eyes glittering. "Perhaps we should speak to the principal."

The boy looked scared. "Hey, man, I'm not bullying anybody! Honest! Come on, guys, we're going to be late." He and his friends almost ran. Bernadette gave Colby a wicked smile as she followed after them down the hall.

Sarina and the clerk were smiling.

"Have you ever thought about a career in education, Mr. Lane?" the clerk asked.

He cocked an eyebrow. "I don't do dangerous work," he replied, tongue-in-cheek. He glanced at his watch. "We'd better hurry," he told Sarina. "I've got a meeting at ten."

"Of course. Thank you, Miss Dawes," she added, smiling over her shoulder.

"It was no trouble at all!" Miss Dawes replied, sighing over Colby.

Sarina felt a twinge of jealousy, which she carefully hid before Colby could see it. Miss Dawes wasn't bad-looking.

They went back to the SUV. He noted the lack of a ticket with relief as he pulled out of the school parking lot and back toward the highway.

"Thanks for what you did back there," Sarina said in a husky tone. "That boy has caused us some problems. He upsets Bernadette."

"He won't anymore," he said decisively.

She smiled. "Probably not." His protective attitude toward her daughter both delighted and disturbed her. It wouldn't be wise for him to get too close to her, in case Bernadette let something slip that she shouldn't. She recalled curiously the remark Colby had made to the boy about Bernadette's ancestors being shamans, or medicine men. He didn't know about her ancestry. He couldn't. Where had the remark come from?

He tried to close his left hand around the steering wheel and it locked. He cursed under his breath when he tried again with the same result.

"What's wrong?" Sarina asked, curious.

"The prosthesis locked down," he muttered. "Damned state-of-the-art twitchy piece of junk," he added furiously. "I was better off with the hook. It drew stares, but at least it was dependable!"

"Do you…have a spare?" she wondered.

"Yes. It's not high-tech, but it's fairly realistic and dependable. I'll have to stop by my place and get it. Sorry," he added, glancing at her. "We'll be even later. But I can't work without it."

"I don't mind," she said, and meant it.

HE PARKED IN FRONT of his apartment. It was surprisingly elegant, a quiet gated community with good security and lighting, and even a front porch. It was far better than her own.

She'd planned to sit in the SUV, but he opened her door, and helped her down.

"It takes a few minutes to get it in place," he said. His face tautened. "And I may need a little help, if you don't mind." He was thinking of the harness that had to span his chest and be buckled in place. He could do it himself, but it was time-consuming and they were already late.

"Of course I don't mind," she said easily.

He unlocked the door and ushered her into the living room. It had Mediterranean furniture, and earth-toned drapes and carpet.

"Want coffee?" he asked.

She smiled and shook her head. "I'm fine."

"I won't be long."

He went off down the hall. She looked around, noting that there were no personal touches at all to the décor. There wasn't even a photograph. His barren life was quite evident and he probably didn't even realize it.

She got up and looked at the small stash of books on a side table. He liked the Greek classics, she noted, in the original Greek. She'd forgotten what an educated man he was.

"Can you help me with this?"

She turned, and her breath caught. His shirt was off. His broad, muscular chest with its sexy covering of black, curling hair, and his shoulders and flat stomach were on blatant display.

His face tautened. "I know it's distasteful…"

"What is?" she asked, genuinely surprised by the comment.

"This!" He held up the stump, which ended just below his elbow.

"Oh," she faltered. "Is it?"

"What were you looking at?" he demanded hotly.

Her eyes went to his chest and stomach involuntarily and she flushed as she averted them back to his face.

His expression was odd. He had the prosthesis in his right hand, but he put it on the side table and went to her, his heart pounding like mad as he realized that it wasn't his arm that was making her so unsettled.

He paused just in front of her, scowling at the way she flushed and stepped back. She might have gone farther, but the wall stopped her retreat. He moved until he blocked her in there. His dark eyes searched hers in the hot, tense silence.

"The first time I took my shirt off, you had that same look in your eyes," he said huskily. "I'd stripped you to the waist and kissed your breasts, and you gasped when you looked at me. When I took you in my arms, I thought you were going to faint. You moaned…"

"Please," she whispered frantically, trying to look away from him.

He stepped right up against her, his good hand going to the wall behind her, his hips levering down against hers. His arousal was instant, painful. He actually groaned.

"Colby!" she protested. Both her hands went to his chest, but she couldn't make them push. He felt good. His body smelled of soap and cologne, that sexy brand he'd worn so many years ago. The thick hair under her cold hands felt good, too, like the warm muscles it covered.

"Seven years," he whispered, holding her gaze, "and I still go hard as a rock the minute I touch you."

"Please!" she protested, embarrassed enough to push. She couldn't budge him.

"You haven't changed, Sarina," he said in a soft, husky tone as his gaze fell to her mouth. "You're as innocent as you were then, despite the birth of a child." He frowned. "How did you get Bernadette? Did you really give birth to her?"

Her eyes widened. “What a question!”

“I know I gave you scars,” he persisted. “Emotional and physical. I can’t believe you were able to give yourself to another man, after what happened.”

She swallowed hard. “This is…not your business!”

His face contorted. “I destroyed you as a woman, don’t you think I know?” His eyes closed as desire pulled him tight as a rope. “I had two neat whiskies before I came to you. I thought they’d sedate me. But nothing did. I couldn’t stop!”

The fear subsided. He looked tormented. “Excuse me?” she faltered.

He met her searching, curious gaze. He drew in a long breath and slowly, deliberately, moved his hips against her so that she could feel him intimately pressed to her belly. “Can you feel me?” he asked somberly.

“For God’s sake…!” She tried to shift away. He caught her hip with a powerful hand and held her still.

“I never meant to hurt you deliberately,” he said softly. “I wanted you so much that I lost my self-control. That’s why you had to have stitches. I’ve always had to be careful with women. One even refused me, a long time ago, when she saw me aroused.”

The blush was fuchsia by now. All those long years, she’d been so certain that it was revenge on his part. She said so involuntarily.

He shook his head. “It was never revenge.” He

bent his head. "And if I'd known you were a virgin," he whispered against her soft mouth, "despite the circumstances of our marriage, I'd have taken all night with you…!"

Just as she started to remind him about Maureen, to save herself, his hips moved gently against her. His mouth covered hers, penetrating it with slow, easy thrusts that created odd, frightening sensations in her slender body. She wanted him to stop. She didn't want him to stop. She moved, moaning, as the threat of him became a sensual promise instead. Her arms lifted helplessly to curl around his neck. His hand slid to her full breast and teased around it until she shifted, coaxing it to the hard tip that ached to feel it under the cloth of her blouse and her bra.

She felt the clasp give, but she was far too intent on the slow, hot crush of Colby's mouth to care. When she felt his fingers moving on her bare skin, she moaned again, her body slumping against him as desire uncurled inside her and began to throb in the most secret places.

The years fell away. Colby's knee invaded the tight clasp of her long legs and he moved into total intimacy with her. She shivered, sobbing as the heat and power of him began to knock down her defenses.

His mouth grew more insistent as his hips dragged sensuously against hers, the exquisite hardness of him rubbing against her in a way that made throbbing little waves of pleasure shiver through her. Before she realized it, she was opening her legs to let him closer, into a rhythmic, insistent intimacy of movement that threatened to satisfy her right through her clothing.

He heard a noise, but he was too far gone to identify it. It was insistent. He lifted his head, drowning in the scent and feel of Sarina, in an arousal more powerful than he'd felt in years.

"No," she whimpered, tugging at his neck. "Colby, no…"

He kissed her again, but tenderly this time, ignoring the painful need of his taut body as he heard the strident ringing of the telephone.

He lifted his head slowly, dragging in a harsh breath. She was his. He could have pulled her down on the sofa and done anything he liked. He cursed as he realized the damned telephone was going to make that impossible.

A groan escaped his tight throat as he moved back, his arm sliding around her waist to pull her with him as he reached for the phone. He couldn't bear to let her go. His mouth closed on hers again in a brief, hungry kiss.

"Lane," he bit off into the phone, breathless.

There was a pause. "Colby?"

He cleared his throat, staring at Sarina's face. "Hunter?"

"Where are you?" Hunter asked. "And where's Sarina?"

"We're putting on my prosthesis," he said, sounding dazed.

"Uh, could you put it on a little faster?" Hunter said, amusement in his tone. "We're all waiting for you in Ritter's office."

"Waiting for me," he echoed, his eyes lost in Sarina's.

"The meeting? The ten o'clock meeting?"

"Meeting. Right." His eyes widened. "The meeting!" He cleared his throat, letting Sarina go all at once. "At ten." His eyes went to the clock. It was ten past ten. "I'll be there in five minutes. Sorry!"

He hung up. "That was Hunter," he said huskily, staring into her misty eyes. "We're late."

"Yes. Of course." She flushed, reaching behind her to find the loose clasp of her bra and refasten it. She straightened her blouse and tucked it in, breathless.

"Here. Help me." He paused to slip the sock over his stump. Then he put on the harness that held the prosthesis in place and drew her hands to the clasp. They were cold and trembling, but they managed to buckle it in place. He tested the artificial fingers and the grip. "Thanks."

"You're welcome."

He tilted her flushed face up to his eyes. "I'll apologize, if you want me to," he said softly. "But I won't mean it," he added huskily.

She swallowed. "It's okay."

He touched her swollen mouth. "I've messed your hair up again. There's a brush in the bathroom."

"Thanks."

He let her go with obvious reluctance and finished dressing, his body still poised on the edge of anguish. He hadn't meant to touch her. They went back to work in a taut silence and parted company at the entrance. He went to his meeting in a fog of emotion, barely aware of Hunter's amused glances.

CHAPTER SIX

COLBY FELT as if he were in a daze as he listened to the discussion around the boardroom table. His body throbbed painfully from recalling the exquisite taste of Sarina's mouth.

"I said, where are you monitoring Vance's car?" Alexander Cobb repeated.

Colby suddenly realized that the DEA agent was speaking to him. He cleared his throat. "Sorry. The unit's in my office."

Cobb nodded. "Can you get tape?"

"Of course."

"There's one other thing," Hunter added. "Cy Parks told us that there's been some activity around his ranch, where Lopez tried to set up that distribution center. The holding company still owns the land."

Cobb's eyes narrowed. "It might be worthwhile

for one of us to go down there and do a walk-around."

"I'll go Saturday," Colby volunteered.

Cobb nodded. "The sooner the better," he added.

"Congratulations, by the way," Hunter told the agent, who looked sheepish.

Colby's eyebrows arched curiously.

"He married Jodie Clayburn over the weekend," Hunter informed the other occupants of the table.

"I don't remember telling anybody," Cobb said after a minute, frowning.

"I used to be a spy," Hunter said blandly. "I know everything."

Cobb only laughed. He went back to his office and phoned Cy Parks, to make sure he and a couple of guests would be welcome Saturday. They were.

COLBY STOPPED by Sarina's office at lunchtime. "I'm going down to Jacobsville to see a friend this weekend," he told her without elaborating, having just made the decision. "He owns a ranch. Would you and Bernadette like to come along? She loves horses. We could go riding."

She looked up at him with wide, soft eyes that still held the excitement of the morning. "Uh, well, yes. When?"

"Saturday. We'll leave early."

She nodded slowly. "Okay."

He leaned against the doorjamb and looked at her, his dark eyes glittering with emotion.

Her face colored. "Was there anything else?"

He shook his head. "I like you in pink," he said softly. "But I like your hair down."

The force of her unsteady breathing parted her lips. She felt flustered.

His own breathing was rough. He wanted her. The years rolled away and she was young again, vulnerable again.

"Have lunch with me," he said huskily.

She swallowed, hard. "I…well, that is…"

Rodrigo walked in, smiling at her. "Ready to go?" he asked gently.

Colby's eyes blazed with anger. "Do you hang from the ceiling, waiting to drop on people?"

Rodrigo gave him a cold glance. "Don't you have doors to check or something?"

"I was asking Sarina to lunch," Colby replied coldly.

Rodrigo smiled icily. "She's having lunch with me." He caught her hand in his, noting its sudden coldness.

That action made Colby tense like a spring. His eyes began to glitter dangerously.

"Colby, I'm sorry." She managed to get between the two men, both of whom towered over her, without seeming to interfere. "I promised Rodrigo."

He was breathing through his nose. His mouth

was a thin line. He was suddenly violently jealous of the other man and barely able to contain a physical response to that insolent smile.

"Sure," he bit off. "Some other time."

He turned and walked out. Sarina gave Rodrigo a speaking glance.

He shifted, puzzled by her expression. "Surely you didn't want to go out with him, after the way he's treated Bernadette?"

"He rescued us from the flood this morning and took Bernadette to school," she said huskily.

His dark eyes narrowed. "He has a drinking problem," he said abruptly.

"He had one," she corrected.

"Do you know anything about his background?" he persisted. "He was…"

"A spy," she interrupted. "I know that, Rodrigo."

He hesitated. "I think he's hiding something," he said worriedly. "We need to check him out."

She cocked her head and looked up at him curiously. "Do you have something against him?" she wondered aloud.

Oddly he averted his eyes. "Nothing personal."

"We're both regulation types," she pointed out. "Maybe we wouldn't work out as secret agents, considering some of the things they're expected to do in the field, but there are people without our brand of scruples, you know. It's not a black mark, exactly, is it?"

He frowned, as if worried about something he didn't want to put into words. "No, of course not." His eyes narrowed. "You're not going soft on him? He's a total stranger, Sarina."

She sighed. "Not really. I was married to him."

He looked absolutely shocked.

"It was a long time ago. The marriage was annulled," she added quickly. "He guarded my father, when I was still in school."

"When, exactly, were you married to him?" he asked pointedly.

She glanced at her watch. "We're running out of time for lunch. We should probably go."

"You're avoiding the question."

She smiled. "Yes, I am. Nice of you to notice. Come on, before the phone rings and I get trapped!"

He followed her out of her office with a dark, cold suspicion that he couldn't overcome.

SATURDAY MORNING, Colby helped Bernadette into the back seat of the SUV and buckled her in. She was wearing old boots and older jeans, with a red checked shirt. Her eyes were bubbly with excitement.

"I love to ride horses! It's nice of you to let us go with you! Is it a big ranch?"

He chuckled, feeling more relaxed than he had in years. "Yes, it is. He runs cattle as well as horses. I think you'll like it."

He opened the passenger door for Sarina, who was dressed similarly to her daughter, except that her long blond hair was in a braid hanging down her back. He had on jeans and boots, too, with a chambray shirt. Sarina's was lightweight denim, with embroidered pink roses on it. She looked trim in those tight jeans, very feminine, and she made him ache in all the wrong places.

He got in beside her, buckling his seat belt. "Do you ride, too?" he asked her.

She nodded, smiling. "Rodrigo taught me."

His face closed up like a clam shell under siege. He started the engine and pulled out of her parking lot with muted violence.

Sarina wondered at the force of his anger. It had been the same way when Rodrigo had taken her to lunch. He couldn't possibly be jealous of her...

"How much do you know about your liaison officer buddy?" he asked curtly.

She didn't dare answer that. She cleared her throat. "He's been a good friend to us, Colby."

He hadn't. It ate at him like acid. He hated knowing how much she'd suffered since their brief marriage. It wasn't his fault, not really, but it hurt him just the same. If he'd been around, he'd have done what he could for her, despite the way they'd parted.

"You used to have horses, didn't you?" she asked, trying to divert him.

"Yes, some years ago I bred quarter horses on a

ranch in north Texas and had a man who showed them for me. We won ribbons," he said. "My father raised them in Arizona when I was a boy. He wasn't keen on quarter horses. He had a herd of Appaloosas. He bought and sold them to put me through school." He didn't like speaking of the old man. He had some regrets about the distance that had separated them.

Bernadette started to speak, but a quick look from her mother made her keep quiet.

"You still ride?" she asked carelessly.

He glanced at her coolly. "I have to mount offside, but yes, I still ride."

She flushed. "You know I didn't mean it that way."

He grimaced. His eyes went back to the highway ahead of them. "I'm sensitive about it."

She glanced at the prosthesis. It was the one she'd helped him put on earlier in the week. She blushed as she recalled what had happened in his apartment.

He saw it, and began to relax. He liked her response to him. It was surprising, considering how badly he'd hurt her. Impulsively his right hand slid over hers where it lay in her lap. He felt it jerk with surprise as he linked his fingers into hers. He pressed them hungrily and felt, delighted, the returning pressure of her own hand. She looked at him, her eyes faintly hungry, her lips parted. He looked back, aching to do more than hold her hand.

"Look out!" Bernadette called from the backseat.

Colby's eyes went back to the road and he swerved to avoid running off the road. "Thanks, tidbit," he said, laughing as he met her eyes in the rearview mirror. "I got distracted."

She grinned back. "Is it far? Are we almost there?"

"Almost," he lied. It was another half hour. He didn't let go of Sarina's hand, though. In fact, he held it even tighter as he drove, the wheel held quite easily in the prosthetic hand.

Bernadette gasped when he pulled up in Cy Parks's yard. "But, this is where Rodrigo brings us!" she exclaimed. "Mr. Parks has a pretty pinto horse that he lets me ride!"

He scowled, meeting Sarina's surprised gaze. "Ramirez knows Cy?"

She swallowed, choosing her words carefully. "They met a few months ago and made friends," she lied. She'd have to get Cy to one side and caution him not to tell Colby what he knew about Rodrigo.

"I thought Ramirez was from Mexico."

"He, uh, worked in Jacobsville briefly," she lied.

She was hiding something. He stared at her for a long moment until he glimpsed Cy coming down the steps to meet them.

"Glad you could come," Cy said, greeting them. "So this is who your guests are! As it happens, this isn't their first time on the place." He grinned at Bernadette. "Long time no see, sprout," he teased, ruffling her thick hair. "I'll have Harley saddle Bean for you."

"Bean?" Colby wondered aloud.

"She's a pinto," Cy drawled, grinning. He looked over his shoulder. "Hey, Harley, how about saddling Bean and Twig for these two, and Dusty and King for Colby and me? I need to talk to Colby for a minute."

"Sure thing," Harley called back. "Hey, Bernie, come on and I'll show you how to do that diamond hitch again."

"Can I?" she asked her mother.

"Go ahead," Sarina said with a soft smile.

Bernadette ran to join Harley in the barn.

"We've got a situation here," Cy began. "The old Lopez warehouse is still in operation. I had Eb Scott put a surveillance camera out there. I've got some interesting tape." He noticed Colby's sudden glance at Sarina, and added, "Sarina, Lisa's making coffee in the kitchen. Would you like to go and talk to her until we're ready to go?"

Sarina had to hide a smile. Cy was trying not to blow her cover. "Okay, partner," she drawled, "I'll go hide out with the womenfolk. If any varmints come growling around, you just let me know and I'll chase 'em off with my petticoat."

"Sassy," Colby murmured in a deep, sensuous tone, his dark eyes twinkling at her.

She grinned back. "Just being helpful," she replied, giving Cy a speaking glance about being relegated to the sidelines, with her history. Cy knew, but she didn't dare let Colby know. Not yet.

CY TOOK COLBY into the office where his surveillance equipment was kept. He moved switches and indicated a computer screen. Several men, and a woman, were speaking Spanish in what looked like a heated encounter.

Colby's eyes narrowed as he translated mentally. "They're talking about a big cocaine shipment that they've got concealed. It's still in Houston. They want to bring it here, but they can't figure out how to."

"They're also considering trucking it down, but one of the others thinks that's too conspicuous. He wants to do it in old, beat-up vans with lots of kids inside." Cy's face hardened. "That's sick."

"It's just business, to them," Colby replied.

"I'm going to keep the tape running and have some of Eb's men monitor it around the clock," the older man mused. "No way am I going to allow drug smugglers to find a safe haven right beside my own land!"

"I've got one of their colleagues wired," Colby told him. "And I'm getting data of my own. I'll share, if there's anything of value." His eyes narrowed. "How is it that you know Rodrigo?"

Cy's eyebrows lifted. "I met him in Houston," he said with a straight face. "I know Eugene Ritter. He was in the office one day. We started talking and found we had a lot in common. He asked if he could bring Sarina and Bernadette down with him to ride horses and I said, sure."

Colby had been in covert ops for a long time, and he knew Cy from the old days. He knew when he was being conned.

"Just accept what I'm telling you," Cy said firmly. "Everything will become clear down the road."

Colby glowered at him. "I feel like a damned mushroom."

"It's nice in the dark," Cy mused. "I've been there several times myself."

Colby shook his head.

They rode down the same wooded path that Colby and Cy had ridden weeks earlier. The foliage was turning to reds and golds and oranges.

"I love autumn," Colby murmured aloud.

"It's my favorite season, too," Sarina confessed.

"Rein him in a little, baby," Colby called to Bernadette. "You don't want him to run away with you."

"Yes, I do," she teased, grinning. "If he tries to run away, I'll bend him."

Colby pulled in his mount and smiled delightedly at the child. "You know how to do that?"

"Sure. I pull him around with one hand and one

leg, and bend him when he tries to take off unexpectedly and run away with me. I learned it from one of Cy's men, who used to train horses."

He grinned back. "And what do you do if he rears?"

"Hold on to his mane with my hands and his back with my knees until he comes down again. Gravity is our friend," she teased, laughing with her dark eyes as well as her mouth.

"Daredevil," he accused.

Sarina, watching them, was so aware of the similarities between the man and the child that she had to fight tears. It was acutely painful to see what Bernadette had missed in her young life. Rodrigo was kind to them, and Bernadette loved him. But he wasn't her father. She wondered if Colby realized what a changed man he was when he was around Bernadette. He laughed, he teased, he played. The man she remembered did those things rarely. In the past few weeks, since he'd come back into her life, he'd been a cold, unfeeling stranger. But here, with the child, he was very different.

Colby saw her watching him and frowned. "Something wrong?" he asked.

She forced a smile. "Nothing." She turned her attention back to the trail.

On the way back to the ranch, Colby and Cy exchanged mischievous glances, dug in their heels, bent over their mounts, and raced to the gate. Before Cy had time to detour around it, Colby had jumped the fence and was reining in at the barn.

"Slowpoke," he told Cy.

The other man chuckled as he swung down, breathing hard. "And you called Bernadette a daredevil!" he accused.

"I have a friend who'd have jumped the gate, instead of the fence," he replied, indicating the lack of space between the gate and the logo of the ranch on a board above it.

"You'd have done it yourself a few years ago," Cy chuckled.

Colby shrugged. "I'm trying to settle down," he drawled. He gave Sarina a pointed glance as he said it, and noted with delight the faint color in her cheeks.

THEY HAD AN EARLY LUNCH with Lisa and Cy and then climbed into the SUV for the drive back to Houston.

The earlier intimacy seemed to have drifted away. Sarina was pleasant, but reserved. He felt the coolness between them and wondered what had caused it.

Sarina was unusually quiet on the ride home. He dropped them off at their apartment. Bernadette grinned at him and thanked him for the trip, rushing off inside to watch a television program she liked.

Sarina stood on the doorstep with him, hesitant and uneasy. He and Bernadette were finding more and more in common, and there was a visible affection between them. What if he asked the right question and the child blurted out an answer? How was Colby going to react? There was one other complication, too. He had no idea what sort of work she did, and she knew already that he wasn't going to approve of it. She was trying not to look back, but he'd hurt her badly in the old days. The new passion between them was dangerous. She didn't want to risk her heart on him again. She'd backed off in self-defense.

She managed a smile as she looked up. "It was a nice day. Thanks."

He moved close, tilting her face up to his. "I've missed so much," he said huskily, as he searched her eyes in the porch light. "A family, children." His face clenched. "Two marriages, and I've still lived alone most of my life."

"Lobo wolves do," she said, trying to make a joke of it.

His arms slid around her and pulled her close. "No. Wolves mate and protect their cubs, and their mates." He bent and kissed her gently. Her mouth was cool and unresponsive. "What's wrong?" he asked quietly.

She swallowed. "Cold feet," she confessed.

He looked at her long and hard. After a minute he stepped back. "Yes," he said. "I know what you mean." He was thinking about all the things she didn't know about him and the life he'd led. He wasn't being honest with her. Perhaps she sensed it. "Well, good night."

She managed a smile. "Good night, Colby."

He started off the porch, hesitated, and looked back to find her watching him with a soul-deep pain in her dark eyes.

He went back to her, framing her face in his hands. "Tell me what's wrong," he said roughly.

She couldn't hold back the tears. They ran silently down her cheeks, into her mouth. He bent and kissed them away.

He folded her close and held her, rocking her gently. His cheek drew against the top of her head. She smelled of roses. They stood that way for a long time. Finally he eased her away from him and looked down at her with quiet, soft eyes.

He didn't say good-night again. He walked away.

She went inside reluctantly, and locked the door.

RITTER OIL Corporation celebrated its fiftieth anniversary with a staff party the next week on Friday night. A live band provided music. Eugene Ritter had rented a banquet room in a local steak house, and a buffet was arranged on a long table against the wall. Children were invited to attend along with their parents. There were lots of kids. Sarina was amused at them trying to mimic the adults on the dance floor.

She nursed a glass of champagne. She had no head for alcohol, so she limited herself to one drink on a full stomach.

Colby joined her at the drinks table, asking for a tall glass of ginger ale. He grinned at Sarina. "I've been on the wagon for almost three years," he confessed. "I don't want to fall off again."

She nodded, searching his dark eyes. He was still handsome. Her heart ached every time she saw him.

He looked around for Bernadette and found her excitedly talking to Nikki Hunter and a little boy.

"She mixes easily, doesn't she?" he asked Sarina.

"Not really. She's comfortable with people she knows, but she's shy in groups she doesn't know."

"I used to be like that," he mused. "I still am, to a degree." He kept staring around the room with narrow, cold eyes.

She looked up at him curiously. "What are you looking for?"

"Ramirez," he said curtly.

She hid a smile. "He said he was going to be late."

"He must have needed a quick nap," Colby muttered. "All that tiring liaison work must be hard on a man his age."

She turned a giggle into a cough and covered her mouth.

He glared at her. "He's too old for you."

"He isn't," she replied. "He's just thirty-five."

His dark brows met. "He looks older."

She turned her eyes to her drink. “He’s had a difficult life,” she said, averting her gaze.

He was going to question that when Bernadette walked up to him trailing Nikki and the little boy she’d been talking to, as well as three other children of comparable ages.

“This is him,” Bernadette told them, pointing at Colby. “He carried us both through the flood to his truck and then he drove us to school! He’s very strong!”

The other children followed her rapt gaze and Colby’s high cheekbones went a ruddy color.

“He can ride a horse, too, and even jump fences with it!” Bernadette added, her dark eyes wide and soft as they looked up at him. She smiled shyly.

He smiled back.

“Let’s go watch the drummer,” the little boy enthused. “He’s playing a solo!”

They followed him. Bernadette looked back over her shoulder, grinning at him, as she joined the children.

“You’re a hero,” Sarina said amusedly. “You rescued us from the great flood.”

He chuckled. “Well!” Not for worlds would he have admitted how it touched him to be Bernadette’s hero. He sipped ginger ale, watching the couples on the dance floor. He glanced down at Sarina. “Do you still dance?”

Her heart jumped. “Sort of.”

"Sort of?" He took his glass and hers and put them on an empty corner of the drinks table.

"I haven't danced in a long time."

"Neither have I. Maybe we won't crash and burn." He pulled her gently into his arms and folded her close while they shifted around the floor to the lazy, seductive Latin rhythm of the band.

Sarina was closer to heaven than she'd been in seven years. The feel of his tall, lean body, the warmth of his arms, went to her head a little. She relaxed into his powerful body with a trembling little sigh.

Colby felt it and his body went rigid with desire. It had never happened with any woman that quickly, except with Maureen at the very beginning of their turbulent relationship. It shocked him that he was still so attuned to Sarina, despite their years apart.

She moved back a little, hiding her eyes from him.

"Still shy of me?" he murmured deeply, chuckling. "All right, chicken, I'll try to behave myself."

He let her shift her hips back from the press of his, but he rested his cheek on her soft hair.

"The music is nice," she murmured as the music worked on her mood.

"So it is. It's been years since I've been in this sort of situation," he confessed. "I don't go to parties."

"Neither do I, as a rule," she replied. She hesitated. She was remembering Bernadette's birthday the following day. She had to remind Rodrigo to bring the cake with him, because the bakery was on his way to her apartment. She wondered if it would be reckless and stupid to invite Colby. So far, he had no idea of Bernadette's exact age.

"You're very quiet," he remarked. His fingers curled into hers and his lips moved against the top of her head. "I've been busy this week with internal security upgrades, but we could go down to Cy's tomorrow and go riding, if you like?"

"I can't," she said softly.

He stopped dancing and looked down at her with intent dark eyes. "Why not? Cold feet?"

She shook her head. "No, it's not that." She grimaced. "Bernadette's having a party," she said.

"What sort of party?" he asked suspiciously.

She hesitated.

"Well?" he persisted.

"It's her birthday."

He was silent for several seconds. "I see."

"I would have asked you to come, but you and Rodrigo…well…"

"You don't have to spell it out," he said, but he relaxed a little. She wasn't trying to push him out of her life at all. He looked down into her dark eyes, and he smiled. The arm with the prosthesis drew her gently closer. "Suppose I come late?"

She smiled back, her eyes twinkling. "That would be nice. Bernadette would enjoy having you there."

He nodded. His gaze fell to her soft mouth and he eyed it with pure speculation.

"Colby," she protested huskily.

"What?" he whispered, and his head actually started to bend.

A big hand came down on his shoulder. "My turn, I think," came a Latin accented voice from behind.

Colby stopped and turned, his eyes wide. "How the hell do you do it?" he asked icily. "You're like the creeping fog, you appear out of nowhere."

Rodrigo smiled icily. "Keep that in mind, won't you?"

He danced Sarina away deliberately, without looking back at Colby, who stood on the sidelines smoldering quietly.

"That was wicked," Sarina told Rodrigo.

He chuckled. "It keeps him on his toes, doesn't it? What time do you want me there tomorrow?"

"About eleven, and are you going to bring the cake?"

"Certainly." His dark eyes narrowed on hers. "You're letting the rent-a-cop get too close," he cautioned. "He's going to start figuring things out anyday now. It's a risk we can't take."

She grimaced. "I know that. It's just…"

"Don't be a fool, Sarina," he cautioned, his eyes narrowing with concern. "He's already thrown you over once for another woman."

Her free hand traced a pattern on his jacket. "I haven't forgotten."

"He's done some questionable things over the years."

She looked up. "How do you know that?"

He cleared his throat. "Cy told me," he said. "I went down to his place to check on a few things today. He said that Lane took you and Bernadette riding down there last weekend."

"Cy can mind his own business," she replied hotly.

The fury in her tone caught his attention. It didn't take a mind reader to know that she was falling in love with Colby Lane all over again. It disturbed him that he couldn't think of any way to stop it. He wanted to tell her what he knew about Lane, but it seemed low and cowardly to fight the other man that way. They were sort of on the same team, and he and Sarina certainly were allies. It wasn't altogether business, either, that made him want to interfere. He had feelings for Sarina that he couldn't contain. Lane was a train wreck that threatened to rip his cozy relationship with Sarina and Bernadette to shreds, and he couldn't find a way to stop it.

"Lane's bad news," he said curtly.

"I know that."

"But it isn't stopping you from going out with him, is it?" He stopped dancing and looked down at her. "Sarina, exactly when did you know him?"

She couldn't look at him. "Seven years ago."

He could add. And subtract. He drew in a long breath and muffled a curse under it. "He's Bernadette's father, isn't he?" he asked, icily blunt.

CHAPTER SEVEN

SARINA MANAGED to lift her eyes to Rodrigo's. It was impossible to lie to him. She shrugged. "Yes. But he doesn't know," she added gently. "And there's no use telling him. His second wife convinced him that he's sterile. He doesn't believe he can have a child."

He let out a long breath. "That explains a few things."

"So it wouldn't do any good to mention it," she continued. "The past is truly dead. I couldn't have a relationship with him now, not only because of Bernadette, but because of my job. He'd be livid if he knew about it."

He saw the misery in her face and felt guilty for bringing it up. He shook her gently and grinned. "Dance," he teased. "We're attracting attention."

"And we're doing it without guns," she exclaimed under her breath. "Wow!"

"Stop that," he muttered.

"Sorry. Couldn't resist it. Don't forget the cake, okay?"

"You've been reminding me for a week," he pointed out. "Once would have done it."

"Point taken."

"I hope she likes what I got her."

"What is it?"

"Oh, no," he teased. "I tell you, and you let the cat out of the bag. I'm not telling you any secrets."

"Well, pin a rose on me…!"

A big hand came down on Rodrigo's shoulder. "And now it's my turn again," Colby said, twirling Sarina back into his arms. He gave Rodrigo a smug grin, which in turn, infuriated the other man.

Rodrigo's dark eyes flashed. "Why don't you take your attitude and shove it right up…!"

"Could you control yourself? There are women and children present!" Colby said with mock horror.

Rodrigo looked as if he might actually implode. His olive tan reddened under the force of his anger.

"Pitiful self-control," Colby said, clicking his tongue as he danced Sarina away, leaving a silently cursing Rodrigo behind. "Are you *sure* you want to get mixed up with a man like that?"

She wouldn't laugh, she wouldn't laugh…!

He drew her head to his chest, amused at her efforts to hide her reaction from her Latin friend. "Don't spare his feelings, for God's sake."

"You're horrible!" she exclaimed breathlessly.

He shrugged. "I try. If you're going to do something, you should do it well, I always think."

She let out a long breath. "Poor Rodrigo!"

"He'll get over it," he mused, smiling down at her. "The world is full of unattached women."

"I *am* unattached," she pointed out.

He shook his head slowly, smiling down at her. "I've got squatter's rights."

She met that soft gaze and her heart did a flip. Past and present merged, and she wanted nothing more than to be held close to him and loved…

The big hand came down on his shoulder again. "And it's my turn again!" Rodrigo purred, as he spun Sarina into his arms and danced her away.

Colby glared after them. But a minute later the music ended and Rodrigo had to stop, because the band was taking a break. He went to retrieve his ginger ale with a smug grin.

He paused to speak to Hunter and Jennifer for a minute. When he looked around, Sarina and Rodrigo were missing. Bernadette was still playing with Nicole and the little boy who seemed to be part of their group.

Curious, he spotted the two against a wall, talking seriously. There didn't seem to be any romantic feeling between them, at least not on Sarina's part, and they looked as solemn as morticians.

He managed to move a little closer, his keen eyes going to Sarina's lips as she spoke to Rodrigo. What a good thing, he thought amusedly, that he was taught lip-reading as part of his covert training.

He frowned as he picked up disjointed phrases, because she kept turning her head as she spoke. There was something about a stakeout, and surveillance, and an upcoming operation in which she was involved.

It made no sense to him. What sort of operation would involve a clerk in an oil corporation? Had Rodrigo involved her in some sort of project? Worse, had Hunter taken him at his word that Sarina was cut out for something better than menial work? What if Hunter had her watching the drug suspects?

His heart stopped at the thought that she might be involved in something dangerous. Bernadette had nobody except her mother. Surely she wouldn't risk her life when she had a child to raise? He was furious at himself for even mentioning Sarina's potential to Hunter.

He moved away, frowning. He was going to have to talk to Hunter about that. Sarina had a child. She couldn't be involved in dangerous work.

He had another sip of ginger ale and waited for the music to start up again, but it didn't. Apparently it was time to leave. He was vaguely disappointed. He'd hoped to have another dance with Sarina.

Holding her in his arms, even on a dance floor, was addictive. But very quickly, she and Bernadette were heading for the back door.

He intercepted them outside.

"I'll see you tomorrow afternoon," he told Bernadette.

Her dark eyes brightened. "You're coming to my birthday party?" she asked excitedly.

Her enthusiasm warmed the cold places inside him. He smiled with genuine affection. "Yes, I am. But I'll be late. About four o'clock. Is it okay?"

"It's great!" she said enthusiastically.

"If you have cake," he stipulated with mock seriousness. "I love cake."

"Chocolate, as I recall," Sarina said without thinking.

His dark eyes met hers. "Yes."

She flushed. She hadn't meant to say that.

"And you like strawberry ice cream," he added with a faint smile.

Her eyes danced. She'd never imagined that he'd remember trivial things about her.

"See you," he added.

"Are you two ready to go?" Rodrigo asked, ignoring Colby as he fished his car keys out of his slacks' pocket.

Colby gave him a dark look, which was returned with interest.

"Good night, Colby," Sarina said.

"Good night," he replied, winking at Bernadette.

"See you tomorrow. At four," the child added with a grin.

"We'll probably run out of cake before then," Rodrigo said blandly.

"No problem. I'll bring another with me."

"Going to bake it yourself?" Rodrigo muttered under his breath.

Colby glared at the older man. "Sure I am. Did you knit that suit yourself?" Colby added with a speaking look at the other man's dark jacket.

"Let's go," Sarina said quickly, getting between the two men. She literally led Rodrigo out by one hand just as he had his mouth open to answer Colby's mocking taunt.

COLBY DIDN'T SLEEP well. Something Sarina had said kept nudging at the back of his mind. Something about Bernadette's birthday. Resolutely he refused to listen. He got up before daylight and made coffee. Later, he dressed and went to the mall to shop. He had no idea what to get a little girl of seven. But as he was passing one of the science shops, he stopped suddenly. He couldn't get the thought of a microscope out of his mind.

He walked into the shop and talked with the salesman about a particularly expensive one that connected to a computer, so that specimens could be saved on CD-ROM.

"It's a bit extravagant for a seven-year-old," the salesman said dubiously.

"She's not your average seven-year-old," came the tongue-in-cheek reply.

He produced his credit card. The store provided a sedate wrapping, but added a colorful ribbon to offset it.

With the present.wrapped, and secure in the SUV, he went to have a leisurely lunch and then went walking around the mall. He was uneasy about what he'd "overheard" when Rodrigo and Sarina were talking privately. Something was going on between those two, but nothing of a particularly romantic nature. It was driving him crazy. She was driving him crazy. He kept remembering how she felt in his arms, that morning in his apartment. He'd thought of little else since then. She didn't hate him. She wanted him. But it wasn't going to be easy, getting her back into his life. She still had hidden fears of intimacy, and he had a few of his own. If he got closer to her, and lost control, as he had all those years ago…

He turned away from the clothing store window he'd been looking in and walked back down the mall. It was almost four. Time to go. He climbed into the SUV and drove toward Sarina's apartment. He hoped Rodrigo was there. He was looking forward to helping the man headfirst into what was left of Bernadette's cake.

THERE WERE COLORFUL balloons tied to the worn wrought-iron railing on the front porch, and scattered bits of pretty paper and ribbon in the trash can next to the door. He tapped gently and Bernadette came running to the door, pretty in a pink striped dress with white stockings and pink sneakers that looked new. She had a jaunty chiffon bow clasped in her newly short, dark hair.

"Hi!" she exclaimed. "You came!"

"I promised I would," he reminded her, with a glance at Sarina, who was washing dishes at the sink.

"Come on in," she called. "I saved you some cake and ice cream. Want coffee?"

"Please." He looked around. No Rodrigo. He grinned as he took off his jacket. He was wearing gray slacks and a long-sleeved shirt and blue patterned tie that highlighted his dark good looks. He didn't often wear short-sleeved things—the prosthesis, for all its realistic look, was more noticeable in them. Newly repaired, the high-tech prosthesis was back in place.

"This is for you," he told Bernadette, handing her a beautifully wrapped rectangular box.

"Can I open it?" she asked, all eyes.

He smiled. "Go for it."

She put it down on the coffee table, frowning. "It's heavy," she murmured as she tore at wrapping and ribbon.

Sarina brought his coffee in a white mug and stood beside him.

"You'll think I've lost my mind when you see it," he said without looking at her. He was beginning to have second thoughts about the present. "I don't know why I bought it…"

The last of the paper came off and Bernadette looked at her mother with quiet dismay. Sarina wore a similar expression.

They both looked at him, without speaking.

A faint ruddy flush colored his high cheekbones. "I can return it," he began slowly.

"No!" Bernadette exclaimed, wrapping her arms around it with horror.

"Then, what…?" he began.

Sarina went to the small desk in the living room and opened a drawer. She pulled out a colored sheet and hesitantly gave it to Colby. It was a color ad for a high-tech microscope; the one he'd just given Bernadette.

"I told her we couldn't afford it," Sarina began slowly. She flushed.

Bernadette was touching it as if she still couldn't believe it was real. There were tears in her eyes, too. "I love to go to school because we have a microscope like this in our classroom," she said. "I go early sometimes so the teacher will let me look at paramecium in it." She turned to Colby. "Thanks," she said huskily, and held out her arms.

The expression in her eyes hurt him. That affectionate gesture hurt him. He'd been horrible to the child, but she hadn't held it against him. He went down on one knee and gathered her close, feeling her small arms tight around his neck as she hugged him. He sighed, kissing her dark hair. Seven. She was seven years old. It was October.

Seven? He went rigid. It was October. She was seven years old. She'd been conceived seven years and nine months ago. In January. Seven years ago. He and Sarina had been married in January. Seven years ago.

A flash of pain hit him so hard that he shuddered. He drew back from Bernadette with the horror in his eyes. His mind was a jumble of half-finished thoughts. Maureen had lied. He wasn't sterile. Bernadette's father had deserted Sarina when she was pregnant. She was in dire straits, sick and alone, her father had thrown her out of her home because she refused to have an abortion. The father of her child had deserted her. He'd…deserted her!

"Oh, sweet Jesus!" he choked, in a tone that was painfully reverent.

Bernadette looked at him for a minute and then moved away. She went to a cabinet and pulled out a photo album.

"Bernadette, no!" Sarina said, horrified.

The child looked up at her with Colby's eyes. "It's all right, Mama," she said softly. "He knows."

Sarina almost fell into a chair, her eyes wide with pain and sick knowledge.

Bernadette took Colby's hand and pulled him to the sofa, and pushed him down on it.

"Look," she said in Apache.

He stared at her helplessly, seeing himself in the shape of her eyes, her mouth, her nose. She was his child. His child!

"Look, Father," she said again in Apache.

The words had passed by his numb brain, but now he realized that she was speaking to him in his own tongue. She wasn't Hispanic. She was Apache.

"My child," he whispered, in Apache.

She smiled at him. "This was my granddaddy."

She pointed at the photo album. As he focused on it, he realized that he was going back in time. There was Sarina, very pregnant, smiling with joy radiating from her face. There she was in the hospital, looking very ill and despondent. There she was, with several people including Eugene Ritter, home from the hospital in a small apartment with lots of presents for the newborn. She was holding Bernadette in her arms. Beside her was an old, stooped man with white hair and a big grin. His father!

He looked at Sarina, shocked.

She moved her shoulders uncomfortably. "I'd given up," she said huskily. "I was all alone. I couldn't get help…from anywhere. There was no food, except what my coworkers brought occasionally, and I was too proud to tell them how little I had. I couldn't even work. Then your father showed up at my door, with his suitcase. He said that the child was a girl. He'd take care of me until she was born, and he'd take care of her after she was born, so that I could work."

"How did he know?" he managed.

"I don't know. He just did. He provided for us out of his social security check until she was born. Eugene Ritter paid my medical bills. He hardly knew me except as an employee, but I'd become friends with Phillip and Jennifer. I suppose they told him." She made a gesture with one hand. "Your father could cook, and he did. Once I was back on my feet, and could go back to work, he stayed with Bernadette. Years later," she said, skipping her night classes at college and the new job she took later, "when he had cancer, I nursed him. When we lost him," she added unsteadily, "it was a blow."

Bernadette was watching Colby closely. Her grandfather had told her something to tell him, and said she would know when it was time. She was certain that it wasn't time now. The man beside her was in great pain. His eyes were blind with it.

Sarina bit her lip, hard.

He looked into her dark eyes, barely seeing them. "Maureen told me nothing about any phone call from you," he bit off. "I was in Africa…" He got up blindly.

She stared at him. He hadn't known?

"She convinced me I was sterile," he said, his voice choked. He looked back at Bernadette, at his daughter, with eyes so full of pain that they seemed black. "All these years…"

Sarina got up. "Colby…"

Before she could get the words out, there was a scream, high-pitched and carrying.

Colby's first thought was that his pistol was in the glove compartment of the SUV. He was out the door in a flash, his eyes searching for the source of the scream.

He found it quickly. An old woman, stooped and silver-haired and buxom, was outside on the grass in front of another set of apartments, pleading loudly in Spanish with a violent young man who was raining violent blows on her with both fists.

Without hesitation, Colby broke into a run. Sarina almost took off after him, until she realized how it would look, and that she didn't dare get involved.

The boy saw Colby coming and looked up with a vicious laugh. He started toward Colby, but it was already too late. Colby aimed a roundhouse kick at his head and brought him down. He rolled and got to his feet, but before he could raise his fists, Colby aimed another kick at his diaphragm and brought him down again. He flipped the young man onto his back, whipped out a handkerchief, and, using his knee to hold him down and his arms in place, quickly tied the boy's thumbs together behind his waist. The boy was screaming curses, violently thrashing, his eyes clouded and glazed. Sarina watched with fascination. She'd never seen him in action. Now she realized with a start how professional and capable he was. The loss of part of an arm hadn't slowed him down one bit. That military training, she decided, never wore off.

The boy was still cursing blindly. Drugs, Colby noted with fierce anger. He knelt beside the old woman, wonderfully gentle. "Are you all right?"

She was sobbing helplessly. "Why? Why?" she choked. Bruises were coming out all over her bare arms, her face.

"Come with me," he said gently, helping her to her feet. "Can you walk?"

"Yes," she whimpered.

He led her gently back to Sarina's porch, where she and Bernadette were waiting. "Keep her here, while I get the police, will you?" he asked softly.

"Of course," Sarina said at once. "Señora Martinez, come inside and let me clean your face."

"No police, oh, please," she choked, pleading with Colby. "You no understand. He all I got, *todo mi familia en este pais.* You give him to police, they put him in jail, he learn much and never be the same boy again! I no have the words…!"

Colby held her hand and assured her, in Spanish,

that he would take care of the boy and he wouldn't go to jail. She kissed his hand, her wrinkled old eyes still pouring tears.

"I'll be back," he told Sarina, noting her faint surprise that he was as fluent as she was.

"I'll take care of her," she promised, and tried not to worry about him, because he still had the aftermath of that terrible shock in his eyes.

"I know you will," he replied. He reached toward her cheek and abruptly drew his fingers back and turned away. He had no right to touch her, after what he'd done to her life.

He walked back toward the boy, pulling out his cell phone on the way. It was going to be tricky if any witnesses had already dialed 911. He had to trust to luck.

The boy was still yelling obscenities and struggling like a beached fish on the sidewalk. Colby stood over him, dialing the phone.

An older boy came running. He stopped short of Colby. He was wearing a bandana over his head and he had tattoos on both arms. Colby instinctively moved into a relaxed fighting stance, just in case.

The boy noticed. He hesitated. "You come to see Miss Carrington," he said.

"Yes."

"You calling the cops, huh?" he asked belligerently.

"No. I'm not."

The boy hesitated. "Then who…?"

"What's your stake in it?" Colby asked coldly.

"I'm Raoul. He's my cousin, Tito." He looked toward the open door of the apartment. "You seen my grandma?"

"She's with Sarina and Bernadette," Colby said. "She's pretty roughed up."

He groaned. "Tito, you idiot!" he groaned at the boy. "You *estupido!*"

"He can't hear you. He's bombed out of his mind."

The boy ran a hand over his face. "She's got nobody but me and Tito. He's her nephew, and he lives with her," he said harshly. "He goes to the store for her and keeps her safe. I told him that stuff was poison…!"

Colby held up a hand. He had the man he'd phoned on the line. He spoke in fluent Spanish, telling the man that he had a young boy high on drugs, he'd battered his grandmother and he needed help. He nodded, aware of the older boy's wide-eyed surprise as he continued to listen. He answered, telling the man where he was, and adding that he'd better bring help. No, the police hadn't been informed. He was hoping the neighbors hadn't phoned for help. He nodded, spoke again, and hung up, closing and repocketing the cell phone.

"Who'd you call?" the older boy asked.

"A friend of mine. An old…colleague, you might

say," he added with a faint smile. "He runs a halfway house downtown. He'll take your cousin and dry him out. Afterward, he'll try to get him in treatment."

The older boy let out a hoarse sigh. "It's more than he deserves, after what he's done," he said coldly. "But he's family, the stupid idiot! You sure Grandma's all right?"

"Go see about her, if you want to. I'll wait here for Eduardo."

"Okay." He hesitated. "Thanks."

Colby shrugged. "If he doesn't shape up, it's just postponing the inevitable," he added. "And next time, he might kill the old woman."

"Yeah. I know that. I'll keep close to Grandma for a while. And I'll do what I can for him."

He went off in the direction of Sarina's apartment. Colby stood above the hog-tied drug user and closed his ears to the profanity. He looked around at darkened windows and a couple of fluttering curtains. These people knew that it was dangerous to know much about crime. He didn't imagine that the police would be called in, this time.

Ten minutes went by before a beige van pulled up in the parking lot between the apartment units. A man in a priest's habit got out with two strong young men and walked toward Colby. He grinned as he held out his hand.

"*Compadre,*" he greeted. "How long has it been?"

"Eight years, as I recall," Colby said, returning the firm hand clasp.

"You look well."

"So do you, except for the strange-looking camo outfit," he chided, indicating his old friend's white collar that denoted a priest.

Eduardo chuckled. "It did take some getting used to."

Colby nodded toward the boy writhing on the ground. "I don't know what he took. Judging by the contortions and the glazed look, it's either acid or crack cocaine."

"Not much to choose between," Eduardo said with clinical interest, "although acid's easier to kick." He nodded to his companions, who hefted the boy like a tiger on a pole between them and carried him off, struggling and cursing, to the van. "We'll take care of him, don't worry."

"What a waste," Colby muttered.

"Drugs always are," the other man said heavily. "Does it occur to you, *compadre,* that our world is long on pressure and short on relaxation? Too much stress, too much responsibility, too much worry, and this becomes the answer." He indicated the boy being put in the van. "The old woman?"

"Will be all right," Colby said. "She's only bruised and hurt. But apparently he takes care of her, buys her groceries and looks out for her. She'll be alone."

"We'll do what we can to get him back on his feet. Meanwhile, I'll make it my business to keep an eye on her. Any other family?"

"There's a grandson, he's with the old woman. He seems responsible enough."

"Tell him we can provide what the old woman needs. All he has to do is call me."

"I'll do that. Thanks."

Eduardo shook hands with him. He shook his head, his black eyes sparkling. "What a long time ago we made our living with violence."

"We were younger," Colby replied. His eyes began to lose their light. "And unaware."

"Yes. Take care. Come and see me when you have time. I'll bet I can still beat you at chess."

"You and a chess master, maybe," Colby chuckled. "See you."

The priest threw up his hand and walked back to the van.

Colby went back to the apartment. The old woman had been given coffee and cleaned up. Sarina was sitting beside her, looking warily at the young man in the bandana who still held a cloth with ice in it to his grandmother's head.

They looked up as Colby entered the apartment.

"He's on his way to the halfway house. Father Eduardo said that if you need anything at all, *señora,*" he told the woman, "he'll do whatever he can for you. He's a good man."

"He must be, to take my Tito and save him from jail," the *señora* said heavily. Her eyes were swollen with tears. "Thank you, for what you have done."

Colby shrugged. *"De nada,"* he said easily.

She got up, with her grandson supporting her. "You're all right, man," the boy told Colby with a solemn look. "I won't forget."

Colby walked out with them. The boy hesitated on the porch. "You need anything," he told Colby, "anything at all, you ask me. Anything. I owe you."

Colby moved closer, so that Sarina couldn't overhear him. "Then look out for Sarina and the child. This is a dangerous neighborhood. I know that gangs operate here. I can't be with them all the time."

The boy gave him an odd, puzzled smile and extended his hand. Colby shook it.

"I give you my word," he told Colby. "Nothing will ever happen to them here."

"Thanks."

The boy managed a smile. "I love my grandma," he said. He helped her along the sidewalk, back toward her apartment.

Sarina came out onto the porch to stand beside Colby.

"He's going to keep an eye on the two of you," he told her quietly. "You'll be all right."

"Oh." She nodded. Her eyes were dark with

shock and exasperation. "You've just asked the leader of the biggest gang in the projects to take me on as a dependent, and you think it's all right?"

CHAPTER EIGHT

COLBY GAVE HER an odd look.

"Didn't you know?" she asked.

"How would I have known?" he returned.

"He's wearing the colors and tattoos of the Serpientes," she told him.

One dark eyebrow went up. He stared down at her through narrowed eyes. "Learned that at work, did you?" he asked softly.

She hesitated for a second. She cleared her throat. "All right, Rodrigo told me," she said, averting her eyes.

"The liaison officer?" he chided.

"He has a friend in law enforcement locally," she said, which was no lie.

"I see." He didn't, but his mind was whirling again with new knowledge of her and of Bernadette. Bernadette. His daughter. He moved closer to the door and watched the child hooking up the microscope he'd bought her to a small laptop computer.

"She knows how to do that?" he asked, surprised at her intelligence.

Sarina nodded. "She's very smart with electronics. Like… you were."

He turned and looked down at her with troubled dark eyes. "I told Hunter that Bernadette's father was a cold-blooded bastard," he said huskily. "I was right. I am."

"You didn't know."

"No. I didn't know. Maureen never said a word about your phone call." He shook his head. "I was blinded by lust," he bit off. "I wanted Maureen so much that I couldn't see past her. What do I have to show for that marriage? Years of hell, when the excitement wore off. And look at your life, and Bernadette's." He sighed. "You told me that Maureen and I went along leaving broken lives behind us. I didn't realize what you meant until now." Her flush made him frown. "There's more?"

She hesitated.

"You'd better tell me," he said bitterly. "It seems to be the night for confession."

But he looked as if he couldn't take much more. Still, he wasn't budging. She grimaced. "Maureen was married when you were going with her."

"Married?!"

She swallowed. "While you and I were dating, she was busy trying to get a quickie divorce in Reno. He fought it. The day you married me." She couldn't bear to look at him. "He… killed himself. So she came home free, after all."

He actually leaned against the wall for support. Of all the horrors of the night, that was the absolute last straw. He closed his eyes. He felt a cold chill. It was misting rain and he was out in it without his jacket. Chills were dangerous. He still had the fevers he'd acquired in Africa, and they recurred if he was careless with his health, but he was too upset to think about the risk.

"He killed himself," he said huskily. He looked at her, seeing the pain and anguish of her pregnancy far more vividly than he wanted to. "You lost everything, almost lost your life having Bernadette. She grew up without a father. An innocent man died so that Maureen could marry me. And I expected a happy life, after all that destruction. God! I got what I deserved."

She didn't know what to say. She'd had no idea that the revelation would hit him so hard. In fact, she'd often dreamed of seeing his face when he knew the truth about his daughter. But it didn't give her the satisfaction she'd once expected. It hurt.

"Colby…" she began, trying to find the words.

He turned away from her. "Tell Bernadette good-night for me, will you?" he asked roughly. "I've got to go."

"Thank you for her present," she faltered.

He couldn't even answer. A present. He'd missed her whole little life, made an enemy of her the day they met, and here he was bringing her a single present when he'd missed giving her dozens. Birthdays, holidays, special days, he'd missed them all. While he was trying to get Maureen to come back to him, his daughter had been living in poverty and growing up without a father. He kept walking blindly toward the SUV.

THE WORDS HAMMERED in his brain until he thought he'd go mad, long after he was back at his apartment. He was glad that he didn't keep alcohol, because there was a great temptation to blow years of abstinence and tie one on, royally.

But that way lay disaster. He took a shower and fell into bed, so worn-out by the stress of the night that he actually slept. But by morning, he was feverish and sick as a dog.

He took some aspirin and went back to bed, certain that it was just a chill. But by late Sunday night, he was delirious with fever. He couldn't even get to the phone to call for help. In fact, he didn't want to. If he died, maybe the pain would stop…

"MAMA! You have to wake up now!"

Sarina opened her eyes immediately, accustomed to having to look after Bernadette during her attacks. "Are you okay, baby?" she asked as she sat up.

"I'm fine, but Daddy isn't," she replied. "We have to go to him. He's very ill. Mama, I think he's dying!"

"Go to him..." She looked at the clock by her bed. "Baby, it's three o'clock in the morning! I have to get up at seven..."

"Please!"

"But, I can't find my way to his apartment in the dark," she argued. "And I'm sure he's fast asleep. We could call him," she offered, because the child was visibly upset.

"No! You have to come, right now, or he's going to die, Mama!"

The urgency in the small voice decided her. Bernadette did seem to know things that other people didn't. What Colby was going to say when she knocked on his door was unsettling, but she allowed herself to be convinced.

She threw on jeans and a sweatshirt while Bernadette got into her school clothes and gathered her books.

"Why are you doing that?" Sarina asked, puzzled.

"You'll have to let me go home with Mr. Hunter and go to school with Nikki," she said matter-of-factly. "Daddy's in really bad shape."

"Will he be all right?" Sarina asked reluctantly.

"Yes. I think so," she added worriedly.

Sarina let out the breath she'd been holding and locked the apartment behind them. There was no doubt in her mind that Bernadette knew what she was saying. She had a link to Colby. Apparently he had one to her as well, she thought, remembering the expensive microscope he'd brought the child. But she hoped Bernadette was wrong about the danger he was in.

THE SECURITY GUARD on duty at the gates let them into the apartment complex because of Bernadette's tears. He even walked to Colby's apartment behind the child, who went straight to his door with serene confidence—even though she'd never seen Colby's apartment in her life.

"He's very sick," Bernadette told the security guard worriedly.

With a grimace, he unlocked the door. "Let me go in first," he said firmly.

He went into the apartment while Sarina mentally compiled a list of good defense attorneys…

But the guard was back suddenly, his face worried. "Do you know who his doctor is?" he asked.

She went in past him, almost running. Colby was lying in his bed wearing only black boxer shorts, shivering and wet with sweat. He didn't recognize her. His skin was blazing hot to the touch and his eyes were blind with fever.

Sarina jerked up the phone and dialed the Hunters' number. Only seconds later, Phillip answered.

"Colby's very sick," she said at once. "He's running a high fever and he doesn't know me..."

"Malaria," Hunter said at once. "He's had it before. Go look in the medicine cabinet. There should be a prescription bottle of quinine."

She went into the bathroom and looked through the usual over-the-counter medicines until she found two prescription bottles. One was high-powered pain medication. The other was quinine, recently filled and full.

She ran back to the phone. "I found it."

"See if you can get two of them into him. I'm on my way."

She went to the kitchen and got a glass of water. Bernadette and the guard looked on as she got his head up and his mouth opened and forced him to swallow two of the tablets.

"It's malaria," she told the guard.

"How do you get malaria in Houston?" he wondered aloud.

"He got it in Africa," Bernadette said in a worried, subdued tone. "He was in a conflict there."

"A war?"

"He worked for the military until recent years," Sarina said dully.

"You can never tell about people, can you?" the guard wondered aloud. "But he's a tough sort of guy. It's not all that surprising."

Bernadette reached out and touched his dark, wavy hair. "Oh, Daddy," she said, and her voice broke.

Sarina reached down and picked her up, hugging her close. "He'll be all right," she promised the child, praying that she was right. He looked bad.

"His best friend is on the way over," she told the guard. "Phillip Hunter. They work for Ritter Oil Corporation with me. I think Hunter's nursed him through this before." She described Hunter, just in case.

"I'll wait for him at the gate and let him through. You staying?" he asked Sarina.

She nodded.

He ruffled Bernadette's hair. "Hope your dad gets better."

"Thanks," she said, wiping her eyes.

He went out, closing the door behind him. Sarina hugged Bernadette close and rocked her. It was painful to see such a healthy, vital man like that. She knew instinctively that the emotional shock of the day before had helped revive the disease in him. He'd left his jacket behind, and it was cold and wet outside, even today. She put Bernadette down and looked at her worriedly.

"I'm okay," Bernadette said softly. "You mustn't worry. I can breathe all right."

Sarina let out a worried sigh. "Okay. Did you use your medicine this morning?"

"Yes, I did, while I was getting dressed." She smiled. "This new stuff really works, Mama."

"It does, doesn't it?"

There was the sound of a vehicle pulling up outside. Sarina went to open the door.

Hunter looked half-awake, but he smiled at her. "How is he?"

"Bad," she said, not pulling her punches. "He knows that Bernadette is his daughter. He had several shocks yesterday, and he was out in the cold rain without a jacket last night. He got chilled."

"That's what happened last time he got it," Hunter said on a sigh. "Too much stress and no relief. He won't take a drink."

"I don't blame him."

Hunter walked into the bedroom. Bernadette was sitting in the chair by the bed with one hand on Colby's good arm, singing something softly in Apache.

"No need to ask if you spent time with a shaman," Hunter mused, having recognized the chant.

Bernadette looked up at him and smiled. "Granddaddy used to say that medicine was okay, but it never hurt to say a prayer while you gave it."

"He was right."

Hunter moved to the bed and examined Colby, who was still burning with fever. He sighed and took off his coat. "It's going to be a long night."

HE AND SARINA took turns sponging Colby down to reduce the fever. Hunter called a doctor who was apparently also a good friend. The man lived in Jacobsville, where Cy Parks also lived, but he seemed more than willing to drive up to Houston to see about Colby.

"Couldn't you get somebody closer?" Sarina asked curiously.

Hunter nodded. "Yes, I could, but Micah's known him a long time and he's familiar with the fevers. He was with us in Africa. In fact, he saved Colby's life by amputating that arm when he was shot."

Sarina was very still. She was remembering something that she'd heard Cy Parks say, about going with a group to Africa and fighting in a conflict there. She stared at Hunter with her suspicions in her eyes.

He was quick. "Don't make assumptions," he cautioned.

"You and Cy Parks were in Africa," she said slowly. "So was Colby."

"A lot of people were, and some of them were sanctioned by government agencies. It's classified," he added. "I can't talk about it."

"Oh," she said, relieved. She laughed softly. "Sorry. I was remembering something I heard about a group of mercenaries who helped restore the government in an African state. Rodrigo told me, in fact."

Rodrigo had been with them, Hunter recalled, but he wasn't telling Sarina that. Or about Colby. When Colby wanted her to know about his past, he'd tell her. On the other hand, he wondered how Colby was going to react when he knew about Sarina's line of work…

He left her sponging Colby's face and chest and casually mentioned going outside to get something out of his SUV. But when he got out into the darkness, he phoned Micah back and warned him about saying anything to Sarina about Colby's past.

THE BIG, BLOND MAN looked far more like a wrestler than a doctor, Sarina mused as she watched him working on Colby. But he knew what he was doing, that was obvious.

"Well, he doesn't get any smarter, does he?" Micah mused after he'd given Colby a thorough examination and an injection. "He knows what stress does to him."

"Hey, at least he's got malaria instead of a hangover," Hunter pointed out.

Micah's dark eyes twinkled. "Who's got the medical degree here?"

Hunter glared at him. "I know malaria when I see it. I've had it three times myself."

Micah harrumped and closed his medical bag. "As it happens, you're right, it is malaria. The fever will break in a couple of days. Keep shoveling quinine into him. I could give you Mepacrine, but I think he'd rather have a buzz in his ears than turn yellow."

"He'd agree with you," Hunter said, smiling.

"Try not to let him get chilled again," Micah said. He glanced curiously at Sarina. "Are you staying with him?" he asked her.

She exchanged glances with Hunter. "I guess I am, for the next day or two," she said.

"Keep him warm and full of liquids," he said. "Quinine every four hours. The directions are on the bottle."

"Okay," she said.

His eyes narrowed. "You're not Maureen."

Her face closed up and her dark eyes glittered angrily. "No, thank God, I'm not."

"Amen," he replied, ignoring Hunter's worried look. "She almost destroyed him."

"Sarina was his first wife," Hunter inserted.

Micah's dark eyes widened. "Excuse me?"

"The mother of his daughter," Hunter emphasized. "The little girl sitting in Colby's living room," he added.

Micah felt his own forehead and looked at Hunter. "I must need a long rest. I thought you said he had a daughter. How, when he's sterile?"

"He isn't," Sarina said firmly. "And if you've seen my daughter, you couldn't have any doubts. She looks just like him."

"I noticed. I wasn't doubting you," Micah replied. "But if you knew Colby as I knew him," he began.

"I'm sure you haven't got time to go into that," Hunter said firmly.

Micah glanced at him and got the point. "Yes. Right. I do have to get home. Our own daughter is a year old now," he told Sarina. "Nothing like children to make a marriage happy."

Sarina's face closed up and Micah grimaced.

"I'll walk you out," Hunter said.

"Thanks." He glanced at Sarina and smiled. "He'll be all right."

"Thanks," she said softly.

He shrugged. "All in a day's work. I like Colby."

She managed a smile. "Me, too."

"I guess so, if you had a child together," he chuckled, noting her flush as he picked up his bag and followed Hunter out.

Bernadette jumped up from the sofa and ran to the big man. "Is my daddy going to be all right?" she asked quickly.

Micah looked down into the worried dark eyes, so like Colby's, and he smiled. "Yes," he assured her. "He's going to be fine."

"Thank you," she said with a shy smile.

He ruffled her hair. "You're very welcome. You can go in there, if you like."

"Thanks!" she replied, running toward Colby's room.

Micah glanced at Hunter and nodded. She was, indeed, the image of her father.

WHEN THEY WERE STANDING beside Micah's Porsche, the physician gave his old comrade a strange look. "Why did you keep interrupting me?"

"Sarina doesn't know about Colby's past," Hunter emphasized. "When he's ready, he'll tell her."

He glared at the other man. "There's nothing so bad about what we did. We were idealists. We did a lot of good."

"I know that, but you don't understand the situation. She's not what she seems," he added, and left it there. "Take my word for it, there are going to be fireworks when they know the truth about each other."

"Callie and I had our own fireworks," he said reminiscently. He grinned. "Now we think she's pregnant again."

"Congratulations," Hunter said, grinning. "We think Jennifer is, too."

Micah whistled softly. "Must be the water," he mused.

Hunter chuckled. "Maybe it is!"

IN COLBY'S BEDROOM, Bernadette sat with her mother until Hunter came back inside, alone. She kissed her father softly on the forehead and went to get her books, because Hunter was going to drive her to his house, to stay with Jennifer and Nikki until her mother was home again. Sarina wasn't leaving, despite Hunter's belated assurances that he could take care of Colby if she'd rather go home.

"You have other things going on," she reminded him firmly. "I nursed Colby's father and worked at the same time. I can be spared for a couple of days easier than you can."

He gave her a knowing look. "And your interest is totally indifferent?"

She swallowed, avoiding his knowing gaze. "He was my husband once," she said softly.

"In his mind, he still is," Hunter said surprisingly. He met her shocked eyes with a smile in his. "Don't believe it? Mention Rodrigo around him and wait for the explosion."

She cleared her throat. "They just don't get along."

"Bull. He's jealous. That's part of what's wrong with him." He was serious again then. "Listen, the fact that he met what had to be a major crisis in his life without turning to the bottle should tell you something. Years ago, a bad day was enough to put him on a roll with a bottle of neat whiskey. He won't risk addiction again, because of you and Bernadette. He'd rather die."

"He won't…?" she asked quickly, the fear in her eyes.

He grinned. "Not Colby," he replied. "He's just discovered a reason for living. Lately all he talks about is Bernadette."

"Really?" Bernadette asked from the doorway, wide-eyed.

"Really," he told the child. "You can draw and sing like an angel and speak Spanish. He's very impressed."

Bernadette grinned.

Sarina hugged her. "Be good for Jennifer," she told her. "I'll take care of Daddy. Okay?"

"Okay," Bernadette replied.

"Got your breather and your rescue inhaler?" she added.

Bernadette nodded.

"Off you go, then."

"Good night, Mama," she said.

"I'll be back as soon as I get Bernadette settled," Hunter told her.

"I can manage the next few hours," Sarina said gently. "You have to work. They can do without me. I'm not that essential at Ritter Oil. And I'm not that essential for the other reason just yet."

Hunter grimaced. "Okay, then, we'll take it in shifts. If it gets really bad, I'll call Cy and have him come up. Or I could call Rodrigo…"

She raised an eyebrow. "He'd sponge Colby down with boiling water and give him hemlock to drink."

Hunter chuckled. "Rivals to the bitter end."

"We're partners," she emphasized.

"That's what you think. Come on, Bernadette,

let's go. I'll be back in the morning. Need me to pick up anything on the way back?"

"Yes," she said. "Some orange juice and aspirin."

"Will do."

HE AND BERNADETTE left, and Sarina sat down in a straight chair beside Colby's bed. He was tossing and writhing on the bed, his powerful body wet with sweat, his hair limp with it. His eyes opened, but they were sightless. When she got up and put a gentle hand on his shoulder to test his temperature, he groaned. High fever seemed to create pain with the lightest touch. She frowned, worried. Everybody said he'd be fine, but it was terrible to stand by and watch him in such agony. She felt responsible. He'd had so many blows, in so small a space of time. Long ago, she'd dreamed of hitting him in the head with the truth of his cruelty. But now that it had happened, she took no pleasure from it. He hadn't told Maureen to say that he wanted nothing to do with Sarina and her unborn child. He hadn't even known about the phone call. Her eyes closed in pain. Maureen had lied. The woman had destroyed lives and walked over bodies without a hint of compassion or regret.

Colby had loved his second wife. She knew that knowledge of Maureen's cruelty had added to the emotional scars he was already carrying. It hurt her to see what a price he'd paid for his infatuation with the other woman, because it was patently infatuation. Perhaps raging desire had played a part in his devotion to Maureen, or pride that wouldn't admit the terrible mistake he'd made in marrying her.

He rolled over onto his back and groaned again, his eyes half-closed, his lips parched. "Thirsty," he choked. "So…thirsty."

She went to the kitchen and added water to crushed ice from the refrigerator. She went back into the bedroom, sitting beside him to gently lift his dark head from the pillow and let him sip the cold water. He moaned, swallowing thirstily. She let his head back down and put the glass aside.

The pillow was slipping. She slid her hand under it and froze. Quickly she pulled out the pistol and opened the bedside table's top drawer. She checked to make sure the safety was on, and put it inside the drawer. It was a .40 caliber Glock, probably the one he carried at work, and it was loaded. She hadn't suspected that he might sleep with a weapon under his pillow, but it wasn't overly surprising. Many ex-military men and police officers did.

She went to get another basin of water and a clean washcloth and towel. She bathed him with cool water, pausing to towel him dry so that he didn't chill. She drew the cloth over his broad, muscular, hair-roughened chest and down to his stomach. He arched sensuously and moaned. She noticed a sudden change in the contours of his body. Her own skin felt hot. She waited a minute, and then switched her attentions to his arms and neck.

"I didn't know," he whispered, clenching his teeth. "Didn't know…!"

She dabbed at the wetness on his forehead with the wet cloth. "It's all right, Colby. It's all right."

He moved restlessly, his breath coming quick and hard. "Damn Ramirez!" he bit off. "He can't…have her…she's mine!"

"Colby," she whispered, faintly shocked.

His eyes opened and looked up into hers blindly. "I'll never let go," he said harshly. "Never again! My child…my baby…she should hate me—!" His voice broke, and he arched again. "Damn me!"

"Oh, Colby, don't," she groaned softly, reaching down to touch his lean cheek.

All at once she was lifted, rolled, flung onto the bed beside him. He threw a long leg across her hips and looked down at her, blinking. "Sarina?" he whispered, dazed.

"You have malaria," she whispered back, reaching up to touch his chin.

"Malaria." He hesitated, breathing deliberately. "Malaria." His eyes closed. "I'm so weak…"

"You'll be all right," she promised. "A doctor came. He gave you more medicine. It will pass."

"So…hot." He let go of her and rolled onto his back. "So thirsty."

She scrambled off the bed on the opposite side

and went back around it to grasp the glass of water. "Here," she said, sitting down on the bed to lift his head again and offer the water.

He sipped it slowly. He shivered, as the chills bit into him again. "Cold," he groaned. "So cold." His eyes opened and he watched her put the glass down. "Warm me," he whispered. "Lie with me."

She hesitated, but again he reached up and coaxed her down onto the bed with him, wrapping her up against the length of him. He shivered again, a harsh ripple of motion down his body. "Hold me."

It wasn't wise. But then, when had she ever been wise? With a long sigh, she slid down against him, hoping that the embroidery on her neat jeans wasn't going to be too abrasive on the bare skin of his thighs. She let him fold her close and she slid her arms under his and around him, pillowing her head on his shoulder. He shivered one last time and then relaxed with a long, shuddering sigh. Seconds later, his breathing became regular and she realized that he was asleep. She should get up at once, she reasoned. She meant to. But the warm, tender clasp of his arms, the novelty of lying against him, was too much for her. She closed her eyes and slept, too.

THERE WAS A MUFFLED LAUGH. Sarina's eyes slid open. There was a broad, hairy chest below her eyes and a wall beyond it. She wasn't at home in her own bed. She was…where was she?

She started to lift her head, and Colby's fever bright eyes were above her.

"If you have plans to ravish me, I'd enjoy it more if you'd wait until the worst of the chills and fever pass," he said in a husky tone, studying her with dark intensity.

She pursed her lips. "I guess you're wondering what I'm doing here," she began.

"In the apartment, or in my bed?" he asked with a feeble attempt at humor.

"Well, both, I guess."

He drew in a sharp breath. "I got chilled," he recalled. "Do I have malaria again?"

"Yes," she said. "Hunter and I are taking turns nursing you. I took his place early this morning with your treatment."

He lifted an eyebrow and looked down their bodies, locked together under the sheet. "Has he been sleeping with me, too?" he mused.

"Stop that," she muttered.

He smiled slowly. "I never liked mosquitos before," he murmured, tracing a path down her cheek to her full mouth. "But malaria seems to have at least one unexpected benefit."

"You were cold," she began quickly.

He cocked an eyebrow, glancing toward the covers rolled down to the end of the bed.

"Don't look at me," she protested. "You jerked me down here and refused to let go!"

"Am I complaining?" He bent and kissed her nose. But the aching misery came back with a vengeance when he moved. He groaned, shuddering. "For a minute, I felt better," he said roughly.

She pulled out of his arms and got up. "Could you eat something?"

"I don't know," he confessed. "The fever seems to be better, but the aching and nausea is back." He closed his eyes, shivering.

"Maybe some milk?"

"I can't drink milk," he replied. "I'm lactose intolerant."

"So is Bernadette," she said without thinking.

"Bernadette. My child. My little girl." He groaned again as the emotional pain came back full force.

She grimaced, not certain what to say.

His eyes opened, bloodshot but penetrating. "Why do you live in the projects? And don't hand me any bull about discrimination."

"Bernadette has asthma," she said bluntly. "Until just recently, any upset has involved trips to the emergency room. They have her on a new medicine that seems to prevent attacks. At least, so far. Medical bills have crippled my budget."

He studied her quietly. "I had asthma as a boy. I grew out of it. Perhaps she will, too." He searched her eyes. "Upsets. Like the ones she had with me, when I first went to work at Ritter's company?"

She flushed.

He groaned again. "My God, the sins just keep piling up, don't they?"

She sat down on the bed beside him, her eyes quiet and soft. "You've had too many shocks. You have to stop looking back. Bernadette cares for you a great deal. She's looking forward to having a father of her very own. You have to look ahead."

His chest rose and fell heavily. "Coals of fire, Sarina."

She smiled gently. "You're not as bad as you make yourself out to be. You didn't know what was going on. I did try to tell you," she added.

"I should have gone looking for you, just to make sure you were really all right," he said. "But Africa changed me. Afterward, I drank so much…"

"But not anymore," she pointed out. "If any man ever had a valid excuse to look for a bottle after last night…"

"I'm tired of crutches," he interrupted. "I have responsibilities now."

Her eyebrows arched.

He glowered up at her. "The first order of business is to get you out of that hellhole you live in. Then we go shopping, for both of you."

She put her fingers across his mouth. "First you get well," she corrected. "Then we can argue about whether or not you'll take over my life and Bernadette's."

His eyes twinkled. "Look out," he mused. "I like arguing with you."

"You think you know me, dear man," she teased. "But you don't."

"Think so?" He swallowed another burst of nausea and shivered again. "Damned disease. I picked it up about the time you were carrying my daughter. There are several different kinds of malaria, but I got landed with the one type they can't cure. I'll always have recurrences if I do stupid things like standing in the cold rain without a coat."

"You won't do it again," she promised him.

He liked that assertiveness. He smiled through the misery. "I would have walked all over you seven years ago, Sarina," he said softly. "Do you realize it now?"

He was strong-willed, and she'd been submissive and worshiping in her youth. She nodded. "Yes. I think I do."

He frowned. "How did you know I was sick?" he asked suddenly.

"Bernadette woke me out of a sound sleep at three in the morning," she replied solemnly. "She said that you were very sick and we had to come see about you. She charmed the security guard into letting us through the gate, and then she came like a homing pigeon to your front door. He let us in and I called Hunter. Bernadette's with Jennifer and Nikki for the foreseeable future."

"I would have let me lie here and die," he pointed out, "if I were you."

She touched his tanned, muscular shoulder. "Not with Bernadette crying her eyes out, you wouldn't. She sat here and sang to you while Hunter and I got the doctor."

"Chanted?"

"Have you forgotten? Her grandfather was a shaman," she pointed out. "He taught her healing skills. Or do you really think that quinine alone got you through the night?"

He chuckled. "Did you ever know where she got that beautiful singing voice from?" he murmured. "My mother sang like an angel. She used to sit beside me when I was sick and chant healing words. She died when I was six," he recalled huskily. "My father drank to excess and didn't realize that she had pneumonia. She died while he slept off a three-day bender. I helped my cousins gather her possessions and burn them, after she was buried. My father crawled back into the bottle and I went to live with a cousin. We were enemies my whole life after that."

"Yes, I know," she said. "He told us all about it. He knew why you never contacted him. He said," she added huskily, "that he deserved it, for letting her die and deserting you. He also said that maybe what he did for Bernadette would make up for it, a little."

CHAPTER NINE

COLBY DIDN'T SPEAK. His eyes closed. He was fighting chills again, and trying not to show how Sarina's explanation hurt him. He'd never made time to make peace with his father. Now, he wished he could change that. But it was far too late.

Sarina let him drift off to sleep, and when Hunter came back later that morning, she went back to her apartment long enough to take a bath and get a change of clothes to carry back with her.

Colby's seeming recovery was a false start. By afternoon, his fever was up again and he was having chills and aches again. Sarina and Hunter kept the vigil between them. He went to work briefly, to make sure the man he'd left in charge at work was doing what he was supposed to. He gave in to Sarina's refusal to leave Colby. She took catnaps at the foot of his bed, and ladled medicine and orange juice into him, bathed him when the fever went up, and worried incessantly. He moaned and talked in his sleep. There was a lot about Africa and some firefight he'd been in. There was more about Bernadette. He raged and cursed as he lived through some sort of interrogation with what sounded like a terrorist. None of it made sense, unless he was remembering his government work.

Sarina talked to Bernadette on the phone, reassuring her that everything was going to be all right. She only wished she could believe it. She'd never seen a major attack of malaria in her life. She knew she'd never forget it.

But on the fourth day, Colby suddenly rallied and the fever went down. He was past the crisis, Hunter said with relief. Now, it was just a matter of rest and food.

Colby became aware of the grunginess of his hair and body and he groaned. He had to have a shower. It reminded him too much of the way he'd been when alcohol had taken its toll on him, when he didn't care if he lived or died, or stank. Now things were different. He had a family that he was responsible for.

He dragged himself to the side of the bed and stood up, wobbling. He hadn't realized how weak he was until his long, powerful legs started shaking.

He made it to the bathroom and turned on the shower, leaning against the tiles to stabilize himself while he took deep breaths and cursed his own weakness.

"What in the world do you think you're doing?" Sarina exclaimed, pausing at the open door with a cup of coffee and a plate of buttered toast in her hands. "I was bringing you coffee and toast!"

"It can wait," he said huskily. "I have to have a bath. Can you change the bed linen for me?" he added. "Sheets are in the linen closet."

She went past him and turned off the shower, put the seat on the toilet down, and coaxed him to sit on it. "You stay right there while I do it." She turned off the shower and went to work.

Colby sat quietly, amused at her assertiveness. When she came back, his dark eyes were gleaming with craftiness, although he didn't let her see it.

"I'll wait outside the door," she began, "in case you're not as strong as you think you are…"

"I can't stand up in the shower alone, much less prop and bathe with only one hand," he added, indicating the stump of his left forearm. Actually he could, but he had ulterior motives.

She blinked. "Well," she hesitated.

"You'll have to climb in with me. If it's not too much trouble," he added with downcast eyes. "I realize that a man in this condition might be repulsive to you."

Her heart twisted. "Of course you're not!" she protested at once.

He felt lighter than air. "Well?"

She cleared her throat, hesitating.

He got up from the toilet seat and moved toward her. "Tell me."

She swallowed hard. "I haven't taken off my clothes in front of anybody except my doctor in my whole life. Not even with you, that time. It was in the dark."

His face softened magically. "I haven't, either," he confessed. "Perhaps you don't remember that Apaches are inherently modest. I swam in trunks even as a boy, when I played in the river with other boys during the monsoon season." He smiled, recalling how rarely the rivers actually contained water, on the reservation.

Her strained expression lightened a little. But she was still hesitant.

He moved closer, his dark eyes quiet as they looked down into hers. "I hate feeling grungy," he coaxed. "Besides, I've got nice clean sheets. Wouldn't it be a pity to climb back into them like this?"

She managed a smile. "I guess so." Her heart was beating double-time. She wondered if he knew.

He traced a path down her cheek. "We were married," he reminded her. "You gave me a child."

She drew in a fatalistic sigh. "Okay. Try not to notice how red I get."

He chuckled, reaching inside the shower stall to turn on the flow and check the temperature. He unsnapped the boxers and let them drop, climbing in under the water, with his hand propped on the tiles and his back to her. "Don't take long," he said. "I'm pretty wobbly." Which was true.

She took off her blouse and slacks and shoes, hesitating. But he swayed and cursed huskily, and she became more concerned than embarrassed. She dropped her lingerie along with her clothes on the vanity. She pulled two dark blue washcloths from the towel holder and climbed in with him.

He glanced down at her, his dark eyes fascinated with the pink perfection of her body, from her high, taut breasts with their dusky crowns to the indentation of her small waist and the flatness of her stomach. Dark color flooded along his high cheekbones and he hoped that he was too weak to let his upsurge of desire for her show.

It was a forlorn hope. He'd been too long without a woman.

Sarina's gaze dropped shyly from the heat of his eyes and encountered the major physical difference between them. Color flooded her face as she averted her eyes to the muscular wall of his hair-roughened chest.

"You must have seen a centerfold from time to time," he chided gently.

She swallowed as she handed him the washcloth. "Not like you, I haven't."

He chuckled, delighted. He laid the washcloth

over one broad shoulder while he popped open the lid on the bottled body wash. "It's a more masculine scent than you're used to, I'm afraid," he indicated. "But we'll manage. Can you soap my cloth for me and do my back?"

"Of...of course." She took the body wash and the cloth and got to work. His back was broad and heavily scarred. She winced as she drew the soapy washcloth over the taut muscles. "You carry the story of your life on your back," she said sadly.

He'd forgotten the scars. His body tautened. "Are the scars distasteful?" he asked.

"Don't be silly, Colby," she said quietly. "You know they're not."

He relaxed. The lacerations made him self-conscious. "That's something, I guess," he said heavily.

His insecurity made her feel funny. It was such an odd quirk, in such a very self-confident and masculine man. She smiled as she drew the cloth down to the taut line of his buttocks. Her hand hesitated.

"Chicken," he teased.

She sighed. "Anatomy was never one of my best subjects."

"This is a perfect opportunity to pick it up," he mused.

She laughed. She drew the cloth down the backs of his legs. It was like touching wood, the muscles were so hard. "You must still work out every day," she commented.

"I have to. Even if I'm in a different line of work, much of what I do is still physical. When I worked for Hutton, I had to go after thieves and even terrorists a time or two. We had a firefight with a group of would-be assassins barely three years ago, right outside Washington, D.C."

She gnawed her lower lip. "I didn't realize it was that risky."

"It's only risky if you let down your guard," he commented. "I drank heavily in the old days. I forgot several doses of quinine when I was in Africa, which is why I got malaria there. It's also how I lost my arm."

"But you didn't take a drink at all after you found out about Bernadette."

His chest expanded on a long breath. "I couldn't do that to her," he said huskily. "I'm not much of a father, Sarina, but I'm never going to take another drink and put her at risk in any way at all. Her, or you." He turned around, his eyes dark and somber as they met hers with the shower spray all around them. He took the cloth from her. "My turn," he said huskily, and went to work on her own body.

Her breasts tautened instantly, from the brush of his hand and the abrasion of the cloth against her skin. She flushed as well.

"You aren't used to being touched," he said softly.

"I'm not," she agreed in an unsteady tone.

He smiled slowly. "The poor liaison officer. No wonder he has such a lean and hungry look."

The flush worsened as he worked his way down her flat belly. "I don't…feel like that with Rodrigo."

The cloth hesitated. He met her eyes. "Ever?"

"Ever."

"You feel like that with me," he added quietly.

"You're sure about that, are you?" she mused, trying to make light of it.

His hand moved again, spreading soap and scattering nerves as he watched her face. "Yes. I'm sure."

He turned her gently to do her back. The feel of him behind her, the spray of the water, the intimacy of what they were doing made her feel swollen all over. She wanted so badly to turn around and press her body hard against his. The desire was almost painful.

He was experienced enough to know it, but he wasn't going to risk rushing her. He handed her the washcloth, so that she could rinse and hang it, and he reached for the bottle of shampoo.

He eased her back into the shower spray and, holding the bottle cap in his teeth, squeezed shampoo directly into her hair. He replaced the bottle cap and began to work the shampoo into her long, wet blond hair with his fingers.

"You manage that very nicely," she commented.

He chuckled. "You learn how to cut corners with a disability."

"Of course."

He guided her back into the spray to rinse her hair. Then he exchanged places with her and drenched his own hair. "Your turn," he said.

She squeezed shampoo into her hand, replaced the bottle, and then realized that she'd have to stand on tiptoe to get to his hair. He was much taller than she was. She found that it involved an intimacy they hadn't shared since the night they'd created Bernadette.

His reaction was a little disconcerting. The second her breasts touched his chest, as she lifted against him to shampoo his hair, he went taut and groaned audibly.

She froze in position, her hands in his hair, her eyes faintly surprised as they met the glitter of his own.

"I haven't had a woman in a long time," he ground out.

She still hesitated. "Is this…painful?"

His hand slid to the base of her spine and pulled her hard against him. "This is," he said huskily as the threat of his body pressed hard into her belly.

Her lips parted. She shivered at the blatant capability that was just faintly threatening.

"You had Bernadette normally, didn't you?" he asked in a strained tone.

She nodded.

His cheekbones flushed again. "Maybe you could

take all of me without pain, after that," he said in a soft, sensuous tone.

Erotic images flooded her mind. She was already vibrating with desire, this close to him. The look on his face, added to the vivid images of the statement, made her color and a faint shudder that he could feel eased through her body.

He backed into the spray of water, rinsing the soap out of his hair. Seconds later, he bent, and his hard mouth moved very gently against her parted lips. He was hesitant, careful with her. He brushed at her upper lip and slid just the tip of his tongue under it, teasing, arousing. One powerful leg inserted itself slowly between hers in a sensual motion that made her want to ease his passage. Her legs slipped apart and she gasped as she felt him move, so that his body was pressed intimately to her own.

He felt her immediate response. His mouth opened and hardened urgently on her soft mouth. She moaned as the kiss built to unmanageable proportions and her body began to shiver with the force of her hunger for him.

He drew back, turning off the shower. He reached for towels and blotted the moisture from her body while she did the same for him. He handed her the hair dryer wordlessly, his eyes making threats and promises with equal blatant meaning.

She could barely breathe. There was a lingering

fear of remembered pain, but her body didn't care. She ached to lie in bed with him and let him do anything he liked to her.

And he knew. It was in the taut lines of his body, the glitter of his dark eyes as she finished drying both his wavy dark hair and her own long blond tresses. He took the hair blower from her and unplugged it. She made one hesitant move toward her clothing. He blocked it by pulling her against him.

She couldn't resist him. Curiosity and desire mixed, making her helpless.

"It won't hurt," he bit off. "Come here."

He kissed her hungrily, his mouth urgent and ardent on her own. His hand caressed her, testing the soft weight of her breasts, the softness of her skin. He pulled his mouth from hers, bent and put his lips over a hard nipple, easing it completely between his lips.

She gasped out loud and arched toward him. The pleasure was maddening, narcotic. She couldn't stop. She didn't want him to stop. Desire seeped into every cell of her taut body as his mouth found her soft belly.

Seconds later, he had her by the hand and he was pulling her along with him to the bedroom. He barely had the presence of mind to close and lock the door on his way to the bed.

"Colby, we...shouldn't," she faltered as he eased her down on her back and followed her onto the clean sheets.

"I would try to be rational," he whispered as his mouth began to work its way down her soft, taut body. "But I don't think I have time…Sarina!"

It seemed almost indecent, the way he touched her, the aching hunger of his mouth on her skin. Pleasure built on pleasure as she writhed under his expert touch. It had never been so urgent, so desperate, not even in the first few ecstatic minutes of their wedding night, before he hurt her.

Despite his own aching need, he was slow and tender with her, making sure that she was completely aroused and ready for him before he eased down over her trembling body.

"I won't hurt you," he whispered at her mouth as he moved into complete intimacy with her. "No matter what it takes. Trust me."

Her nails bit into his broad shoulders as she felt him teasing, pressing, penetrating softly. He lifted his head and looked into her dark, frightened eyes.

"I wouldn't deliberately hurt you to save my own life," he whispered tenderly. "I won't take my pleasure at the expense of yours, either. Especially not now." His eyes closed on a wave of pleasure as he moved higher against her and felt her gasp and pull at him. "You gave me a child," he bit off, shuddering with pleasure.

The feel of him stretching her intimately was a delight beyond expression. Her short nails bit into his shoulders as she arched her hips toward his, enjoying the contact as it became more and more intimate. In spite of his reassurances, she'd expected some pain. There was none. Only pleasure that fed on itself as his motions, tender and slow, became relentlessly more intimate.

"All right?" he whispered, smiling as he felt her eager response.

"It's…incredible," she choked, shivering with every slow thrust.

"And we've barely started," he replied huskily.

Her eyes opened wide. Barely started? The pleasure was already taking her. She was reaching toward something intangible. There was a high place, somewhere above, and she strained to reach it. She saw him, but his taut face hardly registered. She was intent on the deep motions that began to spiral, the tension that grew until she was openly shuddering with every lift and fall of his lean hips. Her mouth opened soundlessly and she moved with him, aggressive now, demanding, as she tried and tried to reach that high level of delight that was surely going to kill her.

"Slowly," he whispered, his hand staying her thrashing hips. "There's no rush."

"I'm dying," she choked, sobbing. "Please…!"

He smiled tenderly. She had no idea what was about to happen. She thought in terms of momentary satisfaction. He was thinking beyond these few seconds to the next few minutes, as he taught her the soft, rocking motion that escalated the pleasure second by throbbing second.

Resting on his elbow, barely aware of the missing hand in his blind passion for her, his hand moved between them into intimacy. He touched her, stroked her, while his hips levered even closer.

She stared up at him incredulously as the soft motion of his fingers shot her right over the edge of sanity into a hot, swirling agony of satisfaction that she sobbed out against his warm, hard mouth.

Her body relaxed and she stared up at him, embarrassed.

He shifted all at once, moved higher on her body, and her sensitized flesh reacted with an even more explosive climax than he'd just given her. She convulsed under his delighted gaze, both hands going to the back of his powerful thighs to hold him to her, to urge him even closer.

He was sweating. He was still weak, and his legs were shivering with the tension and the expenditure of energy. But for the life of him, he couldn't have stopped.

"Please," she sobbed against his mouth. "Closer…!"

"Risky," he whispered back, but he wanted to be closer, too. He hesitated, reached for a pillow and pushed it under her hips. The elevation pushed her over the edge again, almost at once. He felt her body accept him, the heat and softness of it enveloping him, embracing him. He couldn't hold it any longer. He drove for his own fulfillment in a blind, taut agony of motion. He felt it take him, whip his body into a tension that felt as if it could break bones. Then, in a blaze of ecstasy, it threw him up into the stars in a maelstrom of fiery delight. He cried out endlessly as his powerful body convulsed over and over again in the cradle of her softness.

She watched him, fascinated. Her own body was languid now with satiety, but she still responded to the fierce motion of his hips. The abrasion brought yet another climax, more powerful and frightening than all the others put together. She sobbed and moaned as the exquisite pulsing went on and on and on.

Finally he collapsed heavily on her damp body, gasping for breath.

She cradled him, blind with fulfillment, alive as she'd never been in her life. The weight of him was a pleasure so deep that she shivered with it. There had been no pain, none at all; only an ecstasy that she'd never dreamed existed.

"Are you all right?" he whispered at her ear.

"Oh…yes," she choked.

He lifted his head. His hair was damp, like hers, but his face was more relaxed than she'd ever seen it. His eyes were soft and dark, intense with feeling. He couldn't find the right words to express what he wanted to say to her. He bent and traced her mouth tenderly with his lips. He kissed her cheeks, her forehead, her closed eyelids, with breathless affection.

She shivered delicately. Every time he moved, the pleasure bit into her all over again. She began to shift under him, to bring it back.

He looked down at her quietly and caught her hip in a steely clasp. "No," he whispered. "It will make you very sore. We have to stop."

She colored and stilled. "Sorry…"

"I'd keep it up for hours, if I could do it without hurting you," he bit off, his dark eyes smoldering with passion. "I love watching you. But it will be painful later."

She drew in a long breath. "I'm…new to this."

"I know." He said it with heartfelt feeling. He kissed her eyelids shut. His own body shivered faintly as he began to withdraw from her, very carefully. He rolled onto his back and shuddered. "Just an hour ago I thought I was disabled."

She lifted herself onto an elbow and looked at his lean, smiling face. "Excuse me?"

His eyes opened, quiet and soft. "I haven't made love since I lost part of my arm," he explained simply. "I was afraid to. I didn't know if I could, without the prosthesis."

"That was a long time ago," she said.

"Yes." There were oceans of meaning in the word. He lifted an eyebrow. "You and I fit together very nicely now."

She colored. “I noticed.”

He stretched aching muscles and shivered. “I’m not as in shape yet as I’d like to be,” he confessed.

Her fingers went to his hard mouth. She traced it tenderly. “I hope this doesn’t set you back,” she worried.

“I wouldn’t care if it killed me,” he mused. “It would have been worth it.”

She searched his eyes curiously. “It wasn’t like this before.”

“You were afraid of it, before,” he replied quietly. “And a virgin.” He winced. “And I wasn’t cold sober. It still hurts me, to know how much damage I did to you.”

“It was a painful time for both of us,” she replied. Her fingers traced his arm down to the missing forearm. “Is it, well, normal, to feel so much…?”

“Normal, but not usual,” he told her. His face was solemn. “I’ve never felt anything this powerful. Not with anyone.”

That made her feel better. She smiled softly.

He shifted onto his side and pulled her against him, drawing the sheet over them with a long sigh. “We could both use some sleep,” he said softly, reaching for the light.

“But…”

“But we’re not dressed and it isn’t bedtime. I know.” He chuckled, folding her closer. “Humor me, I’m sick.”

She slid one long leg against his and sighed.

"Quit that," he murmured sleepily, "I'm spent."

She smiled against his shoulder and closed her eyes. In seconds, she was asleep.

AFTER THEY WERE DRESSED and having soup at his kitchen table, she felt guilty and ashamed for what had happened. Despite the fact that they'd been married once, they weren't now. Her conscience hurt.

He noticed her downcast expression and was uncertain of the reason for it, until he remembered how spontaneous their bout of passion had been. He grimaced.

She saw it, and frowned. "What's wrong?" she asked.

"I was careless."

She hadn't realized it until he spoke. Her lips parted on a soft breath. "Oh, dear."

He reached across the table and caught her hand in his. "We'll deal with whatever happens," he said firmly. "Don't borrow worries. Okay?"

She nodded slowly.

He searched her dark, quiet eyes. "We're only now learning each other, in all the ways that count," he continued. "We have to learn to trust each other. No secrets. Ever."

Secrets. She had a humdinger of a secret, and it was going to change his entire perception of her. She wanted to tell him, but she wasn't allowed to. Besides that, she was hesitant to shatter the new and delightful intimacy that had happened between them so unexpectedly.

She didn't know that he was silently thrashing himself for his lack of honesty about his past.

"No secrets," she agreed after a minute, and smiled at him.

He smiled back. He had to tell her, he thought. And soon, while there was still time. He hoped she could live with his past.

SHE WENT HOME that night, reluctantly, but she'd left Bernadette alone too long already, and Colby was more than capable of taking care of himself. She found herself suddenly caught up in a whirl of activity at work, with Rodrigo watching her like a hawk and obviously disapproving of the time she'd spent with Colby while he was recuperating.

"He's going to get suspicious," Rodrigo warned her.

"Then let him," she replied more sharply than she meant to. "The job isn't my life, Rodrigo."

"It was," he pointed out.

"He's Bernadette's father," she said quietly. "I can't shut him out."

"Can't you?" His dark eyes narrowed. "And what do you expect he's going to say when he finds out what you really do for a living, Sarina?" he asked.

CHAPTER TEN

SARINA FELT THE BLOOD rush into her face. It wasn't a question she wanted to face. Colby saw her as a complacent filing clerk with a low-stress job, a shadow of the woman she'd become in the years they'd been apart. She was suddenly frightened. She should have told him, despite the fact that she'd been sworn to secrecy. She should have told him! It would be worse because she hadn't trusted him. On top of that, he wasn't going to like the risks she took. He'd think she should have given it up for Bernadette. Perhaps she should have.

Rodrigo saw the torment in her face and felt guilty for what he'd said to her. He took a long breath. She was falling in love with her ex-husband all over again, and he was caught in the middle, with no way to stop it. Well, he might be able to stop it by telling her what Colby had been in the past. But he hadn't the right to increase her torment.

"Soon, you'll be able to level with him," he said tautly.

She nodded. She looked up at him sadly. "I'm sorry," she said quietly. "I know that you had… hopes."

He shrugged and managed a smile. "I'll still be around somewhere, if you need me."

"If only I could have been honest with him from the beginning," she said after a minute. "I don't know how he's going to take it."

He didn't, either, and he couldn't quite relinquish some hope for himself. "For now, we have other things to think about. We've put in too much time on this case to risk blowing it now."

Her eyes were troubled. "I know."

He got to his feet. "Suppose we go down to the firing range when we get off from work? This is not a good time to get rusty."

"Good point. I'll ask Jennifer to let Bernadette visit Nikki for an hour or two."

"See you later, then."

She nodded, only half hearing him.

THEY SPENT AN HOUR on the firing range, during which she outscored Rodrigo and gave him a mischievous grin.

"Rub it in," he muttered.

She unloaded her automatic. "Despite everything, I've really enjoyed working with you."

"Same here."

"I wish…"

He held up a hand, smiling wistfully. "You can't help what you feel," he told her.

"I suppose not." She touched his arm gently. "Thanks for being such a good friend."

He grinned. "I'll always be that, no matter what."

COLBY HADN'T COME to work all day, and when she went to pick up Bernadette from Hunter's home, neither of them had heard from him. Sarina almost phoned him, but she was uneasy after their feverish intimacy. She was shy, uncertain of her welcome. Perhaps he had regrets, and that's why he hadn't gotten in touch with her. It was disturbing, that intimacy had caused more problems than it solved, that it should have put such distance between them. Maybe he'd had a relapse and didn't want her to know. He might be in bed and unable to get up.

She did finally pick up the phone and dial his number, but the answering machine picked up and she was too uncertain of herself to leave a message. She tried Hunter, but he wasn't available, either. She didn't call back because Bernadette was giving her odd looks. She didn't want to worry the child.

But her own worry wouldn't go away. She baked two loaves of banana bread and put one into a plastic container. She tucked it into her car under a magazine, so that Bernadette wouldn't ask about it. She'd really expected Colby to phone, at least. She'd called Hunter this morning, and she knew now that Colby was all right and that he was planning to return to work on Monday, but that didn't take the place of a conversation with him.

It was Saturday, and after dropping Bernadette off to spend the day and night with Nikki Hunter, she stopped by Colby's apartment.

Hesitantly she knocked at the door, practicing her excuse for coming, just in case he wasn't glad to see her. She clutched the plastic container of banana nut bread tightly in her hands. She was wearing jeans and a sweatshirt, her hair left long because she knew he liked it that way. She hoped he wasn't going to be angry because she'd shown up without an invitation.

But when the door opened, she got the single worst shock of her recent life. A pretty young blond woman wearing a short bathrobe, and nothing else, was framed in the doorway.

"Yes?" she asked with a pleasant smile.

Sarina couldn't manage a single word. So this was why Colby hadn't contacted her. This was why he'd kept to himself lately. And he'd gone from her, to this woman…just as he'd gone from her to Maureen, years ago. Why, why, had she expected him to change? Unfaithful men never changed. Why didn't she know that?!

The scarlet blush and flashing dark eyes made the other woman hesitate. But before she could speak, Colby came into the room, his hair still wet from the shower, his lean hips wrapped in a blue bath towel.

"Cecily, I meant to tell you..." He stopped with a comical look in his eyes. His jaw dropped. A ruddy color came up under the skin of his high cheekbones as he took in the tableau. Cecily and himself having obviously just come from a shower, apparently alone, and a shattered Sarina standing in the doorway. "Sarina...?" he began slowly.

She swallowed hard and regained some of her composure. "Bernadette and I made banana nut bread. She asked me to stop by and give you a loaf of it," she lied through her teeth, forcing a smile. "You look...much better."

He was lost for words. He couldn't even speak. He knew what she was thinking, and also that his chances of making her listen at the moment were about as good as his chances of winning the lottery. She wasn't likely to doubt the evidence of her eyes.

Sarina thrust the plastic container into Cecily's hands. "You can share it," she said roughly, and turned. She almost ran for the safety of her car, leaving a shell-shocked Colby staring after her with tormented eyes.

Cecily and Colby had been friends for a long time. She knew he was very upset and not likely to talk to her about the woman who'd just left. She drew in a slow breath, wishing that her husband, Tate, would hurry out of the shower.

"Who was she?" she asked.

He didn't look at her. "My ex-wife," he said tightly.

Cecily stared at him blankly. "Your what?" she exclaimed.

"I was married twice," he said dully. "Sarina was my first wife." He swallowed hard. "We have…a little girl, Bernadette…she's seven."

Cecily pulled out a chair and sat down. Hard.

Tate Winthrop came into the room rubbing his long hair with a towel. He was Lakota Sioux, and looked far more Native American than Colby. His dark eyes went from his wife to his best friend.

"What's going on?" he asked.

"Colby's ex-wife just showed up and saw us like this," Cecily said, moving to her husband's side.

"Maureen? She can't be here, she and her husband are on their way to Nassau. That's why she asked me to give you those papers she found," Tate said obliviously.

"Not Maureen," Colby said.

"He has two ex-wives, apparently," Cecily told Tate, tongue-in-cheek. "This one's blond and they have a daughter."

Tate leaned against the counter. "A daughter? Maybe I have a fever," he said, touching his forehead.

"Maybe you do," Cecily said blithely, "but he's still got a daughter. Did you know you had a daughter?" she asked Colby.

He shook his head. "Not until a few days ago," he confessed. "It's been a shock."

"Well, go after her, Colby," Cecily insisted. "You can take a photograph of the three of us and explain things to her!"

His face closed up. "Not until she has time to cool down," he said. "She won't listen."

"Make her listen," Tate interjected.

Colby didn't soften. "That's easier said than done." He hesitated. "I'll give her a few minutes to get home and think things through," he decided. "Then, I'll phone her." He didn't add that he'd be lucky if she didn't slam the phone down the second she heard his voice. Cecily didn't know it, but Sarina would be remembering that he threw her over for Maureen. She'd see this as history repeating itself, especially since he hadn't been in touch with her since their passionate night together. She'd be hurt, and afraid, and she'd blame him for all the pain she'd endured in the past, and today. He was already losing her, and they'd barely begun again. He'd compounded the problem by being too uncertain of his footing, and the delicate new feeling between them, to get in touch with her, too ashamed of his blatant seduction of her. He'd meant to call her today and see how things stood. But it was too late.

The look on her face told him so. She'd never believe him about Cecily.

Cecily watched him covertly, seeing his reluctance to phone the woman. She wanted to tell him that he was making a huge mistake by putting it off even just a few minutes, but he'd already turned away.

Tate exchanged a speaking glance with her. Colby had a knack for self-destruction. He'd stopped drinking, but he was still on a cold path.

COLBY DID TRY PHONING Sarina just a few minutes later. As he'd expected, she hung up. He tried her cell phone, but apparently it wasn't turned on. He sent a text message, anyway, hoping it would get through eventually.

He was hesitant to go after her because of their past. He didn't want to admit that to his two best friends, who were leaving early the next morning. He decided that his best bet was just to go to her apartment and make her listen to him. He was still wobbly, but he was certainly strong enough to put his foot in her door and refuse to leave. Surely she'd remember how close they'd been, how much he cared for her. Even if he hadn't said it, she must know it. Everything would be all right.

Except that fate stepped in at the worst time, it might have been. Just after lunch, he had an urgent call from Hunter.

"Are you well enough for a standoff?" he asked his friend.

Colby wasn't, really, but he'd been out of action too long already. "Sure. What's up?" he asked.

"We've had a tip that there's something going down at the warehouse tonight. We've got a joint drug task force set to spring the trap. I'd like to have you along."

"I'll be there," he said at once. "Where, and when?"

He listened, assured Hunter that he'd be along, and hung up.

"I'll have to go," he told his friends. "This is a long-standing problem. We're hoping to have a solution tonight."

"Don't get shot before you make it up with Sarina," Cecily said firmly. She drew a photograph out of her purse and handed it to him. It was of the three of them with Tate and Cecily's little boy. "Show her this. It will explain a lot."

"Okay," he said, sliding it into his own wallet. "Thanks."

She smiled at him. "It will work out, Colby. I'm sure it will," she added.

He chuckled, hugging her and then Tate. "Well, at least I've still got hopes of it," he said. He stood back and studied them both. "I didn't realize how much a child could mean until I had one of my own. I wish you could meet Bernadette," he added sadly.

"Maybe next time," Tate said gently. "We'll be back this way again."

"It's a deal. Now," Colby said, moving a little less strongly than usual, "I'd better get cracking."

"There's just one more thing," Tate said, following the other man into his bedroom. "I spoke with Maureen before we left D.C."

Colby's eyes flashed. "That's all over."

"I know that," Tate said curtly. "But there are things you have to know. We can talk while you dress, can't we?"

Colby drew in an irritated breath, but he nodded.

Tate closed the door. He put a thick envelope down on the dresser. "She gave me that."

Frowning, Colby opened it and found…

"The annulment papers?" he exclaimed. He looked through the pages. "Sarina signed them. But…but I never did!" he added, disbelieving when he saw the blank spaces where his signature should have been. "I thought her father had managed to do it without any help from me. I must have been out of the country when these came. I never knew about them! Maureen said she signed them for me. She lied!"

"Didn't you wonder why it was so easy for you to marry Maureen?" Tate asked, very carefully. "You didn't even have to produce identification, did you? And there was no marriage license."

Colby felt a coldness in the pit of his stomach. "Spill it!" he said impatiently.

"Maureen confessed that you and she were never legally married," he said heavily. "There was a clause in her first husband's will that kept her from inheriting a penny of his estate if she remarried."

"She couldn't have gotten a penny of insurance because he killed himself," he said roughly. "Sarina told me."

"Yes, he did," Tate agreed, "but he still left several thousand dollars and a few oil stocks in a will that named her beneficiary. She wasn't about to give those up."

Colby was trying to take it all in, and failing miserably. "I'm still married to Sarina."

"That's right." He shrugged. "Maureen didn't have the nerve to tell you herself. She said she was sorry, but it wasn't as if she planned to stay with you forever."

"I know. She liked the banker's hours and his father's fortune. He'll inherit one day."

"I understand that a new grandchild was the thing that cinched the deal," Tate added coldly, "because her new father-in-law wanted to make sure she wasn't marrying his son just for his fortune."

Colby only nodded. He didn't add that she'd convinced him he was sterile. No need for Tate to know that. Colby fingered the unsigned papers. This was a new complication. How was he going to tell Sarina that they were still married, when she hated him all over again?

"I wonder why Sarina's father didn't pursue the annulment?" Tate asked.

Colby was only half-listening. "I'm sure he thought the attorney had taken care of it. He never bothered with details that underlings could handle. I was out of Sarina's life. That was all he cared about. At least, until she turned up pregnant. He threw her out and she almost lost Bernadette. She was destitute and very ill. I never knew. She phoned me while I was in Africa, and Maureen told her to stay out of my life, that I wanted nothing to do with her. She never even told me that Sarina called!"

Tate winced.

Colby saw it. His eyes darkened. "Lucky Maureen, that she didn't contact me directly."

"If she'd known that you were in touch with your ex-wife, she might not even have given me those papers," Tate agreed. "Fate works in mysterious ways, doesn't it?"

"Yes."

"Your daughter," Tate said, hesitating. "What's she like?"

Colby's eyes lit up. He smiled. "She's like me," he said with helpless pride. "Stubborn and proud, and she's not afraid of anything. She's smart, too, like her mother."

"What does her mother do?"

Colby sighed. "She's a clerk for an oil company."

"Not a career woman," Tate murmured.

"Lucky for me," Colby chuckled, reaching into his closet for his clothes. "I could never settle with a woman who had a profession."

BY THE TIME Colby was dressed, Tate knew all about the pint-size female version of her father. He grinned at his former partner's enthusiasm for the child. He'd always thought Colby would make a good father. He was afraid some years ago, though, that it was Cecily whom Colby had seen as the mother of his children. But Cecily had eyes only for Tate, as he'd learned to his delight, and the two of them had been very happily married.

"What does Sarina look like?" Tate asked.

Colby smiled. "She's blond, slender, very lovely. Dark eyes. And she's a terrific mother."

"Maybe Cecily and I will get to meet her one day under better circumstances."

"I'm sorry about the way it worked out today," Colby said ruefully. "I had plans to storm her apartment tonight. But I can't let Hunter down. We're setting up a drug bust, and I'm essential personnel."

"Shoot straight and remember to duck," Tate cautioned.

"I remember how," Colby chuckled, and patted his friend on the shoulder. "I hope to be back tonight."

"If you're not, we'll lock up on our way out of

town. But I want to hear how it went with Sarina. And the drug bust."

"I'll make a point of telling you, even if it has to be by phone."

COLBY DROVE to the office, parking in front where he saw Hunter's SUV. He checked his sidearm, pulled an extra clip from the pocket of his vehicle, locked up and went inside.

Hunter, old man Ritter, two DEA agents including Alexander Cobb, and five members of the Drug Task Force from other law enforcement agencies were gathered in Ritter's office. Hunter introduced Colby, and then pulled him to one side.

"You still look pale," Hunter said quietly. "If you're not up to this, say so."

"I wouldn't be here if I wasn't," Colby said. "I'd never risk anyone else's life by showing up half prepared. You know that."

Hunter smiled. He clapped the other man on the back. "Okay." He reached in his belt and handed Colby an HK MP-5 automatic weapon.

"I miss my old Uzi," Colby told him, tongue-in-cheek, as he handled the weapon. "Is it legal for us to have these?"

"When you're backing up government agents, it is," Hunter chuckled. "Never mind, just use it. And don't ask where I got it," he added, with a quick glance at the Houston SWAT team that was already gearing up to give support.

"Okay." He holstered his Glock and checked the magazine in the MP-5 before he cocked it and put on the safety.

Alexander Cobb, a senior DEA agent, moved to the front of the group. "We've got two of our people supposedly working in the warehouse. They're known to the employees and apparently just checking out a shipment for Mr. Ritter, so they won't raise eyebrows. If they see anything suspicious, they'll…"

He stopped as his cell phone jangled. He flipped it open, put it to his ear and listened. "We're on the way," he said at once, closing it up. "It's a go," he told the others. "They're just beyond the first line of pallets, and shots have been fired. Don't shoot each other," he added with a faint smile.

Which was a cue for the others to shrug into their jackets, which identified them in large white letters. Colby and Hunter exchanged glances. They weren't wearing ID.

THEY WENT OUT THE DOOR and piled into their various vehicles, Colby sharing Hunter's, and gunned the engines on their way down the block to the main warehouse.

The parking lot was well lit, and there was a van backed up to the loading dock. Nobody was near it. As the group exited their vehicles, with weapons drawn, and started into the warehouse, more shots were heard.

Colby hesitated long enough to draw his firearm and cock it. As he paused by the door, a local policeman came up beside him.

"Hold it right there! You're not wearing ID," the man said curtly, his pistol menacing. "Who are you and what are you doing here? We were told to wait for orders."

"I'm Ritter security," Colby replied.

"Oh. A rent-a-cop," the man said with faint contempt. "Well, don't get in the way when we go in. You might get hurt."

Colby gave the man a glare that could have stopped traffic. "You wait for orders, if you like. I'm going in." Before the policeman could say another word, Colby darted inside the warehouse with his MP-5 raised in position.

Two men with automatic weapons opened fire at once from behind boxes stacked on wood pallets down a long aisle.

Colby dived, rolled, and fired two quick shots. One man fell. He was on his feet again and down the aisle in a heartbeat. This was old hat to him, after all the long years in counterintelligence and covert ops. He was vaguely aware of the policeman following in his wake, and shadowy figures against the opposite wall of the sprawling warehouse which were probably the drug task force.

He wondered where Cobb's undercover agents were, but he didn't have time to look for civilians.

He was up to his neck in drug smugglers. They seemed to come out of the woodwork.

He tapped his earpiece, but the unit that connected him to Cobb and the others wasn't working. Hastily he felt behind him and his fingers touched a dangling wire. The connection was broken, but he didn't have time to fix it. Another smuggler was firing at him.

He dodged behind a stack of boxes and closed his eyes, listening for sound. He heard a board creak above his head and loud breathing from just behind him. He whirled in a heartbeat, the MP-5 suddenly leveled calmly at the policeman's nose.

The other man had time to gasp before Colby cursed and drew the weapon up into a forty-five degree angle pointing at the ceiling. He snapped off several quick rounds at a moving shadow, paused and fired several more shots just ahead of the second creak his ears detected. There was a cry of pain from above and a faint thud.

He turned, avoiding the policeman's curious gaze, and eased down the aisle as softly as he could, with a determined lack of rhythm. He'd learned as a hunter that rhythmic steps always denoted a human, especially in the forest. Even here, it was a giveaway, despite his rubber-soled shoes. The footsteps behind him quickly followed in his own pattern.

He drew a long breath as he continued. There was

another shot, and another. He hoped Hunter wasn't in trouble. Damn the stupid electronic ear that wasn't working! He had no idea where the other members of the drug unit were, or where the undercover agents were—he didn't even know who they were, or what they looked like! The whole situation was a tragedy in the making. It would be a miracle if it worked out.

He thought briefly of Sarina and Bernadette, and how lonely his life was going to be without them if he couldn't make things up with Sarina. But such thoughts were dangerous, right now. He had to concentrate on the situation at hand.

Two men in sweats darted across the aisle, firing as they ran. Colby quickly dropped one with a shot in the leg.

"Get the other one!" he called to the policeman behind him, who darted across the aisle with his pistol raised next to his ear, ready to fire. A shot from nearby shattered the sudden silence. But it was followed by two more shots, each from a different gun. Colby had long ago learned to tell the difference.

As Colby rounded the next corner, he was just in time to see a man in a dark suit running down the aisle and vanishing into another stack of boxes. On the floor, doubled over, was a figure in a baseball cap and a black jacket with DEA in big white letters on its back. The figure seemed to be in pain.

Colby ran to the downed agent and knelt beside him, still scanning the area for other armed men.

"Are you hit?" he asked curtly.

"Just…a flesh wound," came an oddly familiar female voice. "Don't sit there, get after him! Don't you dare let that son of a bitch get away!"

He turned his head toward her, gaping as he met flaming brown eyes in a flushed face. The baseball cap concealed a head of long blond hair. "Sarina?" he exclaimed, shell-shocked. "Sarina! What the hell are you doing here?" he exploded.

She glared at him. "Never mind that. It's Brody Vance," she said angrily. "He's with the smugglers and he shot me. Go get him!"

"You're wounded!" he bit off, staring at the torn upper arm of her jacket as he tried to reconcile what he was seeing with what he'd known of Sarina's job.

"It went through, clean. I tell you, I'm all right, Colby. Don't let Vance get away! And don't shoot Rodrigo—he's with us."

The policeman joined them, whipping off his tie. "I'll take care of her," he told Colby solemnly. "You're better armed than I am." He indicated the MP-5. "Go!"

Colby spared Sarina a last, anguished glance, before he jumped to his feet and rushed down the aisle in the direction Vance had gone.

CHAPTER ELEVEN

COLBY HAD TO FORCE his mind to work again. The shock of seeing Sarina wounded was bad enough, without the knowledge that she was almost certainly working with the Drug Enforcement Agency. She had a pistol and apparently knew how to use it. She had skills she hadn't shared with him, even when they'd been the most intimate. The implications hurt him. She'd lied to him. She'd made him believe she had a dull, safe job, and here she was participating in a dangerous raid. She had a child! What was she thinking?

The more he thought about it, the angrier he became. Faint gunfire from the back of the warehouse caught his attention. He moved toward it, the MP-5 raised and ready. His eyes were almost black with fury. God help the smuggler who moved into his path right now.

With his back to the high pallet of boxes, he eased around another corner and cautiously peered into the aisle.

Rodrigo Ramirez was there, his back to Colby, his hands raised. He was also wearing a DEA jacket, and suddenly everything made sense. Rodrigo and Sarina weren't lovers, they were partners. They were DEA agents! In fact, he was certain that they were the two out of state undercover agents Cobb had been so furious about. They'd been right under Colby's nose, and he hadn't known. He wondered if Hunter had.

He clenched his teeth with muffled fury. But there was no time for speculation now. He had a situation developing right in front of him. As he watched, it became clear that one of the drug smugglers had the drop on Rodrigo. The man with the gun was speaking in rapid Spanish into a cell phone, and nodding as he stared at Rodrigo.

While he was diverted, Colby darted into the aisle and dropped the man with one quick shot into his hip. Even as the smuggler fell, groaning, Colby moved relentlessly toward the downed man with his gun leveled at him. He paid no attention whatsoever to Ramirez.

In rapid-fire Spanish, he questioned the wounded man, who was holding the bleeding wound tightly.

"Tell me!" Colby demanded in a calm, icy tone. "Where is Vance?"

The man grimaced and Colby kicked the cell

phone out of the way, dropped to one knee, and put a thumb squarely over the man's carotid artery. "Tell me," he said softly, in a voice that cut like a knife, "or die here."

The man saw in Colby's eyes that he meant it. He managed to swallow and then said that Vance was headed for a barge anchored in the canal just behind the warehouse.

Rodrigo moved to join him, bending to retrieve his .45 from the smuggler's waistband. "That means we'll have to work our way through a civilian crew," Rodrigo said coldly as he checked and cocked the weapon, putting on the safety.

Colby got to his feet and looked at the other man for the first time. "You're DEA. So is Sarina," he said coldly.

Rodrigo looked back at him with the same controlled anger. "Yes. And you're no military man. I knew you looked familiar, but I couldn't place you until I heard the way you spoke to that *pendejo,*" he added, nodding toward the downed man. "I was in Africa six years ago, when Cy Parks brought you in to interrogate a prisoner. I could never forget the technique you used. The intel you got from the man saved our lives. Even if your methods were, shall we say, eccentric," he added, tongue-in-cheek, "we owed you for the favor."

Colby remembered a man in fatigues who wore sunglasses and was part of another paramilitary group headed by Dutch, Archer, and Laremos. His eyes narrowed. "You were with Archer," he said abruptly.

Rodrigo nodded curtly. "And you were with Parks. Both of us were mercs."

"Does she know?" Colby asked.

"No," Rodrigo replied, his eyes cold with dislike. "Not about either one of us."

Colby didn't say a word. It was surprising that Ramirez hadn't blown his cover.

"Think you've got me over a barrel, don't you?" Rodrigo asked. "Well, Sarina won't mind, even if you tell her. We've been partners for three years."

"DEA field agents," Colby said icily. "And she's got a little girl!"

It had occurred to Rodrigo that Colby was going to be so upset when he knew what Sarina did for a living, but the man was more than upset, he was livid.

"The hell with it," Colby bit off. "I don't have time for personal problems. We've got drug smugglers to catch."

"Where's Sarina?" Rodrigo asked.

"Back there with a local cop," Colby said, averting his eyes. "She caught a bullet. Just a flesh wound."

Rodrigo had to fight the urge to run back to her. But he knew his duty. He had to do it.

He pulled out the .45 and glanced at Colby. "Why do you get an MP-5 and I only have a pistol?"

Colby gave him a superior glance. "Hunter gave it to me. He likes me."

"He likes me, too," Rodrigo said curtly.

"Yeah? Well, he likes me better," Colby shot back. "Let's go." He hesitated as they rounded another corner. "If your earpiece still works, better tell the task force where we're going."

Rodrigo did.

THE CANAL WAS FULL of vessels, everything from boats to barges. The Houston channel ran between warehouses and shipping offices all along the waterfront. Civilians were everywhere, and there were at least three barges snuggled up against the piers.

"Damn!" Colby exclaimed. "Which one?"

Rodrigo was thinking. He noted the names of the barges and mentally compared them against cargo lists he'd been checking earlier that day. "The black one," he said at once. "The Bogotá."

"Are you sure?"

"No. But it's not a bad guess," Rodrigo replied, walking quickly toward it. "Cara Dominguez is from Colombia."

"Not bad," Colby had to admit, but he did it grudgingly.

Rodrigo holstered his weapon. "You'd better put that away as well," he told Colby. "If they know we're looking for Vance, we'll never get aboard."

"He'll tell them we're after him," Colby said.

Rodrigo shucked his DEA jacket, leaving only his suit coat showing. He placed the jacket on the side of a box near the docks. "He'll be hiding below. He probably won't even see us coming."

"Got any idea about how we're going to board that vessel?" Colby asked.

Rodrigo smiled. "Wait and see."

The older man ignored Colby's glare and walked elegantly to the ship, where its captain was going over a cargo list with two other men.

"Good evening," Rodrigo said in Spanish. "We understand you're preparing to leave port with your cargo."

"Yes," the captain said, frowning suspiciously. "What business is that of yours?"

Rodrigo pulled out his wallet and flashed his badge just enough so that the captain could see it, but not read it. "We're ICE," he said blithely, "Immigration and Customs Enforcement. We have reason to believe that you have two illegal aliens on your vessel. We're here to apprehend them."

The captain, who'd been tense and nervous, suddenly relaxed. "Illegals." He shrugged. "Well, we might have one or two. I don't have time to check backgrounds on every crewman I hire. What are their names?"

"We don't have names," Rodrigo said smoothly.

"Only descriptions. I'll know them when I see them. I have photographs."

The captain frowned, checking his watch. "I have a timetable," he began.

"Fifteen minutes," Rodrigo told him. "That's all I need. My assistant—" he jerked his thumb toward Colby "—and I will find them in no time if you'll allow us aboard." When the captain hesitated, he added, "It will take longer if I have to call my superiors and have them send additional personnel."

Not to mention the suspicion it would cause, the captain was thinking. He cleared his throat. "Very well, then. But no more than fifteen minutes."

"Of course," Rodrigo said carelessly.

He motioned to Colby and they walked right aboard the vessel without a single hitch.

"You're handy," Colby mused.

"I do a lot of undercover work," Rodrigo replied. "Which is why they have me on this assignment." He glanced at Colby. "I infiltrated Lopez's organization several years ago. I know things nobody else does about how the drugs are transported."

Colby was impressed against his will. "Cy Parks said that he was acquainted with an undercover agent. He meant you, I suppose."

"I had a cousin who worked for Lopez. He was killed shortly after the last big raid, in Jacobsville." He sighed. "Lopez killed my sister as well.

She was working in a nightclub and he took a fancy to her. She resisted him and he killed her."

Colby glanced at him. "I'm sorry," he said genuinely.

Rodrigo shrugged. "It could as easily have been me. I got lucky." He didn't mention that Alexander Cobb had raised hell when he knew that Ramirez was one of the two undercover DEA agents. They had a history. Rodrigo had ransacked his office just after his sister's death.

They were aboard the ship now, and passing easily among the crewmen, who didn't know quite what to make of the two men in suits walking so leisurely down the decks.

"If Vance sees us, he'll run," Colby said. "Especially after wounding Sarina. Assault on a federal officer…"

"…is a felony," Rodrigo agreed. He glanced at Colby. "We want Vance alive," he emphasized.

Cold dark eyes met his. "He'll be alive. Sort of."

"No," the older man said firmly. "We need him to find his cohorts. Cara Dominguez is still free and running things for the drug cartel. Vance can lead us to her."

Colby's jaw tensed. "Spoilsport," he said angrily.

"Don't think I wouldn't like a shot at him as well," came the cold reply. "It's just that we don't dare. Not now."

Colby's mood lightened. "Later, we could pose

as federal marshals and offer to transport him to trial," he suggested.

Rodrigo smothered a laugh. "You have to stop thinking like a merc. There are rules here in the States."

"Even if you can't break rules, you can bend them," Colby offered.

"Isn't that what got you sent home from Africa in the first place?" he asked. "Bending rules with your, shall we say, inventive, interrogation techniques?"

"People talked to me," Colby defended.

"Not willingly. Be careful," Rodrigo added as they hesitated at the ladder into the cargo hold. "He's still armed, and he'll be expecting someone to follow him."

Colby gave him a sarcastic glance, his hand going inside his jacket to the concealed automatic weapon.

Rodrigo glanced at it, frowning. "They should have given me one, too."

"Admitting what a bad shot you are?"

Rodrigo's teeth clenched. "Admitting the same?"

Colby hesitated suddenly as they entered the cargo hold. He put an arm behind him, to motion Rodrigo to one side. He froze in place, not moving, not breathing. He was almost grateful that Rodrigo had a similar background, because a noisy companion would have gotten them both killed. There, just ahead, were two armed men, talking to Brody

Vance, who was pushing back sweaty dark hair and shaking with fear.

"Did they recognize you?" one of the men was demanding in accented English.

"No!" Vance burst out. "I'm sure they didn't. Well, the agent I shot saw me, but not close enough to recognize me, I'm sure of it. He was blond and thin. He looked familiar… Anyway, I…" He hesitated and groaned. "I shot him! He may be dead!"

"That is nothing to us," the second man said, his voice devoid of any accent at all. "If you weren't recognized, you can go back."

"No! They'll know! I'll go to jail!"

The first man pointed a pistol at his heart. "Jail is not better than dead?" he drawled.

Vance put up both hands. "Please! Please don't kill me!"

Colby was thinking fast. He and Rodrigo could wade in, shoot all three men and arrest the survivors. But if Vance didn't know he'd been recognized, he was valuable in place. He could give them Cara Dominguez if he were carefully handled. The man was a coward. He could be useful.

He glanced over his shoulder at Rodrigo and saw the intelligence in the man's dark eyes, and a nod. He jerked his head toward the access ladder. Without a protest, Rodrigo eased backward until he was out of sight and climbed up. Colby followed him, closing his jacket over the automatic weapon.

They walked together down the gangplank to the pier.

"You're clean," Rodrigo told the captain with a grin. "No illegals there. Thanks for your time."

"It was no trouble at all," the captain said with blatant relief.

"Good day," Rodrigo replied. He and Colby walked back toward the warehouses.

"YOU'RE QUICK," Colby said, hesitating outside the warehouse where a SWAT team was mopping up, along with DEA personnel and the task force. "I hoped you'd understand what I meant before they saw us. Vance is more valuable on the job than in jail right now."

"I agree." Rodrigo moved forward. "I'll make it right with Cobb. I owe him a few apologies before he can draw his sidearm," he added enigmatically. "But I want to see how Sarina is."

Colby followed Rodrigo back into the warehouse. He knew that she was right, it was a flesh wound, and not life-threatening. But he felt guilty and outraged and upset, all at once.

She was out front with the paramedics, one of whom was looking at her arm.

She looked up when Colby and Rodrigo approached, but she wouldn't meet Colby's cold glance.

Rodrigo squatted down in front of her, his face

concerned. "Are you going to be all right?" he asked gently.

She smiled at him in a way that made Colby turn to stone. "I'll be fine." She laid a hand on his shoulder. "Are you all right?"

He nodded, catching the hand to hold it tightly in his.

"Did you get Vance?" she asked Colby, her eyes meeting his for the first time.

"No," he replied. "He didn't recognize you and he still has ties to Dominguez and her operation. We're going to pretend he wasn't involved and see if we can use him to lead her into a trap."

She started to protest angrily, but Rodrigo pressed her hand, hard.

"He's right," he told her firmly. "Vance can't be apprehended just yet."

"He shot me!" she raged, her dark eyes fierce and outraged. "Assault on a federal officer is a felony!" She glared at Rodrigo. "And why are you suddenly taking his side against me?" she demanded, jerking a thumb toward Colby.

Rodrigo glowered. "He…saved my life," he said reluctantly. "One of the mules had the draw on me. He knocked him down with a bullet and questioned him about Vance."

"Uh-oh," Colby groaned.

"You feel guilty for saving my life?" Rodrigo mused.

"Not that. I used Vance's name in front of the mule," Colby corrected. "We'll have to have Houston PD find a way to hold him incommunicado until we wind up this case." He turned away from Sarina's accusing eyes. "I'll go talk to them."

"Calm down," Rodrigo told Sarina when Colby was out of earshot. "Smoke is coming out of your ears."

She almost shuddered with anger. "Ouch!" she protested as the medic put on a temporary bandage.

"Sorry, ma'am," he apologized with a grin, "but we have to get you ready to transport."

"It's a flesh wound," she growled at him, her dark eyes sparking with temper. "I don't need to be transported anywhere!"

"Oh, yeah?" he replied. "When was your last tetanus shot?"

She blinked. She couldn't remember ever having had one, unless it was when she was a child.

"If you can't remember, that's another reason to get in my truck, Rambo," the medic said, chuckling.

"A bullet wound can easily get infected," Rodrigo interjected. "I spent a week in hospital some years ago for doing what you're trying to do. You can't go home and wash it out with peroxide."

She sighed angrily. "Okay, I'll go. But I'm not staying," she added as she got into the ambulance.

Rodrigo didn't say another word, but he and the medic exchanged knowing glances.

COLBY, MEANWHILE, had hunted up the policeman who'd followed him into the building. "I need a favor," he told the man, a corporal, judging by his name tag.

"What is it?" the man asked.

He started to reach into his pocket when he noticed that one of the servos in his artificial arm had stopped working. Cursing violently, he took off his jacket, draped it over a nearby rail, and shot up his sleeve, exposing a bullet lodged in the prosthetic arm.

"Damn the luck!" he raged. "This thing is more trouble than it's worth."

The policeman was eyeing it curiously. "How'd you lose your arm?"

"In Africa, doing covert ops," he replied absently, checking the damage. "Well, I'll have to go home and get my spare."

The police officer had straightened. "Listen," he said, "I'm sorry about that rent-a-cop crack earlier," he said genuinely. "It's just that I've had my problems with security guards who thought they were Eliot Ness."

Colby gave him a grin. "So have I," he mused. "In fact, we had one like that in D.C. when I was working security for the Hutton Corporation. He made such a nuisance of himself that we locked him in a closet with one of the terrorists. When he came out, he said he was going back to walking dogs for a living."

"Terrorists?" the policeman queried.

Colby nodded as he replaced his sleeve and put his jacket back on. "They tried to blow up one of Hutton's oil platforms. We turned them over to Interpol."

The man was very still. "Hutton was involved in that kidnapping overseas, the one that almost started a war. It made international headlines."

Colby shrugged. "That was before I went to work for him. I was doing a stint for one of the covert agencies in D.C." He leaned toward the man. "Just between you and me, private sector pays better."

The policeman chuckled. "Maybe I'll hit you up for a job one day."

"Yeah? And maybe I'll hire you," Colby replied, grinning good-naturedly. "Listen, I asked that goon I shot about Vance's whereabouts. We've decided to let Vance go back to work and pretend we don't know how involved he is in the drug smuggling plot. We need to make sure he doesn't pass that information on to any of his colleagues."

"The one you shot? Didn't you know?" the policeman asked.

"Know what?"

"The fool tried to take another patrolman's pistol while he was handcuffing him. They struggled and the pistol went off. The perp's dead."

Colby whistled. "Solves my problem, but not in a way I'd prefer."

"I know what you mean. Better take care of that arm," he added, noting that the servos seemed to be moving without purpose and making a lot of noise.

"Yes, I had," Colby said. "Thanks for the backup, by the way."

"No problem. I like working with the local DEA boys. They never hog the credit when we go along on raids with them. See you."

"Yeah."

Colby made his way back to Hunter and laid his MP-5 alongside the other special weapons that Hunter had borrowed.

"Damn, Hunter, will you and your people stop lifting our stuff?" the SWAT sergeant muttered as he checked the weapons and unloaded them.

"As God is my witness," Colby told the man, hand over his heart, "I have no idea how that weapon managed to get in my belt!"

Hunter dragged him away just in time.

When he was alone, Colby's mood darkened. He'd told Sarina that they shouldn't keep secrets from each other ever again, and she'd agreed. She'd been lying the whole time. How could she be so intimate with him and not trust him? It destroyed his faith in her.

But there was Bernadette, his daughter, his child. He couldn't turn his back on the little girl now, regardless of how he felt about her mother. He grimaced. What did he feel for her mother? He was confused.

Nevertheless, he drove straight for the hospital when he left the warehouse, despite the malfunctioning arm. Certainly the wound wasn't fatal, but he couldn't help worrying about Sarina. He couldn't leave Rodrigo to take care of her, either, despite his changed opinion of the man.

He found Sarina still in a cubicle in the emergency room. The doctor had ordered X-rays and she was waiting for the radiologist to read them.

"I told him it didn't hit the bone," she was telling Rodrigo, "but he wouldn't listen."

"You should have showed him your medical degree," Rodrigo drawled.

She glared at him.

"What did the doctor say?" Colby asked, joining them, his face giving away nothing of his feelings.

"He's a resident," she corrected curtly, holding her arm. "He said that I seem to have a gunshot wound."

Colby couldn't suppress a grin.

"He's busy reporting it to the police," she added.

His eyebrows went up. "Did you show him your ID?" he asked.

The glare got worse. "I didn't get the chance. He thinks I'm an escaped criminal, apparently. I couldn't bear to deprive him of his evening's entertainment!" she scoffed.

Rodrigo shrugged, as if to say, *you talk some sense into her.*

Just as he started to, the resident, a solemn tall

young man with fair hair and thick glasses walked back in with a police officer on his heels.

All at the same time, Rodrigo, Colby, and Sarina produced their badges for his inspection.

The police officer gave Colby's a long stare. He gave the resident a speaking look, apologized for inconveniencing a wounded agent, and left.

Just for spite, Colby allowed the resident a peek at his ID. It was the old one, of course, his "company" card.

The resident cleared his throat. "I am obliged by the hospital regulations to report all gunshot wounds to the police."

Colby folded his wallet. "You can take my word for it that the young woman is not an escaped fugitive. However," he added with narrowed eyes, "if her wound is not treated promptly, I will have a word with the administrator of this hospital."

The resident got busy.

A PRACTICING PHYSICIAN came in to check the resident's diagnosis, and approved the treatment, but would not allow Sarina to go home.

He held up a hand when she began to argue. "We have plenty of empty beds, and better safe than sorry, especially when the bullet passed so close to the bone. If you do all right tomorrow, I'll allow you to leave first thing Monday morning."

"Monday?" she exclaimed.

"See how it feels when people won't let you do what you want to do?" Colby asked.

She glared at him. "You had malaria! You had no business out of bed!"

"Tit for tat," he retorted.

"He's right," Rodrigo interrupted. "You don't need to be in the apartment alone, especially now. And Bernadette wouldn't know what to do if something happened."

Sarina glared at him, too. "She's staying with the Hunters," she said after a minute, when she realized that raging at the men wouldn't do any good. "I'll ask Jennifer if she can stay until Monday. They can drop her off at school with Nikki. But what do I tell her?"

"I'll go by there tomorrow," Colby said quietly, "and tell her you had an emergency meeting out of town for Mr. Ritter."

She hesitated. "All right."

"I could take her to the zoo tomorrow," Colby added.

Sarina's dark eyes flashed angrily. "You and your new lover?"

Rodrigo perked up, staring curiously at Colby's darkening cheeks.

Colby glared at her, ignoring the Mexican. His face hardened. Not for worlds was he going to admit the truth. Let her sweat. "As it happens, she's flying out in the morning," he drawled. "I'll be all alone!"

"Pity," she bit off. "You're good at keeping secrets, aren't you?"

"And you're a fine one to talk," he shot back. "What the hell sort of mother risks her life for a job when she's got a child to raise?"

CHAPTER TWELVE

SARINA'S FACE went white. She'd expected that question from the minute Colby saw her on the floor in the warehouse, but she still didn't know how to answer it. She didn't want to answer it. He'd given her hope that he cared, that he wanted a future with her. And then he hadn't phoned her, and she'd found him half naked with another woman. It was just like before, when he'd had Maureen in the background and pretended to be interested in Sarina. He'd betrayed her once. Why wouldn't he be willing to do it again? He was never going to be a faithful husband. She'd been living in a dream world of happy endings. Here was the reality.

She lifted her face belligerently. "I'm a good agent, and I very rarely walk into situations this dangerous. Rodrigo can tell you that."

"I don't care what he tells me," Colby replied before the other man could speak. "You took a bullet in the arm tonight. A few inches to the left, and you'd be dead!"

"I'm not," she pointed out. She glared at him. "You have a job that's more dangerous than mine is," she added. "Planning to give it up for Bernadette and take a nice safe desk job, are you?"

"This isn't about me."

"You're her father," she burst out.

"You're her mother," he shot back. "Do you plan to raise her in between gun battles?"

"You shot a man!"

"You tried to shoot one!" he returned hotly.

Rodrigo stepped in between both of them. "She's wounded and you're malfunctioning," he pointed out. "Both of you need some minor repairs. It wouldn't be a bad idea to postpone World War III until you're in better shape."

Colby glowered at him. Then he shrugged and drew in a long breath. "I suppose it wouldn't be a bad idea, at that," he had to admit. "I need to go home and find my spare arm."

She held her arm. "I could use something for pain," she confessed.

Rodrigo nodded. "That's more like it."

Sarina glared at him. "You're on his side," she accused.

He shrugged. "He saved my life. Temporarily," he added with a wry glance at Colby, "I owe him."

"You can save my life at your convenience and even things up," Colby said agreeably.

"I still owe you for the other time," Rodrigo said without thinking, remembering Africa. But he stopped short and looked uneasy.

"What other time?" Sarina asked curiously.

"There were two guys in the warehouse," Colby said easily. "I've got to go. Don't let her assault the resident and escape," he told Rodrigo.

"He isn't my type," she said irritably. "I don't like fair men."

"We noticed," Rodrigo drawled.

Colby glared at him.

The resident came back before he could speak. He looked from the men to Sarina, who was giving him a cold stare. Her hand went to the butt of her .45.

"Now see here, I was only obeying the rules," the resident said quickly.

She lifted the pistol out and handed it, slowly, to Rodrigo. "Keep it for me," she told him.

He gave the resident a bland smile. "I wouldn't worry, she missed the last guy she shot at."

Colby was feeling the effects of the night. He glanced at Sarina and tried not to let it show that he was still concerned. "You going to be all right?"

She nodded. "It's just…"

"…a flesh wound. Right."

"Sure," she said.

"We're sending you along to a room," the resident told Sarina, with quick glances at the two men. "There are some papers to be filled out, but we'll send one of the office workers down to your room to take care of all that. Uh, if you're ready?" he added with a meaningful, but nervous glance at her two visitors.

"I have to go," Rodrigo said. He touched Sarina's hand gently. "If you need me, I'm as close as the phone."

"Thanks," she said and smiled at him.

He left. Colby drew in a harsh breath. "I'll keep Bernadette in the dark. I'll come and pick you up Monday and take you home."

"Rodrigo can do that," she bit off.

"Certainly he can. But he's not going to," he replied. "You can go with me to pick Bernadette up at school Monday afternoon, if you're feeling up to it."

She wanted to argue, but her arm was hurting and she felt sick.

He nodded to the resident. "I'll go, so that you can get her settled." He noticed her grimace as she moved off the examination table. "I know how that feels, by the way," he told her, nodding toward her injured arm. "I've been shot several times over the years. Tomorrow, you'll be glad they didn't let you go home."

"Quite right," the resident agreed. "You'll be sick and in a good deal of pain, more than you're feeling now. I'll write up something for that as well."

"Good night," Colby told her.

She glared at him, but she was already wilting. It wasn't much of a glare. He turned away without comment. He had more reason than she did to be mad, but this wasn't the time for it.

He went out of the cubicle still feeling betrayed. He could have shown her the photograph of Tate and Cecily, but he was too angry. Let her think he had a woman on the side. He didn't care. She'd lied to him.

HE WAS ON HIS WAY home when a small, tragic face flashed before his eyes. It was Bernadette. She was crying, distraught. He couldn't get the picture out of his mind. It made no sense. It was almost midnight. She was asleep. He couldn't go to Hunter's house and wake everybody up…

Yes, he could. He did. The door opened and Hunter whistled softly.

"Thank God you're here, although I don't understand why." He stood aside and Bernadette came running to Colby, wearing purple pajamas, her face wet with tears, her eyes red and swollen.

"Daddy!" she exclaimed, throwing herself into his arms. "Daddy, Mommy got shot, just like in my dream! Is she dead?"

Only then did Colby remember Bernadette's premonition, about her mother getting shot in a big place among a group of boxes. He'd promised her he'd take care of Sarina. But he hadn't known about her DEA work then. He drew Bernadette close and walked the floor with her, soothing her gently.

"It's all right, baby," he whispered. "Mommy's fine. Mommy's just fine."

"But she was bleeding," Bernadette whimpered. "I saw!"

Colby's arms tightened even more. The damaged servo was loud in the room, but he didn't notice. He sat down on the sofa with Bernadette on his lap, and pulled out a handkerchief to dry her eyes.

"Listen," he told her, "Mommy's very brave, so you have to be brave, too. They're going to keep her in the hospital until Monday. But I promise that she and I will pick you up at school Monday afternoon. I promise, Bernadette."

She began to calm, just a little. She looked up into his eyes and saw no lies there. She slowed her breathing. "Okay, Daddy."

The word, still rare, made him feel taller, stronger. He smiled at her, brushing back the damp hair from her big, brown eyes. Tears were still trickling from them, but slowing. "I'll never lie to you," he said.

She nodded. "I was so scared." She drew in a shaky breath. "Why do I have to see bad things?"

"I don't know, baby. But your grandfather did, too. He rode all the way to school on a horse one day I was in grammar school because he knew I'd had a bad fall. Nobody told him, he just knew. I'd broken my leg. He showed up just as the ambulance got there."

She smiled. "He told me."

The Hunters, all three of them, were standing beside the sofa, listening. Nikki was in her gown. The adults were wearing sweatpants and robes. Bernadette was in pajamas. Colby sighed. "I guess I'm overdressed," he told Hunter. "I think I should either put on pajamas myself, or go home."

Hunter was listening to the artificial arm. "I'd say the second idea was your best bet," he agreed, noting the arm. "Did it miss everything vital?"

Colby nodded. "Just a badly placed shot," he said lazily, smiling at Bernadette.

"I wouldn't say that," Hunter chuckled.

Colby got up, placing Bernadette back on her feet. "Can she stay until Monday morning? I can take her to school," he volunteered.

"No need," Jennifer said with a smile as she cuddled up sleepily to Hunter. "She and Nikki can ride together."

"Then Sarina and I will pick her up Monday afternoon at school. That reminds me," he added, looking down at Bernadette. "Would you like to go to the zoo tomorrow?"

"Oh, yes!" she exclaimed. "Can Nikki come, too?"

"Sure," Colby agreed, smiling.

"In that case, we'll all go," Hunter said, "and make a day of it. I like zoos myself."

"That's because you've spent so much time around animals," Colby murmured, tongue-in-cheek.

"Present company excepted?" Hunter chuckled.

"Well, sort of." Colby held his left arm. "I'd better get my gizmo home before it self-destructs," he added. "What time tomorrow?"

"About twelve-thirty?"

"That works for me. I can sleep late. I'm still a little rocky from the malaria," Colby had to admit, "and tonight wasn't exactly a picnic." He bent and picked Bernadette up with his right arm and hugged her close. It was getting to feel very natural, hugging the child. He smiled as he kissed her wet cheek. "Go to bed now, okay?"

"Okay. Night, Daddy."

"Good night, baby."

THE ZOO WAS A TREAT for Colby, who hadn't been to one since he was small, and that one had been more of an exotic animal farm than a zoo. This one had very elegant outdoor confinements for the animals, so that they didn't seem to be caged at all. He especially liked the reptile exhibit. Bernadette didn't seem to mind it at all. She held Colby's hand proudly, smiling at other children she met as if to put him on display. He felt her pride in him, and was humbled by it.

They ate hot dogs and walked until his legs ached. Then they went to the park, where the cold didn't seem to deter swinging, and he and the Hunters rested on benches while Nikki and Bernadette ran to the swings. It was a good day, he reflected. Being a parent was nothing like his expectations of years ago. It was better.

Jennifer Hunter phoned the hospital later, since Colby had refused to, without stating any reason for it. She talked to Sarina. Rodrigo had been to see her, but she was feeling vaguely deserted, especially by Colby.

"We went to the zoo," Jennifer told her. "You should have seen Bernadette at the reptile house. She's fearless, just like Colby. The keeper actually let her hold an albino python, and she wasn't the least afraid."

"She likes snakes," Sarina said, smiling to herself. She shifted in the bed and winced, because the arm was really sore and she had some fever and nausea as well. "Did Colby…say anything about me?"

"No," Jennifer replied. "I think he's still in shock. Phillip said he had no idea what you really did for a living. He's taking it hard."

"He might as well get used to it," Sarina said angrily. "I'm not giving up my job!"

"Both of you are going to have to make some major adjustments one day," the other woman said gently. "A child needs two parents. I don't have to tell you that."

There was a brief silence. "No, you don't. I suppose I'm still upset."

"About the shootout?" Jennifer asked.

No, about the almost nude blonde in Colby's apartment, but Sarina wasn't comfortable sharing that with Jennifer. "Yes," she lied, "about the shootout. I'm having some fever and pain today. I suppose they were right about making me stay here."

"I'm sorry you missed the zoo, all the same," Jennifer chuckled. "Bernadette was having the time of her life."

"I'm glad. I've spent so much time working the past few years that she hasn't had as much fun as I'd have liked."

"Now that Colby's around, he'll take her from time to time," Jennifer suggested. "Nikki loves going places with her daddy, and showing him off."

"Phillip's a good father."

"Colby's going to be a good one, too."

There was a pause. "I don't suppose you know that Colby came by in the wee hours of the morning?"

"What? Why?"

"He said he saw Bernadette crying. A vision, Phillip calls it. When he got here, we were all in the living room trying to convince her that everything was all right. Colby told her just a little of what happened, but he reassured her. She was smiling when he left."

Sarina was silent. Then she sighed. "I thought he might have that emotional link with her that his father had with him," she said softly. "Bernadette had a premonition about him getting shot in Africa, you know. They had an encounter the day they met because she told him all about it."

"Yes, Phillip told me. It's amazing, isn't it?"

"Yes. Her grandfather was just the same. He said he always knew when something bad had happened to Colby."

"It must run in families," Jennifer said. "I knew a woman whose background was Scotch-Irish, who had the 'second sight.' She had the same sort of link with her mother. She got on a plane and flew two thousand miles to be with her mother when the woman had a major heart attack. Nobody had even phoned her. She just knew."

"Bernadette's grandfather said it was a gift, but Bernadette is upset by it. She only sees bad things."

"Still, it must be a comfort to know when something's wrong. You might be able to save a life with it, depending on the sort of premonition you had."

Sarina sighed. "I guess so. But I wish the visions weren't so upsetting." She hesitated. "Colby didn't mention another woman, did he?"

"Of course not," Jennifer chuckled. "Why would he, especially now?"

"Never mind me," Sarina said quickly. "I'm just feeling fuzzy. Thanks for calling me. Kiss Bernadette good-night for me and tell her I'll see her tomorrow. The doctor's already promised I can go home unless I get worse. I'm not going to," she added firmly.

"Okay. I will. Sleep tight."

"You, too."

COLBY WENT BACK to work with the spare arm, having overnighted the malfunctioning one back to the lab with a request for hasty repair—just like last time. He was beginning to wonder if the stupid thing was ever going to be dependable.

SARINA HAD A BAD NIGHT, and Sunday was even worse. She dozed between rounds of antibiotic and painkiller, mentally cursing Colby because he'd betrayed her with that woman! It wouldn't have been quite so bad if she didn't keep reliving that night in Colby's apartment. It was the sweetest memory in recent years, and she'd built dreams on it. Now, those dreams were flying away in the face of reality.

She wondered what Colby's new paramour had thought when Sarina showed up at his door with the banana nut bread. She hoped the woman had given Colby hell all day. It didn't make sense that he'd throw her over for someone else just a couple of days after such a tempestuous interlude. But, then, Sarina didn't have much of a track record with men.

She thought how kind Rodrigo had been to her and Bernadette, and she wished with all her heart that she could love him. It just hadn't happened, even before Colby's sudden reappearance in her life. The first time she'd seen Colby, her heart had turned cartwheels. It still did. She hated her feelings for him. Especially now.

He had a point about her job, but she wasn't going to admit it. She'd been wounded in the line of duty. So easily, she could have been killed. Then what would have happened to Bernadette? Colby might agree to take her, but what would he do with a small child in his life? Apparently he was new to security work, and the old life still tugged at him from time to time. Wasn't it possible that he might find a way to leave Bernadette with someone and go back into the military? He'd been a career man. Surely it was hard for him to give it up, especially for a job that must be boring most of the time.

She recalled his easy handling of the wild-eyed drug user who'd sent her elderly neighbor running. She remembered him on horseback, jumping a fence with his dark eyes glittering in triumph. He had a wild streak that had never been quite tamed. Odd, she considered, how he'd fit in with a military lifestyle. Most military men were conservative, businesslike, withdrawn. Colby wasn't a sedate man, and he wasn't particularly conservative. He had a lot more in common with men who lived on the cutting edge of reason, like those in special operations or SWAT teams. She'd read once that no man who could pass a standard psychological test would qualify for outfits like special forces or delta squad.

Maybe Colby had had disciplinary problems, and that was why he'd taken early retirement. She wondered what branch of the military he'd served in. She'd never asked him.

She laid back into her pillows and tried to watch a television program. She missed Bernadette and her own apartment, sparse though it was. She wasn't used to inaction.

MONDAY AT NOON, Colby appeared in her room, accompanied by her doctor.

"You can go home," he told her. "The nurse will have two prescriptions for you at the desk, including antibiotics and a painkiller." He looked at her over his glasses. "Don't take the painkiller when you're using your gun."

She glared at him. "I never take anything when I'm using my gun."

"Good for you. Keep doing that. Well, I'll say goodbye," he added, with an amused smile at

Colby, who looked as if he were trying to swallow a watermelon. "Call me if you need me."

"I will. Thanks," Sarina added, with a smile.

He left and she got to her feet. She was wearing the same clothes she'd had on when she arrived, and there was a bullet hole and traces of blood on the sleeve where she'd been hit.

"I didn't have a change of clothes," she remarked when she saw Colby glancing at her sleeve.

"I should have thought of that, and offered to bring you clothing," he said quietly.

"It's all right. I'm going straight home. I can change before we go to pick up Bernadette."

"I thought we might get lunch and take it home," he said.

She shrugged. "That would be nice."

"Chinese?"

She looked up, surprised. In the old days, when they'd been close and growing even closer, they'd spent a lot of time at Chinese restaurants. They both enjoyed Chinese cuisine.

"Well, yes," she stammered. She laughed self-consciously. "I haven't had Chinese takeout in a long time."

"Neither have I," he said, his tones austere. He picked up her suitcase and she took one last look around the room to make sure she hadn't overlooked anything. Then he followed her out the door.

There was a slight wait at the nurse's station

while they located her prescriptions and then another slight wait at the pharmacy near the parking lot, where they were filled. By the time they got away, it was past the lunchtime rush.

Colby left her in the SUV while he went into the Chinese restaurant and got sweet and sour pork for her and sesame chicken for himself.

He handed her the plastic bag containing their food and climbed in under the wheel. She noticed his prosthesis on the steering wheel.

He sighed. “It’s not as pretty as the other one, but it works very well,” he remarked. “Actually the simple hook is the most efficient. But it seems to intimidate people.”

“Colby, which branch of the service were you in?” she asked suddenly.

He felt his whole body go stiff. He didn’t want to answer that question. Certainly he needed time for the explanations that would follow.

She frowned. “What, was it some top-secret outfit?” she persisted.

“Something like that,” he said slowly. “Are you comfortable? I can turn up the heater if you’re getting chilled. It was cold out this morning.”

“I’m fine,” she said.

“We’ll just have time for lunch before we have to pick up Bernadette,” he added.

She was diverted, and talk was casual the rest of the way home.

HE PUT OUT THE FOOD on the table while she got out plates and found soft drinks for both of them.

She was unusually quiet while they ate. None of their problems had gone away. She was still thinking about the woman she'd found in his apartment, and he was still thinking about her unexpected profession and the certainty that she was eventually going to discover his own jaded past.

"Thanks for coming after me," she said.

He smiled. "I didn't mind."

She took another forkful of rice and carried it slowly to her mouth. "Have you heard any more about Vance?"

He shook his head. "It's too soon. If he's back at work today, we'll know we're on the right track. I haven't spoken with Hunter this morning."

"I haven't, either. I guess one of us should call the office."

He pulled out his cell phone, pressed a number, and listened. "Yes, it's me. I just picked up Sarina at the hospital and brought her home. We're going to pick up Bernadette at school and then I'll be in." He hesitated. "Yes. Yes, I thought he might. Good. Then we're still on track, I guess." He hesitated again. "Yes, I know," he said heavily. "But we're bound to get a break sooner or later." He looked at Sarina. "She's better, but still not one hundred percent," he said. "I'll tell her. Thanks. See you later."

He hung up and put the phone back inside his

jacket. "He said Ritter and Cobb told him to let you stay out until tomorrow, if you're determined to come back in undercover."

"I need to. I can't let Rodrigo down," she said, without looking at him.

"Cobb was chewing up tenpenny nails trying to figure out who the two DEA undercover agents were, and I understand he hit the ceiling when he discovered Ramirez was one of them. They have a history of some sort," he remarked, then glared at her. "You and Ramirez certainly had me fooled."

"We've done undercover work before. I worked for Ritter when I was carrying Bernadette," she said, "and while I was in college. When this problem came up, he naturally thought of me. I brought Rodrigo in as well."

"You picked a dangerous profession," he said.

She looked up at him. "So did you," she shot back. "Or do you think being in the military is a piece of cake?" She lowered her gaze to her unfinished rice. "Is that where you met her?"

"Her?"

"That blond woman in your apartment," she said stiffly.

His breath caught in his chest. He was about to answer when there came a hard knock at the door.

CHAPTER THIRTEEN

COLBY EXCHANGED GLANCES with Sarina and carefully slid his hand into his jacket, against the cold butt of the automatic as he moved to the door and looked out through the Venetian blinds.

She was tempted to pull her own service weapon to back him up, but she knew it was unnecessary. She'd seen Colby in action. She had no doubt at all that he could handle whatever turned up outside.

But he quickly removed his hand from the jacket and opened the door without turning on the outside light.

It was Señora Martinez's grandson, Raoul. He moved into the room quickly and closed the door behind him.

"I wanted to tell you," he said to Colby, "that my cousin is through treatment and himself again, thanks to your amigo, the reformed priest," he added with a grin. "He had a lot to say about the two of you in Africa."

Colby smiled. "He was one of our best, before he took on the collar."

"He is still one of your best," the boy replied. He glanced at Sarina and grimaced. "I was not in time to warn you about the raid. I am very sorry that you were hurt, *señorita,*" he told Sarina.

She managed a smile. "Thanks."

"But I have come to make up for it," he continued, his eyes narrow. "This woman, this Dominguez, is destroying us all. She has no thought for anything except her own profit. She sacrifices us as if we were ants. My second cousin, a boy of fifteen, died in the attempt on the warehouse, and she gave not one word of apology to his mother. She said only that his own stupidity and clumsiness caused his death."

Colby drew in a rough breath. "Even Lopez, as bad as he was, never killed children."

The boy raised an eyebrow. "We understood that your group had something to do with his sudden disappearance."

"A former member of it," Colby said, uncomfortably aware that Sarina was intent on the conversation and knew nothing of his real past.

"Now we are between the woman and a countryman of hers who is only a little less bloodthirsty," the boy said heavily. "So we make a decision that the woman must go. She is intent on profit and has no thought for life."

Colby became somber. "I'm listening."

"It must never become known that I am involved," he said firmly, glancing at Sarina.

"It never will be," Colby promised. Sarina nodded.

He shrugged. "They are planning to move the shipment soon, to a location south of here, in a small town known as Jacobsville. Lopez once had a base there, which is still owned by a holding company in his name."

Colby's eyebrows lifted suddenly. "Doesn't she know that Jacobsville is a hotbed of former mercs?"

The boy grinned. "No," he said. "She believes it was a rumor concocted to make Lopez look stupid."

Colby actually laughed. "Her mistake."

"It will be," the boy agreed. "I know nothing more, but I will tell you what I can." He glanced at Sarina. "I owe you both for my cousin's recovery and the salvation of my grandmother. But I will not betray my comrades, even so."

Colby held out a hand. The boy shook it. "I give you my word," Colby said, "that your part in this will never be revealed."

He smiled. "This I know already. The priest was very forthcoming about you. I must go."

"How is your grandmother?" Sarina asked.

"Very well, thank you," he replied. "The priest

has two men come every week and shop for her. One cleans her apartment. These mercs," he added with a chuckle, "have remarkable skills. *Adios!*"

He left, as cautiously as he'd come, and Sarina stared at Colby without blinking. "How is it that you're friends with a priest who was with you in Africa, and he was a merc?"

He drew in a long breath, and turned, his eyes narrow as they met hers. "I wasn't exactly in military intelligence all those years."

"No?" She stared harder.

He grimaced. "I couldn't settle in the regular military. I was even out of place in the CIA. I became an independent contractor."

Her expression tautened. "That's why you were in Africa," she began slowly, her eyes wide with sudden knowledge. "You were part of a military coup there!"

He nodded slowly. "We overthrew a dictator who was killing hundreds of innocent people daily," he confessed. "We put in a government that was less brutal, and friendly to our country."

"We?" she persisted.

"Okay," he said on a rough sigh. "Me and Eb Scott, Cy Parks and Micah Steele."

Her lips fell apart. "Cy was a merc?"

Boy, was she in for some big surprises soon, he thought solemnly, especially when she discovered that her friend and partner Ramirez was up to his neck in the same work. But he didn't feel comfortable telling her that. Not yet, at least.

"And Micah Steele," she continued, thinking back. "That was why Phillip called him up here. He was with you in Africa. He knew what was wrong with you even before he came."

He nodded. "He saved my life...performed an amputation with only a native intern as an assistant, under combat conditions."

She turned away, unsettled.

"Well," he said irritably, "now you know how I felt when I found out the hard way that you were moonlighting as a field DEA agent involved in shootouts with drug smugglers!" he returned defensively.

She had to grit her teeth to stem an outburst. He was right. They'd both kept dangerous secrets. But her actions were at least understandable. His weren't.

"I had to support myself and my daughter," she said without looking at him, "who had a serious asthma condition that could have killed her when she was younger. I had to get the best paying job I could find. Working as a clerk for an oil company didn't cut it."

"You could have been promoted into management," he shot back, glaring.

"Right," she laughed hollowly. She sat down on the arm of the sofa. "I can't order people around with any sort of success. That's why I'm still a field agent. I don't have what it takes for management. Some people don't," she defended. "That doesn't mean I can't be good at what I do."

"I'll agree with that. You've got grit and you're canny," he said surprisingly. "You're a natural for security work."

"I like what I do," she countered.

He turned and moved closer to her, his dark eyes quiet and questioning. "I don't," he said flatly. "If anything happens to you, Bernadette gets stuck with me. I'm not a good risk."

She didn't know how to take that. Her eyes darkened with pain. Was he telling her that they had no future together, even after the passionate interludes they'd shared?

He saw her expression and understood it. He moved a step closer, his good hand touching her cheek very lightly. He grimaced. "I've made too many mistakes, haven't I, Sarina?" he asked softly. "I've got so much to make up to you and Bernadette. I don't even know where to start."

"Being honest with me would be a start."

He raised an eyebrow. "Look who's talking."

She flushed slightly. "I had orders, strict orders, to keep my identity to myself and share it with no one."

"You shared it with Hunter," he accused.

"I was ordered to, by a regional DEA official who outranks Cobb," she said flatly. "He knew that Cobb had at least one informer in his organization and he wasn't taking any chances with an operation this big. Hunter had to be told. You didn't. You were a relative newcomer here and the official didn't know you from a sponge."

"I guess he didn't."

She backed down a little when she saw his brooding, hunted expression. "I didn't like keeping secrets from you," she confessed. "But after that Saturday morning at your apartment..." Her voice trailed off and she turned away. "Would you like some coffee?"

"Yes," he said.

She moved into the kitchen and made a pot of coffee, checking the time. "We have about twenty minutes before we have to leave and get Bernadette. I could make us a sandwich," she offered.

"I'm full from lunch."

"So am I."

He hesitated. "But we could go by the pizza joint on the way home instead and get Bernadette something with a lot of pepperoni and mushrooms."

She laughed involuntarily. "How did you know...?"

"I keep having these odd cravings," he confessed. "Since I realized I couldn't be pregnant," he added, tongue-in-cheek, "I attributed it to that odd link I've got with my daughter."

She smiled. "She knows all sorts of things about you. I don't understand how it works. But I know that your father had it, too."

"So does my uncle," he said. "He's Comanche. Teaches history at a community college in Oklahoma. His son, my first cousin Jeremiah Cortez, is with the FBI."

"I'll bet he's a keen investigator," she commented as she poured coffee.

"Actually he doesn't have the gift the way his father does. Neither do I. Bernadette puts us all in the shade." He sat down at the kitchen table and accepted his coffee black. "Does she take a lot of heat for it at school?"

"She tries to hide it," Sarina told him as she sat down across from him. "It frightens her."

"I can understand why, if she saw how I was wounded. One of my own men threw up."

She glanced at the prosthesis, trying not to imagine the pain. It must have been terrible. She couldn't imagine his Maureen being particularly sympathetic, either.

"Colby," she began without looking at him, "that blond woman…"

He cocked his head and looked at her, hard. "I haven't changed fundamentally, even if you are finding out things about me that you didn't know. Am I the kind of man who goes from one woman to another without conscience?"

She looked at him worriedly. "You went from me to Maureen that way."

He grimaced and sipped coffee. "I was obsessed

with her," he said after a minute. "Before I ever really knew you. I was attracted to you, hungry for you. But I was blinded by what I felt with Maureen. It was fool's gold," he added quietly. "I only had to live with her to realize how little she cared for anyone, except herself. She found me repulsive when I lost my arm. She couldn't bear to look at me without my shirt." He met her eyes and smiled gently. "You never seemed to notice it was gone."

"It didn't matter," she replied, helpless to lie. Her eyes met his evenly and her heart jumped up into her throat. "You still haven't said…"

With a long sigh, he pulled out the photo Cecily had given him, that he'd kept in his wallet. He pushed it across the table to her.

She picked it up, surprised. "Who's the man beside her?"

"Her husband, my best friend, Tate Winthrop. He's Oglala Lakota. The woman is Cecily. They have a terrific little boy who's just one year old, and they're pregnant again. Tate was in the shower when you came by."

She grimaced. She'd assumed he was cheating on her and acted accordingly. She hadn't even given him the benefit of the doubt. She fingered the photo. "I'm sorry I jumped to conclusions."

"With my track record, you were entitled to," he said. "But from now on," he added, "we have to try to be honest with each other."

She looked up from her cup. "That might be a little difficult."

"For me, too. I'm used to keeping secrets." He shrugged. "Then we start even. We start over."

She swallowed. "To what end?"

"Bernadette needs two parents," he told her quietly. "A father and a mother. I do realize that I'm starting late, but I'm not going to quit on her."

"She's very important to me, too."

"Where does Ramirez fit into your future?" he added suddenly.

She grimaced. "Colby, he's my partner. We've worked together for three years. Surely you know how it is, when you're under fire with people. There's a bond there."

His dark eyes narrowed. "Is there?"

"He needs me," she pointed out.

That was laughable. Ramirez was even more of a lone wolf than he was himself, and he had a history that was going to make future work relations with her very difficult, when she knew them. But it would look like jealousy if he brought it up right now. He *was* jealous, of course. He just didn't want her to know it. Ramirez would gloat.

"Suppose," he began, "we take it one day at a time, for now? Just until this drug smuggling racket is tidied up, and we know where we stand?"

"That's a good idea," she agreed.

"Now that we know the smugglers are going to

move their product to Jacobsville, it's not logical to keep staking out the warehouse. We need to make a move down to Jacobsville and set up operations there with Eb and Cy."

"But, my job," she began. "Your job…!"

"We'll work it out with Cobb and Ritter and Hunter," he said. "It's well-known in the company that you and I are keeping company, and that Bernadette and I are getting close. It would be pretty natural if we went down to Jacobsville, where we both have friends, and took a few days off together."

"Well, it's not bad, as a blind," she considered aloud.

He frowned. He didn't mean it that way. But she sounded serious. Perhaps it was too soon to start making long-range plans.

"I wish we knew where those drugs were hidden," she said after an uncomfortable silence.

"So do I, but at least we have some idea of where they're taking them, if the gang leader wasn't leading us astray," he pondered. "Cy knows the lay of the land around Jacobsville, and he and a few friends put Lopez on the run. If they did it once, they can do it again."

"I guess so," she agreed.

"I like Jacobsville," he said abruptly. "It's small, but that's not such a bad thing. I remember when I was a boy," he added quietly, "and if anyone got sick, the whole community showed up to help take care of them. It isn't that way in cities."

"I wouldn't know much about small communities," she said quietly. "I lived very high. I had everything in the world, except love." She laughed hollowly and didn't look at him. "Money alone isn't enough to make anyone happy."

"Bernadette loves you very much," he remarked.

She smiled. "Yes, she does," she agreed. "And I love her. She's the most important thing in my life."

"I'm beginning to understand that feeling myself," he said slowly. "I'd like to be around for her, when she needs a father."

Her heart was turning cartwheels. Was he was offering her a future, or just pointing out that he'd be visiting his daughter? "Are you going to be around? How about the call of the wild, Colby?" she asked solemnly. "You've been restless ever since you've been at the oil company."

He curled the cup into his big, lean hands. "I won't deny that it's hard to give up the adrenaline rush. But I'm getting too slow for combat," he admitted a little curtly. "I've lost my edge. Besides that, I want to stay alive long enough to become a grandfather."

She smiled slowly, but she avoided his eyes. "Do you honestly think you could settle down in a small town someday?"

"Why not?" he asked. "I might actually enjoy the

security of neighbors and friends in a small community. Especially among a few ex-mercs," he added only half humorously. He glanced at her. "What about you? Have you ever thought of moving Bernadette to a small town? And if you ever did, could you give up fieldwork for it?"

"I don't know. Maybe." She grimaced. "But even if I had a job here and a place to move to, I just don't know how I'd explain it to Rodrigo." She stopped abruptly, afraid she'd made her wishes all too clear.

"I could explain it for you," he offered with a glint in his dark eyes. "I think I still have some bullets in my left pocket..."

"You stop that," she said. "Bernadette loves him."

"She likes all sorts of serpents," he replied. "You should have seen her at the reptile house at the zoo. She even knows the names in Latin."

She grinned. "I taught her. I like snakes, too."

"Well!" he exclaimed, and returned the grin. "Lucky Ramirez."

"Colby!"

He glanced at his watch. "We'd better get going, hadn't we?" he said, finishing his coffee. "We don't want to be late."

She gave up and let the subject go. He wasn't going to take to Rodrigo, even if half his family did. But she wondered if he'd been serious about settling down...

CHAPTER FOURTEEN

COLBY ARRIVED at Ritter Oil just after Sarina did, and he went straight to Hunter with what he'd learned from the gang leader, and his proposal about doing some snooping in Jacobsville.

"The hitch is that we'll have to explain our absence from here, without arousing suspicion," he added. "And you and Jennifer will have to agree to keep Bernadette for three or four days. We have to have a solid reason for being in town there."

Hunter pursed his lips, considering this. "We might stage a conversation for Vance's benefit," he began.

"Not a bad idea," Colby had to agree. "I'll have Cy put it around town that I might be looking for property, with Sarina and Bernadette in mind. Gossip runs rampant in small communities. I remember that from my own childhood," he added, chuckling.

"So do I. Cy would be willing, I'm sure. Micah, too."

"I owe him one for coming all the way to Houston to treat me for malaria," Colby said with a smile.

"You'd have done the same for him, if circumstances had been reversed."

"I would," Colby agreed.

Hunter frowned. "I wonder why Vance is keeping such a low profile lately," he said. "He hasn't made a single wave since the assault on the warehouse."

"He probably thinks we suspect him," Colby replied. "And he's not wrong." His eyes narrowed angrily. "He could have killed Sarina. I owe him one for that bullet he sent into her. If I could get enough evidence…"

"I know how you feel," the older man interrupted. "But we have to keep playing a waiting game here, until we have a solid lead. Your bit of information, if it's true, is a big help. But until we actually see drugs being moved, we can't prove a thing. And if Sarina fingers Vance for shooting her," he added, "there goes any chance of flushing out Cara Dominguez and her lieutenants."

"I guess so," came the quiet reply.

"Don't be so impatient!" Hunter chuckled. "We'll nail Vance, and Dominguez, and the rest of the bunch. I promise you we will. Don't forget how long it took Cy and the others to bring down Lopez."

"I know. Things move so slowly."

"But they do get done. While you and Sarina are in Jacobsville, the rest of us will put a little more pressure on Vance and see what he does. I'll have one of our men monitor that wire you put in his car. So far he's been pretty quiet."

"He'll slip eventually," Colby said with certainty. "They always do."

"Give Cy my regards," Hunter told him. "Maybe one day we can have a reunion and talk about the old days."

"I'll see if I can arrange that," Colby told him with a grin.

TWO DAYS LATER, Colby and Sarina were installed in separate rooms in the Jacobsville Hotel. Colby might have suggested a single room, but he wasn't ready to share what he'd learned about their marriage with her just yet. She was still wary of him and distant, despite their intimacy in the recent past. He didn't want to push too hard. He wanted her to think about all he'd said.

They went together to Eb Scott's training camp. Colby felt right at home with the mercs. He was somewhat easier with his past now that Sarina knew about it. Her reaction hadn't been quite what he expected. She was a straight arrow, very conventional. He'd expected that she might not want anything to do with him once she found out about his past. It hadn't been like that at all.

Not that she was letting him get any closer. She was polite, courteous, and as cool as ice water.

"You're quiet," he remarked as they got out of the car at Eb's ranch.

"I don't have anything to say," she replied.

"You're still mad about Vance," he guessed, nodding when she gave him a startled look. "I wanted to take him in, but Hunter stopped me. He said we couldn't afford a ripple in the stream." He looked angry and frustrated, all at once.

She was vaguely surprised at the anger. She turned to look up at him, her dark eyes wide and quizzical. "I didn't think it mattered to you that he got away."

"He shot you," he said curtly.

She turned away, but not before he saw a faint smile on her lips.

Eb Scott was tall and lean, with blond-streaked brown hair and green eyes. He shook hands with Colby warmly.

"Long time, no see," he said. "You've weathered well."

"So have you," Colby replied. He glanced around the camp, which he knew was state-of-the-art. If there were any advancements in surveillance, Eb had them first. "You've expanded since I was here last."

"That was years ago," Eb reminded him with a grin.

"I guess it was." He turned to Sarina. "You don't know Eb, do you?"

She shook her head, smiling. "I've heard of him, of course. Cy meant to introduce us, but there was never time." She held out her hand. "I'm Sarina Carrington, DEA."

Eb shook the hand, glancing at Colby curiously.

"We were married, once" was all Colby would admit. "We have a daughter. She's just turned seven."

Eb had heard about Colby's marriage, but from what he knew, the woman had been a brunette. This one was a blonde.

"You probably knew his second wife," Sarina said, anticipating the question. "I'm the first one. But we were only married for one day."

Eb raised an eyebrow. "Wise lady, to know so quickly what a rotten husband he'd make."

Colby burst out laughing. Sarina was surprised, because she'd expected him to take offense. Apparently these two knew each other very well, indeed.

"What are you two doing down here?" Eb asked. "I thought you were working for Ritter, in Houston."

"I am," Colby said. "But we've had some drug smuggling complications, and we understand that a big shipment of cocaine is going to be sent down here for concealment. We plan to stop it."

"Good for you," Eb said. "We've had enough drug smugglers here to last us a lifetime. Cy and

Micah and I shut down Lopez's operation, with a little help from Harley Fowler, and put Lopez's men on the street."

"I heard. Good work."

Eb shrugged. "It wasn't that difficult. He underestimated us right down the line."

"His successor is heading in the same direction," Colby told him. "She thinks Lopez's survivors invented the mercenaries to explain their failure."

"Obviously she doesn't read magazines," Eb mused, recalling that his operation in Jacobsville had featured largely in one about the time Lopez died.

"She's a very superior sort of woman, in her own mind," Sarina interjected. "But she depends on the wrong people. One of her operatives spilled the news that she was going to attempt to move the shipment from its hiding place at our warehouse in Houston. He assumed that he was the only man in the company who understood Spanish." She smiled wryly. "His mistake."

"If you know the shipment is in the warehouse, why don't you just do an inventory?" Eb asked.

"You have no idea how big the warehouse is," Colby replied, "or how many cartons would have to be opened and inspected. Besides that," he added with narrowed eyes, "I don't really think the drugs are in cartons. I think they're concealed somewhere else."

"Where?" Sarina wanted to know.

He grimaced. "I'm not sure. Just a hunch."

"Your hunches used to be pretty accurate," Eb recalled.

"They still are," Sarina murmured, without looking at Colby.

"Well, we'll get Micah and Cy in, and hold a council of war. I've got contacts everywhere," Eb mentioned. "And Cy knows a man who went undercover in Lopez's outfit..."

"I know him, too," Colby said, and his eyes spoke volumes to his old comrade.

Eb was quick. He knew immediately that he wasn't supposed to mention Rodrigo in front of the woman.

"We can discuss him later," Eb said, carelessly. "Come on in and I'll give you a tour of the place. Sally will be home from school about four. We have a son who's in day care while mommy and daddy work, but he'll come with her. You can meet him, too."

"You with a wife and son," Colby shook his head. "Who'd have thought it six years ago?"

"I could say the same of you," Eb returned, grinning. "Haven't we changed, though?"

"We have, indeed," Colby agreed, with a warm smile at Sarina, whose cheeks colored just faintly.

EB'S OPERATION was enormous. There were two barracks with electronic hookups and every sort of gadget known to modern science. There was a huge metal building used for martial arts training. There was a gun range. There were exercise trails through the woods, and marked areas, including an urban setting, where mock combat took place. There was even a track where one of Eb's experts taught defensive driving tactics. It was a counterterrorism school of which any country would be proud.

"We do a lot of contract work here for various governments," Eb told them. "I add people as I need to. The defensive driving range is new. So is the combat area. We have to keep up with current terrorist trends. Street fighting is a recent innovation, starting in Iraq. We have an instructor who teaches Arabic and Farsi, along with some Bedouin dialects. I had plans to teach demolition and bomb dismantling, but Sally put her foot down. She hates explosives." He shrugged. "You win some, you lose some."

"She just didn't want you blown up," Colby ventured.

He chuckled. "It was just as well. I'd planned to ask Cord Romero to teach the course, but he got married and has a child on the way. He's going to retire from merc work and raise prize bulls."

"He and Maggie were in the papers a few months ago," Colby recalled. "They shut down a child slavery ring and killed the ringleader in Amsterdam."

"They did, indeed. And just think, she was formerly an investment counselor."

"She," Colby jerked a thumb at Sarina, "was an oil company clerk. She's one of the best intelligence agents I've come across in recent years."

"I got shot," Sarina reminded him dryly, but glowing from the praise.

"Anybody can get shot," Eb said. "I've got a few holes in my hide, too, and not from carelessness. The wounds heal, eventually."

"Eventually," Colby agreed.

SALLY CAME HOME with their little boy, who was the image of his dad. He was shy around the newcomers, but sweet.

Eb's wife taught grammar school. She was blond and slender, and obviously in love with her husband. She and Sarina kept each other company while Eb and Colby talked over old times.

The next day they spent with Cy and Lisa, at their ranch. They arranged for some surveillance at the known haunts of the late Manuel Lopez, with trusted cowboys riding fence lines and keeping their eyes open.

"Did you know that there's a ranch near by that's up for sale?" Cy asked Colby.

"No. What sort of ranch?" he replied.

"It's not a big one, by local standards," Cy told him. "But it has potential. Lots of good grazing land, plenty of water. It could support a nice herd of horses."

Colby glanced at Sarina, who was listening carefully. "Where is it?" he asked.

Cy grinned. "I'll show you."

They left Lisa at the house, because her pregnancy was advanced and she found riding difficult. It made her sick. Cy loaded his visitors into his big red Expedition and drove them over past the D Bar G, Judd and Christabel Dunn's prosperous cattle ranch to the old Hob Downey property.

"Hob was killed by one of the notorious Clark brothers," Cy told them. "He was a good old man, everybody loved him. The property has been deserted ever since." He parked at the front door of the ramshackle ranch house. "The land is the thing," he added when he saw their dubious looks. "The house is a dead loss."

"It is," Colby agreed. "I'd pull it down and rebuild. Maybe a Spanish revival style. It would fit in well with all those agaves and cacti."

Sarina glanced at him with a warm smile. "Yes, it would. And painted a pale yellow, like desert sand…"

"…it would be perfect," he finished for her. "Bernadette would love it. She could ride horses every day."

Sarina's heart jumped up into her chest. Her eyes widened, darkened, as they met his across the backseat. "Yes," she said softly. "She would."

They exchanged a look hotter than a jalapeño pepper. Cy cleared his throat to get their attention.

"And we're here," he said, hiding a smile as he got out at the front door of the ramshackle shack. At the end of the driveway was a dull, lackluster For Sale sign, which had obviously been there for quite some time.

"Andy Webb has the option on it, at Jacobsville Realty," Cy told them. "Since old Hob had no living relatives, there's no one to inherit. Some of the proceeds will go toward his burial and the rest will be invested, with the proceeds to go to our local needy fund. Hob always used to say that poor people needed more help than they ever got from the government. This way, he can go on helping, even though he's no longer here."

"He must have been a nice person," Sarina said softly.

"He was," Cy replied. "Why don't you two look around? I'll sit in the truck and talk to Lisa on the phone." He grinned sheepishly. "We do that a lot, with the baby almost here."

Colby chuckled and drew Sarina along with him. "If you'd known him six years ago," he told her wryly, "you wouldn't think he was the same man. Marriage has changed him."

"He seems very much in love."

He caught her slender hand in his. "He is." He walked to the back of the property, where the yard was thick with denuded rosebushes and shrubs. Beyond was open pasture that ran to a line of trees far on the horizon. "Lots of space here," he mused. "Like back on the reservation, when I was a boy."

"Your father talked about it a lot," she said softly. "He knew he made a lot of mistakes in his life. He was sorry for all of them, especially when he lost touch with you. He felt responsible."

His hand contracted around hers. "I blamed him for every bad thing that ever happened to me," he reminisced. "Even after I was grown." His broad shoulders rose and fell. "But I'm just beginning to understand how he felt. He loved my mother, but he couldn't give up the bottle. After she died, he must have hated himself. It only made the drinking worse."

"He did hate himself, for a long time. But when he knew I was carrying his grandchild, he sobered up and never took another drink. Not even a beer. He liked to think he made up for a little of the past by the way he took care of Bernadette while I worked. He loved her very much."

He turned and looked down at her somberly. "So do I, Sarina," he said in a tone like rich velvet. "More every day."

She searched over his scarred face, up to his dark, quiet eyes. She'd loved this man half her life. She wondered how she ever managed to live without him. Love was a tenacious thing, she pondered. Tenacious and terrifying.

He touched her soft mouth with his fingertips.

"You loved me," he said in a quiet harsh tone. "I knew it, but I still gave you hell. I deserved what happened to me with Maureen. You don't build happiness on someone else's despair."

Her heart jumped. "You loved her," she began.

"Hell," he said harshly, "I wanted her. I never liked her, as a person. She was selfish and grasping, and she never put herself out for anyone. I feel sorry for the child she'll be raising. It will probably be in juvenile hall before it's thirteen. She's nobody's idea of a mother." He shook his head. "And I wanted children with her. Lucky me, that we never had one."

"Didn't you ever wonder, about that night we spent together?" she asked curiously.

He laughed softly, with self-contempt. "I thought you were experienced, remember. I thought you were on the Pill. It never occurred to me that there might be a child." He searched her eyes slowly. "Have you thought about how it might have been if Maureen hadn't deliberately ignored your call for help?"

She managed a weak smile. "I did, occasionally. I couldn't help wondering what you would have done."

"I'd have come to you like a shot," he replied immediately. "I wanted children more than anything in the world," he said with faint bitterness. "I was convinced that I couldn't have any."

"Then maybe you wouldn't have believed she was yours," she began.

He put his forefinger against her lips, to silence her. "It's easy to get a DNA test these days. There wouldn't have been any doubt for long. Especially once I saw her," he added gently. "I never thought of you as the sort of woman who'd go from one man to another so quickly. Especially," he added uncomfortably, "after what I did to you."

She moved into his arms and pressed against him, embracing his waist so naturally that he enveloped her with delight. "Maybe we're not remembering the same thing that you did to me," she whispered. "I was remembering when we took a shower together, while you were getting over malaria."

He actually shivered. His mouth searched for hers, found it, ground into it in the windy chill of autumn that surrounded them. He groaned when he felt her instant response.

"It was glorious," he whispered roughly. "I've never felt anything like it. Especially after..." He stopped dead and lifted his head. "Oh, God," he whispered, his face tautening.

"What?" she wondered.

"Sarina, we didn't use anything," he said heavily. "Baby, you could already be pregnant."

Her delicate features lifted in a warm, comfortable smile. "I suppose I could," she replied, overwhelmed with pleasure at the way he looked—wondering and happy, all at once.

He chuckled. "You wouldn't mind?"

She shrugged. "I love kids." The smile faded. "Except..."

"Except that we aren't married," he said for her. The smile grew softer. "When we get this case solved, we'll make decisions. Okay?"

She felt as if she could walk on air. "Okay, Colby."

He kissed her again and reluctantly let her go.

They walked around the property, discussing its merits. Colby felt her presence, as she seemed to feel his, because her face flushed. He reached beside him for her hand and locked it tight into his. He felt as if he were vibrating with need. He wondered if she felt the heat as he did. He looked down at her and saw eyes almost burning with hunger. His lean fingers tightened almost painfully around hers as Cy joined them at the front gate.

"How much of the land is in pasture?" Colby asked, trying to make his voice sound normal.

"About two-thirds of it," Cy said. "The rest is in hardwoods and a stream runs through it. You'd have good water. Well? What do you think?"

"Where do we find this Andy Webb?" Colby asked abruptly, and smiled at Sarina's obvious delight.

Cy grinned. "I just happen to know where his office is. Climb in!"

JUST THAT QUICKLY, Colby made the decision to buy the property. He didn't know if Sarina would want to live on it with him permanently. There would be hard decisions to make, for both of them, if she did. But Bernadette would have both parents and security. Perhaps he could sell the idea to her on that basis. He knew that he was never going to survive letting her out of his life again. She and their daughter had already become part of his very soul.

Cy drove them back to the ranch, where they had sandwiches and coffee. Then they left, reluctantly, to go back to the hotel.

Colby stopped at Sarina's door, hesitating, because this was a small town and they weren't known. They had separate rooms. It had never bothered him before, taking a single woman into his room during long trips abroad. But now, in this tight-knit community where he was considering setting up house, he didn't want to do anything to sully her reputation. And she didn't know about that so-called annulment. It was a card he wasn't ready to play.

He tugged her against him, liking the clean, sweet smell of her body and her hair, which she wore in a ponytail today.

"How's the arm?" he asked gently.

She smiled, trying to appear calm when her whole body tingled at the contact with his. She wanted nothing more than to drag him inside her room and push him down on the nearest bed. She knew he wouldn't resist. She knew he wanted her just as badly.

"It's much better," she said at once.

He lifted an eyebrow and tugged her closer. "You wouldn't be trying to seduce me?" he drawled with twinkling eyes. "Because I have to tell you, I'm easy."

She smiled back. "What if I am trying to?"

"You're out of luck, pretty girl," he murmured. "I have something a lot more permanent in mind than a stolen hour. Especially with an audience."

"Audience?"

He quirked an eyebrow to their side, where the proprietor of the hotel was sweeping off his porch. Not that it was dirty…

She laughed softly. "Small towns."

"Yes. I think I might like to live here, Sarina," he said after a minute. "I've never really belonged anywhere, except on the reservation. But I've grown too far away from it to be able to go back. Here, I'd be among old comrades, people I've known for years, people who share my own history."

"You mean, give up working for Mr. Ritter?" she asked, a little worriedly.

He met her eyes. "I'd like to give it a try. A real try."

"Oh."

He scowled and tilted her face back up to his. Her eyes were dark, sad. "What's wrong?"

She drew in a slow breath. "I don't actually work for Mr. Ritter. I work for the DEA, out of the Tucson office," she said. "I have to go back."

"Do you? Why?"

She caught her breath. "Because it's my job! I have to make a living, Colby," she persisted.

He slid his hand under her left one and tugged it up to his broad chest. "You might be pregnant," he reminded her. "Do you really want to have another child alone?"

Her eyes were tormented. "Of course not. It isn't that…"

"Then, why couldn't you work here in Jacobsville?"

She blinked. "The DEA doesn't have an office here," she stammered.

"There are several law enforcement agencies here in the county," he said. "Every town has a police force. Cash Grier, Jacobsville's police chief, is especially hard on drug dealers. So is the sheriff, Hayes Carson. Cy says they're both always complaining that they don't have enough investigators."

"You mean, leave the DEA and go to work here?" she questioned slowly.

He nodded. "I could hit Eb for a job at his school. I'm a master interrogator. I use methods that aren't in any book of rules. And I have a reputation with intelligence gathering and martial arts. I think I could find a place for myself."

She could hardly believe what he was saying. But he actually seemed to be serious. "Bernadette and I could come and visit you at the ranch…"

"You and Bernadette could live with me, at the ranch," he replied, very solemnly. "I've made a hell of a lot of mistakes in my life. Most of them have hurt you. Now you have to decide whether or not you think you can spend the rest of your life with me, here."

Her lips parted. It was like a dream come true. There were obstacles. There were concerns, like moving Bernadette to a strange town where she'd have to give up her friends and make new ones. But just the thought of it was tantalizing.

"Think about it for a week or two," he told her. "You don't have to make decisions tonight. As I said before, at Downey's place, we'll talk about it again, after we break up this smuggling operation. How about that?"

She smiled with her whole heart. "Okay," she agreed breathlessly, laughing.

He smiled back. "Okay."

She reached up tentatively and touched his cheek with just the tips of her fingers. "I never even hoped that you might consider something permanent."

He caught her by the waist and tugged her closer. "I like the idea that you might be pregnant, by the way," he whispered, loving her soft flush. "We might think about having several more children while I've got the stamina," he whispered wickedly.

She blushed. "I'd like that," she whispered back.

"I know something I'd like better, just at the moment," he murmured, bending. His hard mouth brushed over her soft one with a lazy, gradually insistent pressure that made her body ache all over.

She reached up and held him close, moaning as his arms contracted and he deepened the kiss.

It was all he could do to stop. He pulled away, his body taut, his face rigid. "Not yet," he ground out.

"Spoilsport," she chided breathlessly.

He burst out laughing. "I'm trying to make an honest woman of you!"

"I'm already an honest woman. We can still have sex. It's okay."

He wondered how he'd lived so long without her. He gathered her up close in a warm, affectionate embrace and rocked her against him, still laughing. "You're going to be a handful," he mused.

"You're going to love it, too," she shot back.

He sighed, putting her slowly away. "I have to get some sleep. So do you. Tomorrow, we're going to put out feelers and see if we can't flush some drug dealers. I'm impatient to get this operation finished."

"Funny," she murmured, "so am I."

He let her go. "Sleep tight."

"You, too."

"Breakfast at seven," he reminded her. "I want to get an early start."

"Suits me. Good-night."

He wrinkled his nose at her. "Good-night yourself."

HE DIDN'T SLEEP. It was a shock to find her willing to live with him. He hadn't mentioned marriage, but he was certain she understood that was what he meant. They were still married, and he had yet to tell her. There was time, he decided. Now, there was all the time in the world.

CHAPTER FIFTEEN

THE WIRE COLBY HAD placed in Brody Vance's car paid off the very next day. Hunter called Colby on his cell phone with news.

"The tip you got was apparently right on the money," Hunter said, alluding to the young gang leader's anonymous conversation with Colby, who hadn't mentioned his identity to Hunter. "The Dominguez woman's feeling safe," he told the other man. "She's considering moving the shipment tonight, or tomorrow night, to Jacobsville. We don't know where it is, but we have some idea of where it's going. Was there a honey operation down there at anytime?"

"Cy mentioned one, at the back of his property," he replied. "He said the holding company still owned it, although it's been derelict since Lopez's operation was shut down here."

"Bingo!"

"Listen, can you talk to Cobb and tell him to take the surveillance off the warehouse, just for today and tomorrow, and make sure that Vance overhears it?" Colby asked.

"Are you nuts?"

"We don't need to know where it is, Hunter, as long as we know where it's going, don't you see?"

Hunter paused. "I suppose you're right. But it's risky."

"Not if we have Eb and Cy and Sarina and myself down here waiting for it, with any backup Cobb feels comfortable sending," he added. "I wouldn't mind having Ramirez along," he said reluctantly. "I don't like the guy, but Cy says there's nobody better in a tight corner, and I found that out firsthand during the last raid."

"Cy's right," Hunter told him. "Okay. I'll send him down to Cy's today. He can get a motel room and be there when the dam breaks."

"Take good care of Bernadette," Colby warned. "I don't think Vance would hesitate to have her snatched if he could get to her. She'd be a great bargaining tool. By now, the outfit is sure to know that Sarina is a DEA agent."

"I spent several years working for the CIA," the other man reminded him, tongue-in-cheek.

"So did I," Colby returned, "but it's still better to spell everything out. Isn't it?"

"I guess so," came the resigned reply. "We'll make sure Bernadette's safe. You and Sarina look to your own backs. This is a dangerous crowd."

"So are we," Colby said with a grin. "But just in case, you watch your own back."

"Got you."

Colby debated whether or not to tell Sarina that he'd asked Rodrigo to come down and join the operation. Some part of him was still jealous of the attention the other man got from Sarina and Bernadette. He decided, finally, to let it be a surprise. It was safer.

COLBY RELAYED what Hunter had told him to Cy and Eb and Sarina as they all sat around the dining room table at Cy's later that day.

"I've made a few phone calls," Eb added, toying with his coffee cup. "We'll have plenty of local law, as well as the feds. It looks like we're going to shut down one of the biggest drug operations in south Texas sometime in the next forty-eight hours, if Dominguez doesn't get cold feet and change her mind."

"I hope you're right," Eb said solemnly. "This is a dirty business. I don't want it in my county."

"Neither do I," Cy added. "Did Colby tell you he's buying Hob Downey's place?"

"Are you?" Eb asked with a grin. "Then how about signing on with me? I need someone to teach martial arts."

"You're as good as I am," Colby replied, chuckling.

"But I don't have the time to do administration and teaching as well, not with a child to raise," Eb replied. "I'll pay you double what Ritter's offering, and you can set up your own curriculum."

Colby pursed his lips. This was more than he'd hoped for. "Autonomy?"

"Complete autonomy," Eb agreed. He cleared his throat. "As long as you don't try to teach interrogation tactics to any of my students."

Colby gave him a droll look. "Spoilsport."

"The deputy director of the FBI had a lot to say about your presence in Africa after the embassy bombings," he replied. His eyes said more than the words did.

"They sent me home," Colby said, shrugging. "Beats me why. I was only asking simple questions."

"It was the way you were asking them, and what with," Eb mused.

Colby glared at him. "I got results."

"And the Bureau got lawsuits," Eb nodded. "No interrogation tactics. Period."

Colby shrugged. "Okay. But if we ever need information from a hostile force…?"

"You'll be first on my list," Eb promised. "Well?"

Colby extended his hand and shook Eb's. "Put me on the payroll. I'll need to give Ritter two weeks' notice."

"All right!" Eb laughed.

Sarina met Colby's searching eyes and smiled so

brightly that his heart skipped. No need to ask if she was pleased with his decision. He felt warm inside.

But before he could speak, there was a knock at the door. Lisa opened it to admit a tall, handsome Mexican with laughing dark eyes.

"Was I expected?" he asked when Colby glared at him.

"You were," Cy agreed, shaking his hand. "Colby asked Hunter to send you down."

Sarina's eyes widened like plates. Rodrigo lifted both eyebrows at Colby and smiled. "You asked for me?" he queried.

Colby cleared his throat. "Yes, actually, I did. Cy told me about your participation in an earlier…undercover operation," he said, without letting on that Rodrigo had been a merc. He had to choose his moves very carefully. Sarina might react badly if he ratted on the competition.

Rodrigo's eyebrows lifted even more. "Yes?"

Colby shrugged. "You have an advantage on all of us about the operation in these parts. It would be stupid to leave you out. Especially now."

Rodrigo tried not to look smug. He couldn't quite manage it.

"And you can drop the smug expression," Colby added with a glare. "Or something might accidentally slip."

Rodrigo knew what he meant. But he only chuckled. "I do not think it would matter much anymore," he confessed quietly, with a knowing glance toward Sarina, who was openly staring at Colby as if he belonged to her. Which he did.

Colby let go of the anger when he saw where Rodrigo was looking. His eyes met Sarina's and she blushed. That amused him and defused the tension. He chuckled along with the older man. "Point taken. Let's get down to business, shall we?"

THERE WAS a comradeship in the group of former mercenaries that Sarina envied. She was good at her job. She'd been in life-and-death situations. But she felt as out of place as a turnip in the gathering.

Her gaze went to the small town's police chief, Cash Grier, who looked as out of it as she felt. He was standing on the sidelines while Colby discussed tactics with Eb Scott, Cy Parks and Rodrigo.

Cash glanced at her and grinned. "Feeling out of place? Alone? Unnecessary?"

Her eyes twinkled. "How did you know?"

He shrugged. "I read minds."

"Nice talent."

"Actually it's the way I feel myself," he confessed. "I was never really part of a group."

"No? What did you do?"

He leaned closer. "Naughty things. Very naughty things. However, I'm reformed now," he assured her with a grin. "Tippy and I are very pregnant."

"Tippy?"

"My wife," he replied. "I want a girl. She wants a boy. But we'll be happy enough with either."

She smiled. "Congratulations," she said, wondering how such a lone wolf sort of man had ended up married. He didn't look the type.

A tall, good-looking man in a sheriff's uniform came into the room, grimaced as he saw the group of men and automatically made a beeline for Cash and Sarina.

"I feel—" Hayes Carson began in his deep voice.

"Out of place and unappreciated," Cash finished for him. "And we know exactly how you feel. This is Sarina Carrington," he introduced. "DEA."

"Hayes Carson, Jacobs County Sheriff," the other man replied, extending a hand for her to shake.

"Hey!" Cash called to the group.

They all turned and stared at him.

"Is this a closed operation, or do you take outsiders?"

They laughed and joined the other three.

"Sorry," Eb Scott said, extending a hand to first Cash, then Hayes. "We were reminiscing."

"Don't tell me," Sarina joked. "You were all together in Africa."

"How did you know that?" Eb asked curiously.

"Just an educated guess," Sarina said, and she was giving Rodrigo a very strange look.

He moved to her side, his hands deep in his pockets. He shot a glance at Colby.

"He didn't tell me anything," Sarina told her partner of three years, with a glare. "But it's hard to miss that you fit right in here."

Rodrigo grimaced. "I was not always a DEA agent," he confessed.

"No kidding?" she drawled.

"Don't give him any heat," Cy told her firmly. "If it wasn't for Rodrigo, we'd never have shut down Lopez. He got a leave of absence from the DEA and actually went undercover in Lopez's operation. He damned near got himself killed in the process."

Sarina caught her breath. "You never told me!" she exclaimed.

"Well, look who's talking?" Rodrigo shot back. "Did you tell me you'd been married?"

"I would have thought you would assume I was, since I had a child," she replied.

He glowered at her. "Plenty of people have children without marriage."

"I don't!" she returned.

Colby stepped between them. "We are all here to fight drug dealers," he pointed out.

"Are we really?" she muttered.

"And you never told me that you were a DEA agent," Colby added. "I had to find out during a drug raid!"

"He has a point," Rodrigo told her.

"You can shut up," she invited.

"Isn't that your boss?" Cash asked suddenly, indicating a tall, grim looking man with dark hair and green eyes striding toward them.

Sarina and Rodrigo turned immediately, snapping to attention.

"So you're both already here. Good. Good," Alexander Cobb said. "I assume all of you are part of the deal?" he added, noting the group.

"We know the layout of the land, and at least two of us were involved in shutting down Lopez," Cy volunteered.

Cobb narrowed his eyes at the other man. "I remember," he said curtly. "You walked right into my operation without my knowledge, thanks to Kennedy—who is now serving time for conspiracy to distribute drugs!"

Rodrigo held up his hand. "May I intercede? I was working undercover in Lopez's operation at the time, and they intervened to keep your men from killing me."

Cobb's lips made a thin line. "Obviously they missed. And lucky for you that I've mellowed since then," he added, and Rodrigo smiled sheepishly.

"Some target practice might not come amiss," Cash murmured dryly. "*My* men are required to qualify on the shooting range monthly."

"Your men don't shoot people," Eb pointed out.

"Well, if they ever have to shoot anyone, we don't want them to miss, now do we?" Cash agreed.

"Who do you have staking out the smugglers' local warehouse?" Cobb asked Cy.

"One of my men with a pair of binoculars and a cell phone."

"And if they spot him?" Cobb persisted.

"He's wearing a Ghillie suit."

Cobb blinked. "Where the hell did you get a Ghillie suit?" he demanded.

Cash raised his hand. "I wasn't using it for a day or two." He glanced down at Sarina's puzzled expression. "I got it at Fort Bragg, years ago," he whispered. "Army Sniper School. But don't worry, it's just my spare." He grinned. She didn't know whether to laugh or run. He couldn't be serious, of course.

Cobb gave Cash a curious glance, but he didn't pursue it. "Okay, then, can we assume he'll let us know the minute he spots traffic?"

"We can," Cy assured him. "It looks like a long night."

"Or maybe two or three of them," Colby added. "Hunter's going to tip off Vance unobtrusively. Then we have to hope that Dominguez will take the bait."

"Absolutely."

THEY SETTLED DOWN to wait. It wasn't long before Cy had a quick communication from Harley.

He chuckled. "It seems the smugglers have just moved in a shipment of bee gums," he said dryly.

"Bee gums." Cobb nodded. "Open or closed?"

He asked Harley. "Closed," he replied. "And get this, there are men with automatic weapons all around the bee gums, making sure those bees don't escape."

The task force grouped together. Everyone started checking guns and ammo, and communications equipment. They synchronized watches.

"Everybody ready?" Cobb asked the group.

There were murmured assents. There was no joking now.

Colby tugged Sarina to one side and looked down at her solemnly. "How's the arm?" he asked with some concern.

"I'm going to be just fine, as long as you and Rodrigo are there to back me up," she said with a tiny smile.

He chuckled, having already decided that Rodrigo was no longer a threat. He winked at her. "I'd kiss you," he whispered, "but we'd never live it down."

She wrinkled her nose at him. "Afraid of gossip?' she mused.

He glanced at Cash Grier, whose eyes were sparkling with gleeful malice.

Colby indicated the other man. "Are you?" he whispered.

She chuckled. "Well, maybe just a little," she confessed.

He cocked his pistol and put on the safety before he holstered it. "Later," he promised with twinkling eyes.

She nodded. "Yes," she said breathlessly. "Later."

"Let's go!" Cobb called.

The various members of the task force melted into cars and set off for the warehouse.

COLBY AND SARINA were almost at the site when Colby's cell phone rang insistently. He glanced at it, saw Hunter's name on the caller ID, and turned it off. He'd call him back after the raid, he decided.

"Better shut off your phone as well," he told her. "We can't afford to have them ring before we're in position."

"Good point," she agreed, and shut her own off.

They pulled up behind Cobb and Cy, on a dirt road several hundred yards from the entrance to the warehouse.

Everyone got out, checked weapons, and gathered for the assault. But before they could act, Eb Scott moved in front and held up a hand urgently.

"Hold on," he said curtly. "There's a complication."

He looked straight at Colby and Sarina as he said it, and Colby cursed under his breath. "Bernadette!" he said at once.

Eb gave him an odd look, but he nodded. "The Dominguez woman has her," he said tightly.

"Hunter took the kids with him and Jennifer to a restaurant. Bernadette went to the rest- room and didn't come back. Hunter is furious with himself, but it's too late for regrets now. The Dominguez woman says either we back off, or…" He let the rest slide. There were murmured whispers.

Colby glanced down at Sarina and gathered her close. "It's all right," he said softly. "Trust me."

"You know I do," she said. "But…"

He pressed his fingers against her mouth. He moved away from the law enforcement contingent and drew aside Eb and Cy. "I need a hostage," he said. "Someone high level." He glanced at Cobb and the others. "You're not here for the next fifteen minutes."

Cobb, alert to what was going on, nodded solemnly.

The three men moved off together into the darkness. Sarina stood with the other law enforcement officers, gnawing her lip, and prayed.

TEN MINUTES LATER, Colby came back ahead of them, his face grim, his eyes flashing. "They've got her at the old Johnson place, near where Sally Scott lived before she married Eb. I need two willing volunteers."

"Me," Sarina said at once.

"Me, too," Cash Grier said, and he wasn't smiling. "I've got my rifle in the boot of my car, with night vision," he added grimly. "Colby and Sarina and I will go in together. When we've got the child in the clear, we'll give you the green light."

"A rifle?" Sarina asked worriedly. "Listen, if they've got her close to them…"

Eb Scott moved to Sarina's side while Cash went to get his gear. "You don't know Grier, and he won't tell you, but I will," he said, lowering his voice. "He was a covert assassin. There isn't anybody better with a sniper kit. But you didn't hear it from me."

Sarina let out a breath. "Okay. Thanks."

Eb nodded and went with Cy and the others to the back of Cy's Expedition, where his own cache of weapons was stored. Cash came back in a riot jacket and a face mask, carrying the rifle over his shoulder. He looked as grim as the others.

Hayes Carson moved closer. "Listen, county enforcement is my jurisdiction," he told Cash.

The older man turned to him. "Can you hit a target in the dark at six hundred yards and not miss, when a child's life hangs in the balance?" he asked curtly.

Carson let out a breath. "No."

"I can," Cash replied with supreme confidence. He motioned to Sarina and Colby with his head. "Let's go."

Colby drove. As they neared the Johnson place, Cash had Colby stop the SUV and let him out with the rifle.

He checked his cell phone. "Turn yours on, if it isn't already," he told Colby. "And don't make a move on the house until I take out whoever's holding the child. I'll send a signal, just one. Go like hell when I do."

"Roger."

Cash took off into the woods, so silently that Sarina was amazed.

"How did you find out where they had her?" she asked Colby as they moved closer, without lights, and stopped just out of sight of the house.

He glanced at her. "You don't want to know. Really."

She pursed her lips. "They won't hurt her…?"

They would, and he knew it. "They won't get the chance," he told Sarina. He closed his eyes, hoping against hope that his odd psychic connection to the child would work this one time when her little life might depend on it. Father, he thought silently to the old man he'd treated so badly in recent years, help me save her!

As if in a dream, he saw Bernadette, her dark eyes solemn and unblinking. He saw through her eyes the room, the window, the man standing behind her with a loaded pistol while a dark woman, Cara Dominguez, spoke on a phone. There was another woman as well, armed with an automatic rifle, and another man with a pistol.

"God," he whispered unsteadily. "Keep your head down, baby. Keep your head down!"

Even as he thought it, he heard the first of three

shots. They were quick, deliberate, and, apparently so accurate that the people inside couldn't even react—because the phone suddenly rang.

"Let's go!" Colby told Sarina.

Both had their pistols out and they were running for Bernadette's life.

Colby didn't stop to open the door, he kicked it in. He went low, Sarina went high, as if they'd practiced the assault all night. The Dominguez woman had Bernadette around the neck and she was crouched, the pistol at the child's neck. The other three members of her group were on the floor, one dead, two badly wounded and useless.

"I will kill her!" she told Colby, screaming. "You will not stop me!"

Colby took a slow, careful breath. He didn't lower his pistol. "Baby, you know what to do," he whispered.

"Yes, Daddy," Bernadette said, her voice shaking, but her eyes full of courage.

"*¿Que?*" the Dominguez woman demanded. Her grip on Bernadette tightened. "What are you…?"

Bernadette's eyes closed and she went completely limp all at once. She was small, but such a dead weight that the Dominguez woman had to shift her weight suddenly. The tiny movement gave Colby a shot and he took it. He got the woman in the chest. She groaned and fell, her lung punctured. The gun fired, but into the floor.

At the same time, the downed man got his fingers around his pistol and raised it, but Sarina was equal to the task. She winged him in the arm holding the gun and it flew out of his hands.

Colby shot forward and scooped up his daughter, holding her so tight that she shivered, her little arms hard around his neck. Sarina disarmed the woman on the floor and kicked the man's pistol aside before she went rapidly to her family. She slid an arm around Bernadette, too, and kissed her hair.

"I was scared to death," Sarina said shakenly.

"Great shot, by the way," he told her, grinning. "I couldn't have saved myself in time."

"Thanks. Oh, Colby!" she groaned. "What a close call!"

He kissed her hungrily. "Bernadette and I knew what we were doing, baby," he told Sarina. "We just couldn't tell you!" He smiled at Bernadette. "God, I'm so proud of you!" he told her. "So proud! You were very brave."

"So are you. I heard you, in my head," she told him seriously. "You said to keep my head down. Somebody shot those men, before you and Mama came, and that other woman…!"

Cash came up on the porch so silently that nobody heard him until he was in the room, the rifle slung over his broad shoulder. He surveyed the damage and nodded.

"I need to get in more practice," he muttered coldly

as he noted the two who were only wounded. They gave him horrified looks.

"You did great, from our point of view," Colby said sincerely. He held out his hand. "Thanks!"

"I'll second that," Sarina said with a tearful smile. "Thanks a million!"

He shrugged. "All in a day's work," he assured them, as he shook Colby's hand, and with a warm smile at Bernadette, who returned it. "But I count favors," he told Sarina. "And I really need an investigator. Making drug cases is the biggest part of what I do here. I've got a missing woman who's up to her neck in the Dominguez operation. She's still out there, somewhere, and she'll probably replace Dominguez. This isn't over, by a long shot."

She looked at him and then at Colby and Bernadette. She smiled. "Okay," she agreed. "I'll give Cobb my resignation today," she said. She glanced at Colby's delighted smile. "Where are we going to live?"

"We'll rent a house for the time being," he said huskily. He cuddled Bernadette close. "How would you like to live on a ranch in Jacobsville, baby, and have your own horses?"

"Oh, Daddy, I'd love it! Can we?"

He looked over her head at Sarina, in a way that could have set fire to dry leaves. "Yes, we can."

"Are you going to marry my mommy?" she persisted.

He smiled. "We'll talk about that later. Right now, we've got a drug bust..."

Cash's phone rang. He answered it, glancing at Dominguez, who was cursing steadily. "Stop that," he muttered, "there's a child present!"

"And she speaks Spanish," Colby seconded, glaring at the woman.

"Right," Cash said into the phone and closed it. He grinned. "It seems that the rest of the beekeepers are now in custody, along with their product. They'll be guests of the federal government for some time."

"How..." Colby began.

"Oh, I phoned them," Cash said easily. "I saw Dominguez go down in my scope and figured you had the situation in hand, so I gave Cobb the green light. He and the rest took out the operation."

"We weren't even needed," Sarina sighed.

"I wouldn't say that," Cash replied, noting the results of their raid. "Nice shooting," he told them both.

"Not so nice," Colby muttered. "I wasn't aiming for her shoulder," he added deliberately, and the woman on the floor stopped cursing and went white.

"You can practice on our local gun range whenever you like," Cash told him. "Sort of a thank-you for letting your wife work for me."

"You're welcome," Colby said, looking past him

at Sarina with warm eyes. He still had to tell her about their marriage. He hoped it wasn't going to be a disappointment.

CHAPTER SIXTEEN

LATER, when Cash found out how Colby got Bernadette to go limp in the nick of time, he took them all to his house and introduced them to his beautiful, and very pregnant wife, Tippy. She had the same gift that Colby and Bernadette shared, and found the successful end to the kidnapping not at all unusual. Despite her fame—she'd been both a model and film star—she was as down-to-earth and charming as her husband, and her young brother who lived with them.

Colby and Sarina left Bernadette with the Griers, and young Rory, while they went back to the motel and talked about the future. But talk was on the back burner the minute the door closed. In the aftermath of terror and potential tragedy, they were both too aroused to need words. They ended up on one of the big double beds in a tangle of arms and legs, throwing clothing over the side as fast as they could release hooks and buttons and snaps and zippers.

They came together in a firestorm of passion, barely capable of rational thought at all. She arched up to meet the furious thrust of his body, clinging as the movements sent her quickly right over the edge of the world. As she fell into what felt like throbbing fire, she heard his harsh groan at her ear. Consciousness eluded her for breathless seconds.

When she opened her eyes again, she was shaking in the aftermath. So was he. They were both wet with sweat.

She managed weak laughter and then groaned as her arm protested the exercise she'd exacted from it.

"Does it hurt?" he asked apologetically.

"Yes, but I don't care," she laughed wickedly. She looked up at him, feeling the throb of him deep in her body. She shivered again. She linked her arms around his neck. "Don't stop," she whispered.

"I'm not sure I could," he replied, grinning back. His hips rose and fell and quickly humor melted into a rekindling of the helpless ardor that had sent them spinning down into oblivion. He heard her voice at his ear, whispering that she loved him, that she'd never stopped loving him. The pleasure was so intense that he actually cried out.

WHAT SEEMED like hours later, they lounged together on the rumpled bed, catching their breath.

"Volcanic," he murmured.

"Feverishly passionate," she replied drowsily.

"I'm running out of good adjectives," he remarked.

"Me, too."

He rubbed his cheek against her hair. "Do you remember those annulment papers that your attorney sent to me seven years ago?" he asked abruptly.

"Yes," she murmured. "I'd forgotten all about them."

"I never signed them," he told her.

It took a minute for that to sink in. "You what?"

"I never signed them."

She drew back and met his dark, soft eyes. "But if you didn't sign them…"

"…they never went through the process," he finished for her. "We never had an annulment. And Maureen and I were never legally married."

She sat up, shocked. "How? Why?"

"Her late husband left a will. If she remarried, she lost every penny in his savings account. There was a lot of money in it. So she got a friend to pretend to be a minister and marry us. I never checked the marriage license. If I had, I'd have realized it was phony."

She was trying to figure it all out. "We're still married."

He smiled. "Convenient, isn't it?" he asked. "Instant family, just add house."

She laughed. Cried. She hugged him close. "Oh, my goodness!"

"I've been wracking my brain for a way to tell you," he confessed. "Especially when it looked like Ramirez was winning."

"I'm very fond of Rodrigo, but I could never feel that way about him," she said softly. "He's just my partner."

"Former partner," he said firmly.

She looked worried. "I know. But I…"

"Former partner," he repeated. "He can still come and see Bernadette from time to time," he conceded. "She genuinely cares about him. And vice versa."

"That's nice of you," she said.

He grinned at her. "Yes, it is, isn't it?"

She curled close to him. "I think we're going to be very happy here."

"So do I, baby," he replied, cuddling her. "So do I."

THE HUNTERS came down to see the new property, with Nikki.

"I'm damned sorry about Bernadette," Phillip told Colby solemnly. "It's not like me to be off my guard like that."

"Dominguez would have found a way, no matter who had her," Colby said sincerely. "Who'd expect a child to be snatched in public view, in a restaurant?"

"I suppose so. I feel bad, just the same. By the way," he added, "guess where the drugs were hidden in the warehouse?"

"You found them?" Colby exclaimed.

"Found where they'd *been*," Hunter corrected, smiling. "Remember the dogs sniffing around the wall? Well, during the tenure of the former guard, the one who was arrested, the smugglers actually built a false wall with plywood and repainted it. Damned good job. Turns out one of those men Vance was protecting was a carpenter."

"I'll be damned," Colby chuckled. "What about Vance?" he added.

"Arrested and charged with conspiracy," Hunter replied. "That should make Sarina's day."

"Indeed it will."

"Domiguez is in the hospital with around-the-clock guards. When she's able, she and her confederates will all be escorted out of Jacobsville by U.S. Marshals. That should be pretty soon."

"I won't mind seeing her go," Colby said curtly. "She was willing to kill Bernadette. One of her henchmen had my baby with a gun to her head. If Grier hadn't been around," he added, "I don't know what we'd have done. I never trained as a sniper."

"Lucky for you that Grier was here," Hunter said heavily.

"You aren't kidding," Colby said quietly. "Imagine, a man with a background like that being able to settle in a small town like Jacobsville."

"He's learned to live with his past," Hunter replied. "Something we've all had to do."

"Some of us are still trying," Sarina pointed out as she joined them, smiling. "Or didn't you hear yet about the smuggler who ran to the sheriff for protection after Colby questioned him?" she added with a pointed glance at Colby.

"I had to know where they were holding Bernadette," Colby defended himself. He put a hand over his heart. "But I'm reforming as we speak," he promised with a grin.

They all laughed. Bernadette, who'd been playing with Nikki, had a sudden change of expression. She went to Colby and took him by the hand.

"I have to talk to you, Daddy," she said solemnly.

"Okay," he agreed with a smile. "What is it?"

She pulled him to the end of the porch at Cy's house and pushed him gently into the swing. She jumped up beside him. "You mustn't interrupt me," she said, "because I learned it all by heart and I have to say it straight through. Okay?"

"Okay," he agreed curiously.

"Here goes." She launched into a short speech in Apache.

Colby's face went white. He knew the words. His father had written them to him, when he was much younger. He'd thrown the letter away, half read. But now he listened, intently, while his daughter spoke the healing words that burned the mist away from the past and made a path for Colby back to the father he'd known as a boy.

Bernadette hesitated only once, just at the end. "You are my son," she told him, "and I will always love you, no matter what you do, no matter what you are, no matter where you go. As my eyes close forever, it is you that I see behind my eyelids, as I walk into the darkness where your mother awaits me. As a father forgives his child, so the great spirit forgives all his children, even me. I will always watch over you, and your child, and her children. And I will always love you."

She stopped speaking, because tears were rolling down Colby's dark cheeks.

She reached up and brushed the tears away with her small fingers. "Granddaddy said that I would know when to tell you. It was the right time, wasn't it?"

"Yes, my baby," he whispered, pressing his lips to her forehead. "It was the right time."

"I love you, Daddy."

He closed his eyes as he held her close, remembering all the loneliness of his life, all the pain and grief and misery that he'd experienced, that he'd caused. It was a long path from there to here, with his child against his heart and a future with her and her mother that looked diamond bright.

"Are you sad, Daddy?" she asked.

He held her closer, glancing past her at Sarina, who smiled at him with misty eyes. "No. I'm so happy that it's overflowing," he whispered. He kissed her cheek. "I love you, too, Bernadette. With all my heart."

"And Mommy, too?"

"And Mommy, too," he agreed.

She grinned, looking so much like him that it was uncanny.

He tugged at her hair. "I could eat a very large pizza right now," he said.

"So could I!" she exclaimed, jumping down.

He got up from the swing, feeling twenty pounds lighter and a foot taller. He hoped that his father could see the small family circle, arm in arm, walking together, wreathed in love. He was almost certain that he could. He held Bernadette's little hand tight in his own, and drew Sarina closer at his side. A man who had love, he decided, needed nothing more. Nothing more at all.

* * * * *